GREEN NECROPOLIS

The Greenway Way

Christopher Cooke

Amazon

This could have done with a
more thorough proof check for
typos before going to print...
However, on the bright side,
it is one of a 'limited edition'
of just ten paperback copies!
Please pass on to a friend
or to a second-hand or charity
book shop. Best Wishes
Chris Cooke

The greater part of humanity who today experience the devastating effects of poverty, war and climate breakdown may take comfort in the knowledge that the end of this present life of torment will bring the prospect of rebirth on a regenerated and peaceful earth.
Where, then, is death's sting?

THE NEW RELIGION

CONTENTS

CHAPTER 1: THE FORBIDDEN SHOES

It was a mercifully mild Saturday afternoon in late November as John set off to his second assignation with Mandy. He would ideally have slipped on his raincoat as an insurance, but preferred to forgo the extra warmth. He told himself: *Better to feel cool literally so as to look cool figuratively.* He muttered the phrase two or three times before dismissing it as an unlikely new entry in the Oxford Dictionary of Quotations.

The reality was that although his raincoat was particularly shabby looking, his regular clothes were only marginally smarter. At sixteen, he had finally achieved full vertical growth. This was a developmental stage every parent eagerly awaited, as it marked the potential end of relying on eternal hand-me-downs for their children. However, despite his repeated protests, John's mum was adamant: he'd have to wait until the end of the autumn term of his Lower Sixth Form before receiving a brand-new pair of trousers and top.

As John joined the high street, fellow pedestrians became more numerous and, feeling self-conscious, he quickened his pace. With only a hundred or so more metres to his rendezvous point with Mandy outside the *Superway* café, he willed himself to relax and slow down. After last weekend's promising encounter, he was confident that she wouldn't stand him up, but instinct told him it was still too soon in their relationship to risk arriving more than half a minute late. It would be far safer to be several minutes early.

Then, disaster! A voice hailed him from behind:

'Steady as you go, young man!'

John stopped in shock so abruptly that he almost lost his balance. *Oh no – what have I done?* was his automatic reaction as he turned to face his accuser - a policewoman.

Officer Margaret Warwick had approached to within barely two metres and was looking him up and down studiously.

A five-second memory scan was all John required to certify his conscience as clear.

'What's wrong officer? To be honest, I'm in quite a rush. I'm meeting a friend in just a couple of minutes!', he pleaded in a tone which wavered between earnest and apologetic.

'It's just something about the way you were walking. Please lift each foot in turn and show me the soles of your shoes....'

Officer Warwick sounded to John not unlike his mother who, in a different context, might well have issued such a challenge. Had house-proud parents struck a secret deal with the local police force to combat inconsiderate teenagers treading dog muck into their hallways? He obligingly turned away from the police officer, stood on his right leg and gingerly raised his left foot, taking care to avoid contact with her face. He needn't have worried for, just as he was about to lose his balance for the second time, she seized his foot and steadied him.

'So that's it then. It wasn't the *way* you were walking so much as the *sound* your shoes made that caught my attention. I do believe we have here a pair of rubber-soled shoes.' She released her grip and allowed John to return to a two-footed posture.

John felt a surge of resentment combined with relief well up within him. He would so like to have sarcastically quipped: *So that's crime of the century solved then. Weren't you going to examine the other foot for complicity?* But nearly seventeen years of State and domestic socialisation quickly obliterated the temptation to challenge authority. Instead, he silently assumed an air of humility signalling a compliant intent to hear out the officer's further questions or instructions.

'How old are you, young man?'

Her second use of the term *young man,* seemed to John a touch warmer than the first.

'Sixteen. Is that important?' he replied, immediately wishing he'd maintained his deferential tone.

'It is, in fact. If you were eighteen, you'd be legally responsible for a breach of environmental law banning all use of articles with a rubber interface on highways. And, before you object that you were on a walkway, there is no pedestrian route into town without crossing at least one road. And technically, pavements are highways in any case.

'Oh dear, I hadn't realised. I did read something about the furore when cyclists had to fit 'new-compo' tyres to their bikes.'

John continued to self-censor against any hint of sarcasm in his tone. There would be little point in claiming ignorance: no Year 7, never mind Year 12 student, could have avoided being force-fed at least one area studies module on the hazards of particulate matter pollution. His younger self had been intrigued when one day his primary school teacher explained that the class would no longer be allowed to correct mistakes using little eraser blocks. These sent tiny particles of rubber and graphite into the environment only to be perilously ingested by all creatures great and small.

Officer Warwick read John's anxious expression and, her empathy growing, felt it would be mean to send him home humiliated in his socks. Any why subject the crestfallen lad to further interrogation? He was a bright lad and, fearing that they could be held criminally responsible, he'd simply deny that his parents had obtained the shoes for him. Maybe they'd been supplied by a young relative or school friend in any case.

'Fair enough, son. Just make sure, wherever you're heading this evening, that you don't drag your feet.' She refrained from adding *like most teenagers.* 'Lift them as you go to avoid any unnecessary friction. Then, as soon as you get home, put them away and don't wear them again until you've fixed them. You may be able to remove the soles and take the uppers to a repair shop.'

John smiled back sheepishly, attempting to look appreciative of the advice. Then he tiptoed round to face his original direction and proceeded as instructed with as much haste as his restraining order allowed. On another occasion, he might have been happy to stick around discussing the fate of his forbidden shoes with a police officer. Today, however, making it to his rendezvous with Mandy on time was a greater priority.

Thanks to his resolve to arrive at the café early, John's encounter with the law had consumed only three or four minutes of his safety margin. He calculated that enforced friction-free walking until out of view of the police officer would lose him a further thirty seconds getting him to his destination with barely a minute to spare. It could have been so much worse. She could have confiscated his shoes on the spot. Then he would have had to make the agonising decision between walking home in his socks or meeting Mandy in the forlorn hope that should wouldn't notice his missing shoes. Or, if she did, her powers of observation would be matched by an equally powerful sense of humour.

At last, John reached the *Superway* café and allowed himself to relax for a moment before a new anxiety set in: would Mandy arrive on time or at all? At first, he convinced himself that this worry was purely the effect of a blow to his confidence caused by a brush with the law.

But when the appointed hour came and went with no sign of Mandy, John's anxieties appeared increasingly rational. For fear of looking uncool, he was loath to stare too hard in the direction she'd be coming from. In any case, weren't women, presumably girls too, entitled to be a few minutes late? Or was that just an outmoded notion he'd picked up from his grandparents?

But the minutes continued to pass with still no hint of Mandy on the horizon. This was one of those exceptional occasions where a mobile phone would have come in handy. His father often reminisced about these, but nowadays only officials like the police seemed to possess them. Armed with one of these, Mandy would surely have sent a message or even called to explain why she couldn't make it after all.

When at last John gave up on his second date with Mandy, he noticed that for the past few despairing moments, he'd been mechanically lifting his feet alternately on the spot, as if practising the walking technique prescribed by the policewoman. As his anxiety turned to anger at Mandy for standing him up, he conceived a plan to give full vent to his frustration. He cast a series of furtive glances over his left and right shoulder, then, satisfied the coast was clear, he proceeded to stride defiantly homewards, scraping the soles of his shoes hard against the pavement as he went. Every so often, he looked round to view the fruits of his labours. There were fewer tell-tale black skid marks than he'd hoped, but he knew he'd find clear signs of wear and tear on the soles of his shoes once he got back home to inspect them.

As he opened the front door, John caught his mother in the hall walking towards the dining room. In order to fend off any awkward questions earlier, he had told her that he was going out to call on a school friend. But seeing her now provided him with another opportunity to let off more steam.

'Mum, you know those shoes you got for me the other day? I wore them for the first time just now and you'll never guess what happened – I got stopped by a cop: she told me off 'coz of their rubber soles!' Only halfway through this announcement did John realise he was rather relishing the prospect of embarrassing his mother or at least giving her a bit of a scare.

'Oh no, dear, I'd never thought to check them for, what do they call it these days...'

'*Illicit composition* is the term you're looking for', John graciously helped her out. 'Don't worry, I'm not blaming you. And when I explained I was only nearly seventeen, she said I wasn't legally responsible. Odd how the age of criminal responsibility is fourteen or fifteen for some things, but the law hasn't caught up yet when it comes to environmental crimes.'

'I guess it's because they assume most people your age aren't likely to be going out and buying their own clothes like they were in my day.'

'In your day? You sound more like gran than my mum!'

'Well, things have changed rather dramatically in recent years....' The anxious look that John had been cruelly counting on now crossed her face. 'I don't suppose she asked who'd got hold of the shoes for you, did she?'

'No, fortunately I thought quickly on my feet. So as not to incriminate you, I told her a friend had passed them to me.' John instantly felt ashamed of his lie and was keen to move the conversation on. 'Trouble is, now you've given my old ones to what's-his-name next door, I don't have any other decent ones to wear...'

'Dad might be able to adapt them somehow. It's about time he applied his old DIY skills in his own home again - not just at the repair shop. Honestly, I can understand them banning rubber tyres after all the pollution millions of motor vehicles must have caused over a hundred years or more. But rubber-soled shoes with their tiny environmental impact. How petty the law can be!'

Emerging from the lounge where he'd been watching TV, dad had overheard the latter part of the conversation.

'That shouldn't present any great difficulty. I'm sure I'll be able to fashion some new soles out of cork. I've got some handy pieces from those awful tiles I pulled up from the bathroom. They're stored away in the garage somewhere. I'll be back in sec.'

'I must say, that's an uncharacteristically quick response from your dad!' mused John's mum.

'Yes, but what's the betting he gets side-tracked once in there and doesn't come out till tea time having completely forgotten what he went in for?' John had now achieved a dig at both his parents. It was now time to withdraw back into himself for a moment of reflection. What would his father use to affix the cork soles onto the rubber ones? What if the glue required was itself a banned substance under such and such an environmental law? What if his dad, rusty DIY practitioner that he was, decided to nail or screw the cork soles onto the rubber and got carried away in the process, rendering the shoes entirely unfit for purpose? And then, thinking at least his mother or sister would be around to hear his outburst:

'Flipping heck – those shoes are going to be damned uncomfortable with cork soles! The whole point of rubber was the elasticity to make walking comfortable! And I thought the government wanted people to walk places these days....'

But neither his mother nor his sister was within earshot and so John had to be content with sulking in silence. This at least gave him time to recall the real reason for his bad temper: he'd been stood up by Mandy.

An hour later, dad emerged from the garage radiant with self-satisfaction. 'Here you are lad. A masterful job, though I say it myself.' He confidently presented the shoes to his son.

John who by now had regained a degree of emotional equilibrium, slipped straight back into irritability mode. He snatched the shoes from his father's grasp and glared at them hypercritically. The odour of chemicals assailed his nostrils and at once caused his eyes to water. So, Dad had clearly gone for the glue solution! John had to steel himself not to appear totally unappreciative.

'Thanks, dad, they look OK. I don't suppose the glue's had a chance to set yet for me to try them out?'

'Well, I'd give them another hour or so, son, but they should be fine. Cork's actually really hard wearing when treated properly and it's really light too, so you shouldn't find them too clunky. When they do eventually wear out, there's plenty more where that came from thanks to the previous house owners who just loved those tasteless cork bathroom tiles! Oh, and Mum's just told me you were worried they'll be uncomfortable. I'm sure they'll be quite nice to walk in, as you'll still get the benefit of the give in the rubber under the cork.'

So, there'd been a parental conference in his absence. John examined with relief the three-millimetre cork layer affixed to the rubber. Thank heavens this would not transform him into the lanky giant he'd begun to visualise. His feigned appreciation turned to genuine gratitude and he was unable to conceal a sheepish grin from his father.

John's relief at reclaiming his footwear was not to be his only source of joy that Saturday. Barely half an hour after the evening meal which had been delayed somewhat on account of the shoe saga, the telephone rang. John's sister, Jenny, who had been washing up and fancied herself to be the most agile family member, sprinted out into the hallway and took the call. A moment later, she reappeared.

'It's for you, John!' As she handed him the phone, her neutral facial expression turned into a quizzical smirk.

It was Mandy. She had been kept in by her parents who were concerned about her falling behind with her homework! Unfortunately, they'd been around all afternoon patrolling the ground floor, so she'd not been able to use the phone earlier to let him know. At last, they'd nipped out for a walk so she'd used the opportunity to give him a quick call. No, she wouldn't be able to meet him tomorrow either, as it was Sunday which meant the morning at church and the afternoon with her nose back to the grindstone in her room.

So, John would have to wait till Monday to catch up with Mandy. Never mind. What did grandad used to say, or even gran before she started going a bit senile? *Separation makes the heart grow softer*, or something like that. His mum would know the exact idiom.

An inexplicable sense of desolation came over officer Margaret Warwick as the young shoe offender gingerly made his way off into the distance, at each step lifting his feet as instructed to what he clearly hoped would be an acceptable height, then bringing them down as gently as one could expect of a testosterone-fuelled teenager. She kept him in view for two hundred yards or so before losing concentration and giving way to an inborn urge to ruminate over any remotely awkward encounter with another human being. As a police officer, she was obviously in the wrong job!

She continued her musings as she cycled her way back to the police station. *Was I too harsh on the lad or maybe too lenient?* She could have lectured him more perhaps from a social responsibility angle. She imagined forcing him to picture the tiny particles of rubber deposited on the walkway being washed down the grid, entering the water system to clog up the innards of some innocent marine creature. They could end up being ingested by an infant human causing a nasty lifetime allergy...

The youngster had appeared intelligent enough, but that just meant he had all the less excuse to be ignorant. Yes, she probably should have been tougher. She should have challenged him over what he he'd been taught in environmental awareness classes at school. But then, she was a community police officer, not an environmental enforcement officer. On the other hand, it was everyone's responsibility these days to protect the environment...

One thing was clear: when giving her report back at the station, if she entertained any hopes of eventual promotion, she'd need to be careful not to portray herself as being too soft with a borderline young delinquent.

As he checked in for the Saturday morning shift at the Ministry, Howard Morton stood outside his office staring for the eleventh time this week at the new plaque on his door. At last, he entered, sat down at his solitary desk and continued his musings. Howard had qualified as an economist over twenty years ago and pursued a career in the Civil Service, moving occasionally between departments, but his work had never until now taken him so far out of his field of expertise. His ministry had been renamed more than once, but its most recent reincarnation as Economy, Finance and Taxation had removed him from his comfort zone. It seemed so much more daunting than in the days when it was simply called the Treasury Office.

Clearly, an ambitious politician had had the brainwave to create one huge ministry by logically lumping together everything to do with money. But in the modern world everything to do with money seemed to Howard illogical, unpredictable, infinitely complex and doomed to failure.

This wasn't just how Howard felt about matters on a Saturday morning when, like most people, he should have been enjoying quality time with his family. It was how he had gradually come to feel over the course of his career.

Governments, pledge as they might, couldn't control the economy whatever they attempted to achieve through fiscal measures and tweaking tax rules. Past administrations had historically just about managed to keep up with their country's economic affairs during the decades of growth and social progress. However, in these days of environmental degradation and ever more frequent natural disasters, forward planning was nigh impossible. All that could be counted on, it appeared, was the progressive destruction of generations of infrastructure accompanied by economic stagnation and decline.

The State had limited options for intervention, most of them reactive rather than proactive. Today, like most days, Howard's task was to consider further means of transferring to the Treasury more of what little remained of ordinary citizens' wealth. What else could be taxed? What new licence fees and fines could be introduced and which existing ones could be increased?

In recent weeks, he had been lying awake at night mulling over a whole spectrum of schemes – some suggested to him by colleagues, others of his own imagining. But today, decisions had to be taken by his political boss, the Minister for Economy, Finance and Taxation, and on the basis of Howard's recommendations.

The environmental crisis and associated rocketing death rate had led legislators to prohibit cremation in one of many desperate moves to reduce global emissions. He was especially dreading the forthcoming conversation about tightening restrictions on use of cemeteries and the related charges associated with garden burials. Despite his broadly conventional civil servants' outlook on most matters, Howard found this topic morally distasteful and ethically challenging. But there was no escaping that part of his job description requiring him to brief and advise the Minister.

CHAPTER 2: TODAY IN EVERY WAY, I'M BECOMING GREENER AND MORE SUSTAINABLE!

The Greenway family were spending their Sunday afternoon like most former middleclass families throughout the land - barely talking to each other. But unlike most other families, at least they were all seated together around the same dining room table. The meal as such was over, but somehow everyone - parents and children alike - felt something substantive and weighty had to be said before each went their separate ways. It was Anne who opened the conversation, prompted by a promo broadcast on the wall-mounted TV which had been running quietly in the background throughout the meal:

'I feel sorry for you kids. When I was your age, by late November, we could start looking forward to the merriment of the festive season and piles of presents on Christmas day. Nowadays, instead of reminders to make an early start on the Christmas shopping, all we get on TV are public education programmes on planning ahead for our New Year's Resolutions. How much less we're going to spend and consume, how much greener we're going to be from January first next year...'

John gave in to his inner sarcastic core. 'Well, I reckon with a surname like Greenway we should promote ourselves as the model family. What about adopting the slogan: *Green is our name and green is our way - Greenway*. The government might hire us to be in their ads...'

Jenny too could rise to the sarcasm challenge when provoked.

'You mean instead of taxing us so hard that poor mum has to cadge some third-hand rubber-polluting shoes from a neighbour? And so, you can be charged with environmental crime for wearing them?'

'Well, it was about time they taught you irony at school, siss. What year are you in now?' John had found Jenny's intervention refreshingly witty. Had she grown out of his view of her as too wet and immature to criticise government policy? He went on:

'I must say, I've not yet given much thought to my own New Year's Resolution. We've got till mid-December to register them anyway. But I think I can guess what mum and dad's is going to be: to *not* buy me my first ever set of new clothes even though I've now officially stopped growing and at seventeen it's even legal! That would be a really worthy sacrifice not just for me, but for them too, as they'd have to bear the shame of watching their only son wander the streets like a tramp. Or perhaps I'm being unfair and they'd deem it a great honour to have me still going around in public wearing clothes so threadbare, they're virtually see-through!'

John stared accusingly at each of his parents in turn, satisfied that referring to them in the third person had heightened the impact of his rant.

Anne shot a glance at her husband in the forlorn hope that he'd step up to the plate to defend the parental corner. As this clearly wasn't going to happen, she assumed the mantel herself.

'John, love, we know how frustrating it's been to have to wait so long for your first ever new set of clothes – well, trousers and shirt - and I know we did kind of promise we'd fix you up in September for the autumn term. But you know how tight things were financially, especially with our family .... bereavement in the summer', she had hesitated, looking across at grannie Mary whose husband had passed away in June. 'But we really are confident we'll be able to scrape together enough cash in the New Year, aren't we, dad?'

Mike wasn't as assertive as his wife and had been hoping up to this point that he wouldn't have to contribute to his own defence. Besides, surely his son's gratitude for yesterday's shoe upgrade couldn't have worn off already? Apparently, it could.

'To be fair, I *have* been earning a little extra these past few weeks, working in the neighbourhood repair outfit. People don't *have* to pay for services rendered, but most folk hand over a pound or two to show their appreciation. It's all getting put away towards your new clothes, son!'

Mike, still only in his late forties, had never felt entirely comfortable in his own skin after relinquishing his 'normal' job as a skilled fitter when it finally disappeared some fifteen years ago. Admittedly, it had been easier to adjust psychologically with two thirds of his colleagues in the same boat and having to rely on the Universal Basic Income. That was the price of automation combined with environmental disaster. Like most of his peer group, he had eventually managed to top up his meagre state subsistence allowance by earning a few extra pounds on the side. In his case, this was by putting in a few hours most weekdays at the neighbourhood repair shop.

Grannie Mary was smiling wistfully and should have liked to join the family conversation, but simply couldn't find the words. Though her mental powers had been steadily fading for some time now, at least she had recognised that her daughter-in-law's reference to bereavement related principally to herself. The pain of her loss was still raw even if she was no longer able to visualise her husband as he had looked in his final years.

She had recently confided her fading visual memory to Jenny whose thoughtful response was to create a collage for her gran out of a selection of photos of her grandad at various ages. The project was of limited success, as the last twenty years were missing owing to the impossibility of printing off digital photos from the defunct family computer, as this would have required using an equally defunct printer. So much, Jenny reflected, for technological progress and all the so-called *control* it was meant to give ordinary people over their lives.

Both parents sensed that, with lunch well and truly over, it was high time to issue the usual command to side the table and retire to the kitchen for the washing up, but neither was inclined to make the first move. Jenny took advantage of the indecision to extend family time a little longer.

'Tell you what, why don't we take up John and mum's suggestion and decide our New Year's Resolutions now rather than keep putting it off right up to the deadline?'

'It was hardly a suggestion. We were just using that to illustrate our points about TV ads and not being able to afford new clothes these days!' John objected.

'Never mind how the subject came up,' Anne supported her daughter. 'I think it's a splendid idea since we've all started thinking about it one way or another. I'll go and get the forms listing all the admissible categories. Won't be a minute.'

'Now it's getting exciting. You're making it sound like we're about to play one of those old-fashioned board games we've all been encouraged to go back to by the Ministry for Education, Culture and wots-its-name,' Mike contributed, hoping the current trend in thinking around the table might lead to this.

'For Heaven's sake,' John saw his chance to administer another dose of cynicism, 'I believe you're all actually going to enjoy seeing what more we can give up on top of literally everything we've given up already over the past god knows how many years! And, by the way, dad, it's the Ministry for Education, Culture and Spirituality, not wots-its-name.'

Anne returned to the dining table scrutinising a couple of sheets of official-looking paper as she regained her seat.

'I thought as much: we're encouraged to categorise our choices under one or more of the following headings: mitigation of environmental degradation, environmental enhancement and waste reduction. Then it lists examples...'

'.... ninety-five per cent of which we've already been doing for the last ten years.' John cut in again. 'After you've not bought any new clothes since the last Ice Age, repaired your existing ones to the nth degree, given up your private car, hardly ever left the house during the last six months, set the heating at max 18 degrees in mid-winter for just forty minutes daily, grown half your own vegetables and recycled two thirds of your own domestic waste – what remains to give up, enhance or mitigate?'

Jenny, being like her father, of a more compliant nature, felt the urge to feed something positive into the discussion:

'We all committed to avoiding food waste last year. I found that challenge really worthwhile as well as saving money, so is there anything else we could avoid wasting?'

Whenever his daughter put forward an idea, Mike's instinct was to support it, often without stopping to consider whether or not it was an especially good one:

'That's precisely what I was going to suggest and it follows on from our chat about clothes a moment ago. Don't worry, John, I've not suddenly changed my mind about buying your new clothes for next term! I mean making the ones we have last even longer...'

Anne knew where this was heading: 'You mean by not washing them so often. We must all have noticed the latest run of government promos featuring celebrities reminding us how washing our clothes is the main factor in wearing them out. I can't argue with that, after becoming the chief manual laundry woman since washing machines were outlawed. But aren't we missing the point here that the main cause of smelly clothes is smelly bodies? I'm surprised there hasn't been a related promo on the value of keeping our bodies clean without soap or water to reduce the need for washing clothes so often in the first place.'

Anne and her son enjoyed a similar symbiotic relationship to that which existed between father and daughter, so John naturally took this intervention as his cue to contribute on his mother's side.

'I can see the logic of clean bodies wearing clean clothes or dirty bodies wearing dirty clothes. So as a typical male teenager not over preoccupied with personal hygiene, I'd tend to vote for the latter. Much less effort in any case. As long as we all strive as a unit to achieve the same degree of smelliness, I think we might pull it off. Besides, going ever greener means effectively returning ever closer to nature. In our natural state humans like other animals would hardly wash at all.'

Mike saw that the game was up and his regret at letting the genie out of the bottle had subsided within seconds. All he could do was attempt to attenuate the appalling spectre of grime and squalor now haunting his family.

'My grandad used to attend a junior school next to a pig farm. The first few times you approached on foot, it seemed to stink out the whole neighbourhood let alone the school. But he reckoned after a couple of days no one noticed the pong anymore, so presumably it was the same for everyone in the surrounding area.'

John interpreted the analogy: 'So what we're saying is – once we've all got our personal hygiene down to near ground zero, after a short while we won't notice how smelly we are anymore. Trouble is, anyone coming in from the outside certainly will!'

'Unless they're doing the same thing. That reminds me of the philosophical conundrum about whether a tree falling in a forest actually makes any sound if there's no one around to hear it. Would we all smell bad if no one noticed the smell?'

Mike had again tried to redirect the course of the discussion.

'The technical answer is 'no', as the vibrations are only perceived as sound when they hit the ear drum and are transmitted to the brain by the nervous system....' Anne offered, hoping to trump the philosophical with the scientific answer.

'It's easy to tell you've not been to school for a long time', interjected Jenny. 'Even in the uninhabited forest there will always be creatures capable of hearing the sound. Your example is anthropocentric and shows the people who thought it up didn't care about biodiversity or endangered species. That's not acceptable in the world we live in today.'

'Well done, Jen, very politically correct', mocked John, though actually quite impressed with little siss for the second time. 'But I'd argue the old forest analogy is even more appropriate today, as there are hardly any species left to hear anything anymore. And the way things are going, we'll disappear soon so there'll be no humans left to pose such deep questions and it won't matter anyway!' A cruel thought about gran suddenly occurred to him which he suppressed at once.

Since his father-in-law's passing, it had fallen to Mike to assume the role of chief reminiscer:

'In the time before daily showering became the norm, ordinary folk just got one or two baths a week, if they were lucky. People used to boast about saving so much water and energy by showering instead of bathing when in fact all they did was use a bit less water more often. And there'd be those who'd shower for twenty minutes, the equivalent to two baths full and still feel virtuous!'

Then he remembered the point he'd intended to make before getting side-tracked:

'There are two main ways to cut down the need for washing so much. The one that comes most naturally to us older folk is sitting about doing very little physical work so we don't work up a sweat.'

Anne spared her husband the potential embarrassment of a clumsy attempt to explain the other she knew he had in mind:

'And the most economical and logical approach to bathing when water is short is to only wash regularly the parts that get the dirtiest. That's easily done with a couple of jugs of water standing in the bath.'

It was settled. They would all undertake to economise on water and energy through less and more judicious targeted bathing and make this official by each family member completing and signing the appropriate government form. Jenny was relieved that the issue of water temperature had escaped attention on this occasion. No doubt the question of reducing the thermostat setting by up to ten degrees would occur to someone for next year's offering.

The conversation didn't end quite there, however, as it was resolved that everyone should add a further personalised sacrifice for the sake of authenticity and credibility. Anne mentioned she'd heard of forms being rejected and individuals or whole families fined for flippant or unrealistic promises. This gave rise to considerable mirth and rivalry between John and Jenny who competed for a while to dream up the silliest examples they could think of: scraping out earwax to make candles (Jenny's idea) or collecting belly button fluff which over time might be sufficiently voluminous to stuff a quilt (John's). Inevitably, the imaginings of the two youngest family members became cruder and ruder as they proceeded with the washing up.

Gran was the only one who had not participated verbally in the conversation over dinner. This was as much due to her hearing impairment as indifference brought on by her incipient dementia. She had tried to conceal her lack of engagement by periodically looking round the table and alternately smiling and frowning as various family members spoke. She was a little offended that no one had courted her views on matters discussed. Had she been asked, she would certainly have attempted to put them across as best she could.

Now, with everyone gone, she could make her way unnoticed out into the rear garden as was her custom just before dark. She had always enjoyed the mystical experience of observing the rising and setting of the sun while breathing in the fresh garden air. Such freshness was enhanced by the array of herbs, shrubs and trees, some of them fruit bearing, which the present family and their precursors had had the foresight to plant and cultivate over the years.

Since the summer, she had another more personal reason for frequenting the garden. Towards the rear fence there was a more open area which had purposely been kept clear of trees. Here, Mary was able to sit down for a moment's rest on the memorial bench her son-in-law had made in honour of her husband who had passed away from cancer five short months ago. It had been too late in the summer for the grass to completely recover around the grave, so Mary took some comfort in discerning its contours. She had vaguely understood at the time that the grave's precise location would need to be remembered for future use – almost certainly her own.

After the children had washed up and retired to their bedrooms, Mike spent a while in the kitchen shoring up several leaks around the door where an annoying draft had been getting through. Also, from the late evening, an array of slugs had been squeezing through invisible gaps and leaving alarmingly circuitous trails all over the floor and walls. No one had ever seen by what precise route they had entered or eventually slipped away. Someday soon, in milder weather, he'd steel himself to spend an hour pointing the external brickwork.

He retired to bed later that night relieved that the latest ordeal facing the family had been tackled reasonably well. The communal New Year's Resolutions were more or less nailed down and the further deprivations would at least be partly balanced out by financial savings. Provided there wasn't yet another fuel and water price hike, which was far from guaranteed.

Anne was strangely ambivalent about how her Sunday had gone. She, like her husband, had been relieved to find an opportune moment to meet the government's ever more oppressive demands on her family. However, she still felt terribly guilty and angry with herself for sending her son out into the hostile world in unsuitable footwear. She suspected he had lied to the police officer in order to conceal her error. Her gratitude and pride in her son made her all the more determined to ensure he got his promised new clothes for the start of next term.

John had been watching his grandmother's wanderings around the garden through his bedroom window and immediately guessed where she was heading once out of view. He wished he'd made an effort to bring her into the conversation earlier, but then so should everyone else. He didn't relax until he saw Mary return some minutes later looking more peaceful and yet at the same time invigorated.

His little sister's remarks this afternoon had brought home to him that at fourteen she was growing into a proper individual in her own right. He'd been unfair to dismiss her as a weak-willed wimp as he tended to view their dad.

He'd sleep well tonight and looked forward to catching up with Mandy after Saturday's disappointment.

Howard's meeting with the minister had been tolerable after all. Sir John Beecham had a knack of making virtually any subject sound the most natural in the world and their conversation around proposed new interment legislation had been no exception. On this occasion, Sir John had lightened the atmosphere with a hackneyed anecdote about how a not very bright junior civil servant had confused interment with internment.

Sir John Beecham's narrative went: Fee increases for various burial services were totally justified in terms of supply and demand. Regulations concerning minimum depths for garden graves and the administration charge payable to the local authorities for registering and archiving relevant records were also eminently reasonable. However, Sir John's idea to make the hire of registered grave diggers compulsory even for garden burials had clearly occurred to the minister spontaneously, as it had not been mentioned in the research brief. Howard deemed this totally unnecessary, but had not felt it was his place to object.

CHAPTER 3: THAT SEVEN-DAY ITCH

John's expectation of a good night's sleep ahead of the school week proved justified. He awoke refreshed and dimly aware that Hypnos and Eros had joined forces to craft him an exquisite sequence of dreams. Most other students in his Year 12 class, he was sure, would be dreading that Monday morning feeling, whereas he, in eager anticipation of meeting up with Mandy at last, was on top of the world.

Anne, like most diligent mothers, felt morally obliged to rise with her children at seven o'clock and today was no exception. At fourteen and sixteen, they were beyond the age where they needed their breakfast preparing, but as a dutiful mum, she felt they both appreciated, Jenny especially, being waved off to school by at least one parent. She dared to hope that this little ritual infused them with a little extra fortitude to face whatever lay beyond the sinister school gates as she recalled them from her own unhappy childhood experience.

Mike and her mother would not arise until after half eight, so with John and Jenny gone, she enjoyed a few quiet moments to herself to reflect on life and where, if anywhere, it appeared to be heading. Like most adults in their forties these days, particularly those with parental responsibilities, she was not engaged in any paid employment as such, and had to structure her own daily routine pretty well from start to finish. Unconsciously influenced by yesterday's great family debate about water economy and energy saving, her first impulse was to head for the shower.

Minutes later, Anne was luxuriating under warm jets of water, rinsing herself all over at leisure and losing track of time. Suddenly, a sharp engine noise snapped her out of her daydream and she realised her shower had run far longer than the acceptable norm.

She jumped out of the cubicle at once, snatched a bath towel and, swirling it round herself, ran to the bathroom window where she spotted what was unmistakably a detector van parking right outside their house. A stream of possible guilt sources instantly beset her. A detector van could be on any one of an ever-growing range of missions.

Of course, there was the old favourite target in the form of the unpaid TV licence. Although the BBC had at last been absorbed five years ago by the Government Department for Broadcasting and Information, the pretence that the annual fee was a licence rather than a plain tax still persisted. There was no way a law-abiding citizen could escape liability to pay it given the BBCs ubiquitous TV and radio broadcasts which often interrupted those of other networks in order to announce the government's latest schemes.

But Anne knew her husband was sure to have kept up the payments, so in all likelihood, the van crew had detected an environmental breach or was snooping around in the hope of finding one. Modern favourites were, of course, energy over consumption or wastage, inadequate recycling or – EXCESSIVE WATER USE! Houses nowadays were all fitted with gas and electric meters which could signal surges in energy consumption to the government-owned energy company and thus trigger a home visit. However, as far as she knew, they hadn't yet introduced similar technology to deal with water usage.

By the time she had dried and made herself sufficiently decent to answer the door, to Anne's relief she could see that the van crew had decided to call on a house on the opposite side of the road. She still felt it wise to keep an eye out by the front room window in case they were doing the rounds of the whole neighbourhood rather than just a single *targeted domestic raid*, as she'd heard them called.

She waited tensely for a good fifteen minutes before three operators exited the house across the road and returned to the van. A further few minutes passed during which Anne imagined sinister conversations taking place within the van and the necessary paperwork being completed.

When the van finally drew off, Anne's tension turned to resentment. So, what if she'd indulged herself a little in the shower just now? Surely, she was entitled to enjoy a few extra jets of warm water to compensate her for all the deprivations of the past year and with even worse to come in January! Her resentment grew into full-blown anger at the government for introducing ever more draconian measures and at humanity in general for getting itself into such a ludicrous position. How could one supposedly intelligent species use up half the world's resources over two or three generations and virtually ruin the planet?

Just as her mental anguish was beginning to subside, Anne became aware of the physical discomfort emanating from her bladder. Surprised by the sudden noise outside, she had been in such a rush to snatch her clothes and get dressed that she had skipped her usual practice of peeing in the shower. This practice gave her the satisfaction of knowing that she was saving money and water as well as increasing her chances of weighing in at just under seventy kilogrammes on the bathroom scales. Still eager to check her weight, she rushed upstairs, used the toilet and undressed again in the bathroom. At last, she was able to enjoy a moment of deferred gratification as she came in at just 69.9kg.

Anne had had a frustratingly short career as a teacher, but still clung on to the hope that she'd be allowed to return to her beloved profession once Jenny hit age sixteen in just over a year's time. At just forty-three, sitting at home for the past seventeen years bringing up the children and looking after the home hardly fulfilled all her aspirations.

Whenever she felt downhearted, Anne had the unhelpful habit of reviewing her curriculum vitae up to when her working life was put on hold. The story ran: University Degree with First Class Honours in English followed by one year's teacher training which brought her to age twenty-two. Then four years of exciting and successful work as a teacher until she met and married Mike. One more year in teaching with promotion prospects on the horizon before the birth of John which sounded the death knell for her career at age twenty-seven.

Each time, on reaching the end of this repetitive loop through time, Anne was beset by doubts as to whether she could ever cope again in the classroom even given the chance to refresh her training. Life had changed beyond recognition over the past sixteen years, her very own children being a perfect example of societal transformation.

Now she had the rest of the morning and perhaps the afternoon to consider her own individual sacrifice to enter on the government form. She hoped the rest of the family had the same sense of urgency and she wouldn't have to nag anyone too much.

Of all the family members, Jenny had been the most subdued as she retired to her room following the Sunday meal. It was all very well everyone agreeing to shower less often and use less water, but unlike her, they hadn't just been taught a series of personal hygiene modules in SRA or Social Responsibility and Awareness classes at school.

It was only last week that their form teacher had given her group a half-hour session on the importance of regular bathing with several references to the consequences of poor hygiene, especially for pubescent youths such as herself. Fair enough: too frequent washing removes the protective oils from the skin.

However, if unwashed by the seventh day, this same skin starts to get rather itchy. And then there was the inequality between the sexes. Adolescent boys' sweat, even after the most vigorous sports exercise could hardly out-stink a girl's period pong. Reflecting on this, she was simultaneously shocked and amused by the grossness of her own musings.

More like her father, Jenny was less rebellious towards authority than her brother and mother, but this washing less and poor hygiene business was a bridge too far. She'd just have to find a way to cheat for the sake of her own sanity and hope to appease her conscience by making up for her deceit through her individual choice of New Year's Resolution. She spent a while considering what this might be and concluded that diet was her best bet. She was sure she could commit to cutting out all foods with a bad carbon footprint and those containing fat, sugar and salt. She had been impressed by the nutrition modules in SRA classes which explained the link between good health and social responsibility, in other words, healthier food leading to better wellbeing hence less illness equals less pressure on the health service. This would also qualify on the government form under the heading 'saving resources' which allowed for broad interpretation.

This latter reflection, however, brought her back to concerns over gran whose deterioration had clearly accelerated in the wake of grandad's death. She sensed that the situation would be easier for gran if her husband had been laid to rest in a graveyard some distance away or even cremated as used to happen until recently. It was disturbing too for the whole family to see gran wandering off to the bottom of the garden at least once daily and often looking more confused and distressed on her return than when she had set out from the house.

Adding to Jenny's torment, was the grisly fear she harboured that grandad might somehow be disinterred, possibly by a wild animal or a freak seismic event such as she vaguely recalled from an old horror film. She tried to dismiss this as childish paranoia, but was defeated by her own vivid imagination. What would happen when gran eventually passed away? Wouldn't mum want to bury her next to grandad in the garden, thus effectively disinterring him for a short while at least? And what if the geology of the earth forced them to rest her on top of grandad? That would mean she'd be lying even closer to the surface. And, to return to freak seismic events, there had been an increasing number of these in recent years and their link to severe and accelerated climate change was beyond doubt.

At breakfast before school on Monday, Jenny impatiently waited for a moment alone with her father and asked, attempting to feign simple curiosity:
'Dad, do we have a record of how deep under the earth grandad was buried?'
'I'm not sure we have an official record. Let me remember, now. I'm sure the regulation was that it had to be at least five feet under. Why do you ask?'
'Just wondered.'

She was more at ease discussing this with her father her as grandad's son-in-law than she would have been with her mother who was his daughter, after all. However, she was too ashamed of her real feelings to reveal them to either parent. At some point, she would endeavour to summon up the courage to talk the subject over with her brother who had at last started to take her more seriously. At least that was one saving grace of maturing into adulthood!

Like most teenagers with ailing grandparents, John had grown up with the realisation that sooner or later he would have to face losing them. They had always lived nearby even before moving in a few years ago and so he was naturally closer to his gran and grandad than most of his peers were to their theirs. Nevertheless, he knew he would not be unduly devastated when they eventually passed away.

On school days, John generally put house and home out of mind within seconds of closing the front door. Today was no exception and the images of his grandmother groping around in the back garden the night before had disappeared without trace. Friday evening to Monday morning had seemed like an eternity and he was savouring the prospect of meeting Mandy again at last.

However, the more he thought about her excuse for not turning up on Saturday, the more he suspected it might after all have been a white lie intended to let him down gently. How bizarre that modern-day parents should insist on their seventeen-year-old daughter staying in to catch up on homework on a Saturday night! Mandy was hardworking enough in lessons and surely if young people went out at all these days, it would be on a Saturday night with homework reasonably left till Sunday.

John was so preoccupied with his Mandy musings that he didn't once give a thought to the performance of his newly resoled shoes until he almost tripped on approaching the bus stop. Seated on the bus, he wondered whether his near fall had had anything to do with his dad's handywork and was relieved to observe that the new soles were still securely attached. Even as a small child, when walking deep in thought, he tended to drag his feet and this trait had led to many a grazed knee or twisted ankle.

During the ten-minute bus journey to school, John mentally reviewed the day ahead. He had chosen a conventional combination of Advanced Level subjects in the sixth form: English, History and Sociology on top of what was now compulsory Citizenship with his form tutor group. It was only for English that he shared classes with Mandy who was in a different form and had opted for French and Information Technology.

When he first became attracted to Mandy back in October, John had considered changing one of his options in order to spend more time in her presence, but had decided against this in case he became too distracted from his studies. A mature and wise decision, he thought, having observed how his parents managed their own relationship by keeping apart most of the time. At least now they were in the sixth form, he could catch up with Mandy in the common room once a week when their private study periods coincided.

John didn't in fact see Mandy until after his History class before lunch and even then, his heart sank as he realised that he'd forgotten the hour-long lesson would consist mainly of a test essay on recent topic work. His homework had been to revise for this essay on late twentieth century environmental movements, but he had ignored this as usual thanks to his powerful retentive memory which had thus far ensured academic success. His memory did not, however, serve him so well in day-to-day matters such as remembering whether he had a test or not! Now was the testing season for most subjects on the curriculum and it occurred to him only now that this was probably why Mandy's parents were so keen for her to extend her home study time.

At last, the lesson was over and John was able to join Mandy for lunch in the canteen. She'd just had a French grammar test.
'How did you find the test?' was John's obvious question as they sat down.
'I think I did okay. I can learn all the verb forms in a table and write them out no problem. I just mix them up trying to use them in a sentence!'

'I'm always getting the dates in History mixed up, but don't reckon they mark you down too much for that, so I just concentrate on getting events in the right order. In history of environmental movements, it's easy to get the names confused: they all contain similar words like *green, earth* and *peace* in various combinations...'

Their conversation continued in a similar vein and didn't get much beyond mundane concerns. However, the mere fact that Mandy was happy to chat over lunch to John without embarrassment in full view of their peers gave him courage enough to suggest a rendezvous later in the week. He was delighted when she agreed to come round to his place after school on Wednesday for a joint study period. She hoped that this pretext would appease her parents.

John got home from school as usual around half four and went up to his room to get the bulk of his homework out of the way within an hour or so. This was no mean triumph of self-discipline given that every few seconds thoughts about Mandy strayed into his consciousness. He then came down for a snack tea in the dining room on his own, as his parents tended to dine together about half an hour later. He knew that Jenny, whose school was within easy walking distance, would have disappeared to her room when she got home much earlier. She would only re-emerge to raid the fridge for a late evening snack after everyone else had been and gone. He'd never bothered to ask what she got up to during the intervening hours.

John dawdled a little longer than usual over his tea-time sandwiches, daydreaming and trying to convince himself that nothing over the next forty-eight hours could get in the way of Mandy coming round after school on Wednesday. His parents came in just as he was getting up to leave the dining room. Surprised to find John still there, Anne spontaneously, though a little hesitantly, sat down by him and asked him to stay for a chat about a serious matter.

'No, I'm not going to interrogate you about your personal New Year's Resolution, though that's important too, of course', Anne began. 'It's about gran.'

John instantly recalled observing his gran's movements the

night before and felt not a little guilt for having put this entirely out of his mind for the past twenty-four hours.

'I know we've all been concerned about how she's deteriorated over the past six months since grandad died,' Anne continued, 'but there's something else we need to be mindful of...' She looked across at Mike who had remained standing, sullenly avoiding eye contact with either of them. After a moment of awkward indecision, he took over the conversation as tacitly agreed.

'The thing is that next week will be gran's seventy-eighth birthday. From then on, she'll only qualify for the minimal treatment allowance under the new NHS rules. I don't know whether they teach you this at school, but the annual treatment budget allocated to each person depends on their age. It means that instead of the State paying more for treatment as people got older as used to happen, now it's the other way round and reduces incrementally year by year. It gets down to just one thousand pounds max per year when you hit seventy-eight...

'So, thinking ahead, we have several options.' Anne resumed where Mike had trailed off.
'We can just try to manage gran's decline ourselves as we are doing now and hope she passes away peacefully as many old folks do. Or, if she does require NHS treatment, once the meagre allowance is spent, try to top it up ourselves. To do that, dad says we would have to borrow on the value of the house and pay back over God knows how many years. What they used to call a re-mortgage...'

'Or move down.' Mike said. 'And it's not easy to move house these days.'

'Or send her to a care home before she becomes ill in the first place....' Anne quickly added in a tone that suggested the idea was utterly anathema to her, hence purely theoretical.

John was quite flattered to have been invited in on this conversation – a mark, no doubt, of his perceived maturity. It was time he contributed.

'Is that not the wrong way round? Wouldn't you send an elderly relative to a care home only once they became too ill to manage in their home rather than before they reached that stage?'

'It *is* rather counter-intuitive. Officially, it's so that they can make a smooth transition and consent to what's happening. From what I've heard, though, it's so the State can manage the reduction in health care expenditure without inconvenient fuss from the family.'

'So, the rule about decreasing treatment costs as people get older still applies even in care homes?'

'It absolutely does. But they would argue that the State is bearing the huge cost of accommodating them in the home.'

'So how do they make that work financially?' John's genuine concern was beginning to show through his habitual veneer of teenage insouciance.

'A lot of very old people in this position have no remaining family ties and so when they die, the State gets their wealth which more than covers the initial cost of minimally looking after them. Plus....' Anne paused, half wishing she'd not begun her last sentence which only begged further questioning.

'Plus what?' John obliged.

'Plus, I think there are cases of doctors somehow being allowed to euthanise old folks who have no or little capacity to express consent.'

Anne delivered this final insight with the relief of someone confessing a dark secret.

The three of them remained in subdued silence until Mike, who had been standing by the door, at last approached his wife and son and sat by them. This was an instinctive effort to display solidarity to compensate for a guilty awareness of his status as Mary's only non-blood relation within the family group.

At this point, Jenny slipped into the dining room on the way to the kitchen. She had left her room to raid the fridge for her routine mid-evening snack. She sensed at once that something more serious and personal was being discussed than a dreary sequel to Sunday afternoon's debate about how to save the planet.

'I guess you've been worrying about gran,' she offered. The others naturally assumed she'd been eavesdropping at the door and exchanged horrified glances.
'I saw her looking so sad and lost in the garden again today visiting grandad's grave. Don't you think we ought to get her a pet to take her mind off things and keep her company?'

The question of a pet was a far more vexed one than would have been the case just five years ago. Recent legislation prohibited dog ownership altogether unless proof could be produced that applicants had adequate private grounds to walk them. The stage before that had been to reintroduce costly licences ostensibly to cover street cleaning costs, but most owners and would-be owners saw through this scheme as a cynical means to make dog ownership prohibitively expensive for most people. And, in any case, the authorities either couldn't or wouldn't coordinate street cleaning services effectively once the licences were introduced.

'It would have to be a very small dog, preferably a lapdog for gran to look after and so it would get enough exercise confined to our back garden. And we'd still have to pay the ridiculous licence fee!' Mike felt guilty for ending on a pecuniary note and wished he could go back and reorder his last sentence.

Jenny had meanwhile gathered more intuitive information by

scanning each family member's facial expression and body language in turn.

'Is gran ill again or something?'

'You're not far off,' John came in. 'I think we should tell her. She's old enough.'

Jenny felt a surge of gratitude and warmth towards her brother for acknowledging her at last. She had always assumed this leap of faith would come first from one of her parents, probably her dad.

The whole family minus gran remained in the dining room for a further few minutes as Jenny was fully initiated into the clan.

By the time the earnest talk was over, Jenny returned sullen to her room. She had completely forgotten about feeling peckish and the meagre barely palatable snack she'd originally come down for.

During the whole discussion about Mary, no one had stopped to wonder where she was. As she rarely ate in the evening these days it was a safe bet that she wouldn't enter the kitchen. In fact, she had been in the garden sitting by and contemplating her husband's grave.

Howard shuffled the papers on his desk that same Monday afternoon. He reflected on how the new burial regulations would no doubt sail through parliament within a week or two. The political process had significantly speeded up since the abolition of the second chamber and any legislation introduced in mid-December was unlikely to cause a public stir. The minds of humble folks would be focused on making the best of what was left of the festive season. If anything did catch the public eye, it would be the far juicier legislation being prepared for the New Year by other government departments.

CHAPTER 4: THE SANTA CLAUS CLAUSE

Tuesday passed without major incident or further heart-rending family discussions, but the next day, December first, impacted all members of the Greenway household to some degree.

Jenny's thoughts immediately turned to the Advent calendar which her mother had heroically conjured up at the eleventh hour by reviving last year's. In fact, the calendar was now in its third incarnation. The reason for Anne's delay in announcing it to the family was that substituting tiny gifts for the chocolates of two Christmases ago required a great deal resourceful ingenuity.

She had just made the deadline by stuffing the last three compartments with recycled contents from even older Christmas crackers. The task at last over, Anne heartily wished that the twenty-four-day advent myth invented by Protestant Germans in the nineteenth century had been suppressed in the same way that the traditional Teutonic tree had been banned on environmental grounds. Her resentment soon passed, however, as she anticipated the fun and excitement her efforts would engender.

The first day of December had another, less welcome, significance. It was a signal to Anne to remind her clan to commit to their personal New Year's Resolutions so she could write them all up and submit on time to the relevant government department for approval. She wasted no time broaching the topic once all the family had assembled for breakfast. Her anxieties proved largely unfounded, as clearly, several nights' sleeping on the question had yielded results.

Jenny was proud to announce her intended renunciation of

fatty, sugary and salty food, though Anne wisely advised her to give up just one of these for now so she wouldn't have to think of something new for the next two years. Though that would stop her cutting down on them all right away to enjoy the health benefits.

John, whose seventeenth birthday was coming up in February, declared he'd renounce all material gifts. To his parents' pleasant surprise and relief, his definition of 'material gifts' included money. Instead, he'd be happy to be treated to a cultural outing to the theatre or a concert, assuming these still existed in two months' time.

Anne had already made her husband's mind up for him. Since he had become much less physically active these days, she saw no reason why most of the remaining clothes in his wardrobe shouldn't last another year. With just a little tailoring, at least one of his now redundant and slightly worn suits could be transformed into casual wear about the house. He already had a fair stock of scruffy but warm garments for working in the garage or garden.

As for herself, she would sell off several items of jewellery containing precious metals which could be melted down and no doubt refashioned into something essential for the modern economy. She just hoped this wouldn't be rejected by the authorities on the grounds that selling even one's own items for personal gain was against the spirit of the exercise. Or – even worse - that she'd be expected to sacrifice their monetary as well as their sentimental value.

Finally, it was time to consider the delicate matter of her own mother's contribution. Unfortunately, and unjustly in Anne's view, having reached the age qualifying for minimal NHS benefits, gran had not been granted a dispensation from taxation or further sacrifices. This included the New Year's Resolution and Anne could not for the life of her think how her mother could conceivably use or consume less of anything than she already was. She hardly ate, hadn't bought anything new for over two years and never used public, never mind private, transport. The only time she even breathed slightly more than strictly necessary was during her periodic ramblings around the garden.

Anne at last decided that she ought to talk the issue over with her mother. It was only fair to try to explain to her what this whole thing was about and give her the chance of retaining some agency over her own fate. Besides, just because nowadays Mary rarely appeared engaged in family discussions or initiated conversation didn't mean she was incapable of grasping anything that was going on around her.

When Anne knocked and entered tentatively, Mary was in her room sitting in her armchair with the television turned on at low volume.

'Mum, we've got to talk about this ruddy New Year's Resolution business that first came up at the weekend. Do you remember? We've all made a family commitment and now we're into December already, it's time to make our own individual commitments to saving….'

'I know dear,' Mary interrupted her daughter looking serious but still smiling gently. 'I've been thinking over very carefully what I could do to…,' she paused in search of the right word '… contribute. I'd like to die early next year to join Arthur. That way, I'd save everyone a lot of trouble and somehow help the planet, I'm sure.'

John walked on air to the stop that morning and daydreamed throughout the bus journey. He mechanically disembarked outside his school and only fully came back down to earth on reaching the entrance.

Ironically, Wednesday was the one day he and Mandy shared

no classes, as their common subject, English, wasn't on the timetable. He didn't even get a chance to speak to her besides a brief mutual greeting as they crossed in the corridor just before lunch. At least this allowed Mandy to confirm she was still able and willing to accompany him home at the end of the day.

They hadn't directly discussed the likely social awkwardness of being seen leaving school together by their peers, but John had made a prior arrangement with Mandy to wait for her by the post office one bus stop away from school. On meeting up at last, the two decided to walk the rest of the way to John's house rather than taking the bus, so they could chat more freely.

'So, your parents didn't have second thoughts about letting you join me for an after-school study session?'

'No, but they have interrogated me a couple more times since the weekend. I just kept my cool and tried to be as matter of fact as possible. They're overprotective, but not stupid. I'm sure they realise they need to give me a bit of space for a social life!'

Over the half-hour brisk walk to the Greenway home, they covered two main topics. The first was talking shop about school – how they found their various subjects and teachers, particularly the ones they shared for English. They both preferred Mr Jacobs who radiated a real love of literature and entertained his students with his original teaching methods. One of these was to regale them with some of his own short works including some ingenious limericks which artfully fell just short of being inappropriate for their age group. As an end-of-lesson treat, he often set them creative writing tasks which were not strictly part of the curriculum. His way of rebelling against the system, Mandy suggested.

This segued into a broader discussion of how they each felt about life and society in general.

John, for whom nothing could feel more uncool than peer chat about New Year's Resolutions, was taken aback when Mandy broached the subject herself. It seemed her parents and younger brother had faced a similar challenge to his own folks, whereas in their case it was Mandy's dad who brought the subject up and convened the family colloquium.

John was initially surprised to hear that Mandy's lot had opted for a similar commitment to cut down water consumption. Then it occurred to him that essentially, everyone was in the same boat except that less well-off families had to cut back on the basics sooner than the better off.

As he brought Mandy to their front door, in a strange way it seemed to John that their respective families had almost already met through similar shared experience and hoped this would make introductions less awkward.

'Hello Mandy, pleased to meet you!' John knew his mum had been hovering around the hallway anticipating their arrival, eager to make a good impression. He wondered if one day he'd get a similar warm reception from Mandy's parents. Mike, predictably assuming an auxiliary role, had moved into position a few metres behind Anne as the doorbell rang. Too far away for a handshake, he greeted her with wave and smile which John adjudged to be as good a performance as could be expected from his dad. But the best performance of all was Jenny's for graciously absenting herself from the welcoming party altogether. She'd choose her moment to peek in at Mandy later on, John was sure.

Not long before his son's girlfriend arrived, Mike had returned home from the neighbourhood repair shop. Here, he'd managed to satisfy a number of supplicants, two of whom he could justifiably call 'customers', as they'd been kind enough to reward his efforts to the tune of five pounds in total. He'd have to surrender twenty percent of his takings – a whole pound – towards the collective's overheads and other running costs, but what was left would buy perhaps the collar and cuffs of John's new shirt.

His most challenging and time-consuming pro bono job of the day had been disassembling and reassembling a twenty-year-old vacuum cleaner. This was all in the cause of fixing a small electrical fault for an elderly couple who, he imagined, might well not live to see the day it failed again. And if they did, they would be hard put to find an adequate replacement. Vacuum cleaners were bound up in history with carpets. All modern flooring surfaces needed was an occasional good old-fashioned sweep. With a dwindling active workforce, it wasn't as though everyone was too busy out at work to accomplish this modest domestic chore.

As he set off home, his batteries recharged by a degree of recovered self-worth, Mike continued to reflect on the old couple's newly repaired machine. It wouldn't surprise him if it eventually met its end at the hands of an environmental inspection team. Once they had finished pulling up the old couple's carpets on public health grounds, they might as well carry off the redundant vacuum cleaner into the bargain!

Mike's hard-earned four pounds went straight into a jar secreted in the garage workshop where it joined the twenty or so he had already managed to put away since he'd resolved to spare John further sartorial disappointment. He'd not yet summoned the courage to quiz Anne on the subject, but assumed she too was managing to save a little from her household budget. He guiltily recalled his first ever real infatuation with a girl over thirty years ago and how much importance as a teenager he attached to 'impressing through dressing'. But Mike knew he was one of that final generation to expect better for their children than they had for themselves.

As a qualified engineer forced into extremely early retirement, the repair shop was the highlight of Mike's day. His hours spent outside the community repair shop were excruciatingly dull and unfulfilling for the most part. Over the past two months, a rare exception to this were the couple of hours spent in his garage refashioning his son's second-hand shoes.

Anne had been more shocked than moved on hearing her mother talk so matter-of-factly about her wish to join her husband in death. It was not, however, a simple matter to interpret her declaration. Did her mother mean that with Arthur gone and missing him so much, she had little interest left in life? Or, as her precise time reference to 'early next year' suggested, was she considering ending her own life?

Voluntary suicide or euthanasia had become a mainstream discussion topic in recent years and had a growing number of advocates both in the medical and wider community, not to mention an increasing number of politicians. Countries across the world had already introduced legislation to legalise and facilitate the practice with England a relative outlier in this global movement.

Unable to decide between asking Mary to clarify her meaning or telling her not to be ridiculous, Anne took the midway course of not responding at all. She left her mother's room and went straight into the bathroom next door to collect herself for a few moments. She then went down to the kitchen and returned to her mother's room with a cup of cocoa which she knew she normally enjoyed at any time of day.

'Mum, you may feel differently in a little while. I know it's hard to imagine when you're going through a bereavement, but I'm sure the worst will have passed in a couple of months' time. Then life will seem worth living again.'

'I've got over the grief pretty well already, love. Yes, I do miss him, but that's not really it. I... I worry about losing my marbles and all the terrible things I've heard about it. Not knowing where

I am, not recognising people, even the family, mixing up my memories about the past with ....'

'What's going on in the present...' Anne couldn't help completing her mother's thought. A teacherly habit. 'Well, you're not showing any signs of losing your marbles today!'

'Today must be a good day. Even this morning, I couldn't remember my grandchildren's names and the more I worried about it, the worse it got.'

'That's just normal. The more you fear something, the more you make it happen.'
Anne knew she was defaulting to denial and reassurance mode which, while it may smooth things over in the short term, really just risked putting off the awkward conversation until too late.
Her mother appeared to have run out of words and sat staring vacantly. This was a signal to Anne to refocus on the here and now, which meant thinking about the children's evening meal or tea as it was now generally called on weekdays.

Jenny was standing outside John's bedroom door eavesdropping on the conversation between him and Mandy whom she was dying to meet. Her hopes of hearing something saucy going on between them were sorely dashed, however. The only discussion alternated between views on school life and the homework they were tackling together. She was torn between politely knocking on the door and barging in uninvited, then pretending to be surprised to find her brother had a guest. She opted for a middle course by simultaneously knocking and entering.

'Oh, sorry, I didn't know you had company,' was Jenny's opening gambit. 'Is this your friend from school I've been hearing about?'
'Yes, she's called Mandy in case you didn't hear while you were standing with your ear glued to the door!'
Jenny felt herself blush slightly, but wasn't unduly disconcerted by her unmasking. John would have probably joked the same

way whether he knew what she'd been up to or not. And he had probably just been guessing...

'You know I wouldn't dream of eavesdropping! Anyway, mum said your girlfriend was coming over to help you study....'

'Well, help each other, actually,' Mandy came to John's defence. 'Do *you* get lots of homework?'

After two more minutes exchanging platitudes, Jenny and Mandy instinctively warmed to each other and John relaxed with a sense of gratitude towards his sister for being far less troublesome than she could have been had she put her mind to it. Another sign of her growing maturity!

Nearly two hours of collaborative homework later, Anne called everyone down for the evening meal as she exceptionally called it in their visitor's honour. Usually, during the week it was a case of everyone fending for themselves at tea time, so John was chuffed that his mum had made a special effort on what was really only a special occasion for himself.

Conversation around the table was remarkably relaxed considering the topics were predictably glum. Whether Mandy's family had considered their New Year's Resolutions yet immediately came to Mike's mind, but the theme was quickly despatched by John who filled everyone in on what he'd learned on their way home. In a world of high and rising unemployment, it would have been an act of gross tactlessness to ask about Mandy's parents' occupations, so Anne skilfully put the question in terms of how her family spent their time.

Mandy's mother did in fact receive a salary working for local government in waste management. Her father, however, like Mike, had been laid off some years ago, but used to work in the building trade. Nowadays, he earned a meagre income picking up odd DIY jobs by word of mouth. Jenny suggested the two fathers would no doubt get on a treat.

Jenny discreetly brought up the issue of first new clothes while complimenting Mandy on the smartness of her outfit. Mandy intrigued all by proudly explaining that her top and skirt had both been her mother's. They had stood the test of time owing to the high-quality tailoring and careful washing by hand over the years. This gave Mike and Anne food for thought, as they'd not expected to invest in their son's clothes for the long term, assuming he'd probably wear them out by the end of the sixth form.

John saw Mandy off on to the bus after nine. At least public transport could usually be relied on since private motorcar ownership had virtually disappeared. They would see each other again in English tomorrow where they'd discuss when John could come home with Mandy to visit her parents.

No one had remarked on Mary's absence that evening despite Anne's efforts to encourage her to break with her usual habit and come down for the family meal and meet John's friend. Mary was sitting listlessly in her armchair in front of her TV which she had turned low mainly to serve as a comforting background hubbub of human voices. She had not consciously decided against joining the rest of her family, but without the trigger of hunger to remind her about dinner, she had lost track of time. Although communication with others had become more challenging for Mary in recent months, she still had a strong sense of self and of her own needs and desires.

Following the morning's cabinet meeting, The Minister for Health and Wellbeing was left in no doubt as to the inevitable future course of public policy and legislation emanating from her department. However, she felt she needed advice from a trusted and more experienced colleague before setting her Civil Servants team to task. She pressed a button on her desk which instantly summoned the PA of the Minister for The Economy, Finance and Taxation who was also her current lover.

'Hello there. This is Hazel Cruickshank. We've just come out of the cabinet office and I was wondering if I could catch Sir John before.....'

'He's just got in this minute from the cabinet meeting himself. I'll see if he's available.'

He bloody well better had be available! The reflex thought shot across Hazel's mind during the split-second wait before the reassuring answer came.

'Hello Hazel. I suspected you'd want to talk this through. Perhaps better if I come over to your office.'

Hazel was ushered into her lover's parlour with appropriate decorum. She took care in her body language to reveal nothing of their relationship to any of the junior civil servants present. Sir John immediately asked the latter to leave the two of them alone as soon as Hazel was seated opposite him at his outsize desk.

'This is a really big ask if not a tall order', she began. 'So far, we've been able to nudge the public more towards accepting voluntary end of life on various rational grounds. Alleviation of suffering and reducing the burden on family were always strong moral arguments. The new religious case is also now getting through to people, but I've always believed that it's the financial incentive that motivates people the most. One aspect, as we all know, is not having to worry about the cost of health care rising as people get older while NHS support declines rapidly. People don't want to admit it, but the other aspect is even more powerful: family members being eager to get their hands on an inheritance.'

'I'm sure that's a pretty accurate analysis even if you do put it rather bluntly, Hazel.'

'And this new pressure we're under to effectively seize half the dearly departed's assets undermines that. It contradicts the broad logic which has so far made it possible to defend earlier measures. And even the existing measures would have been regarded as unpalatable and unethical barely a decade ago. I think this is just a bridge too far.'

Sir John, sat back pensively in his chair. 'What we've found in recent times is that once the public gets over the initial shock of bolder government policies, they become inured to the aftershocks of add-on legislation. So, in this case, the big hurdle to get over was making euthanasia in exceptional circumstances more readily available and acceptable to most of the population. The next step was to broaden these circumstances, let's be honest, by stealth. And this largely got under the radar of the media who were more focussed on criticising the budget cuts for adult social care which were introduced at the same time...'

'Surely, though, taxing the estates of old people who voluntarily end their lives will be perceived as unjust, as they're already saving the State a fortune.'

'Yes, but the saving to the State won't be uppermost in people's minds. It will be seen as more about releasing sick old folk from their suffering and their families from the burden of caring for them. Many won't have substantial savings to pass on to their heirs in any case and it wouldn't be worth our while to try to collect sums under, say, £100. We'd send out an official-looking request, but wouldn't bother to enforce it with the few who refused to pay up. The small minority whose old folk have a bit put aside probably wouldn't know the law's changed and even if they did they'd probably be too embarrassed to bring the subject up or wouldn't be concerned enough to contest the death tax demand. Death taxes have existed for centuries, after all.'

'Yes, but only on the very rich. Now we're talking about anyone whose estate is over a hundred pounds, not half a million!'

'Well, as I said before, once the principle's established, it's a relatively small matter to extend it without provoking a general outcry. We may be governing an impoverished country, but at least we had the foresight to invest in a top-notch Comms team...'

Their conversation on matters of State over, Hazel Cruickshank spent a further twenty minutes or so in Sir John's cabinet office enthusiastically fulfilling her role as his mistress. The thick sound-proofed doors and plush carpet conspired perfectly to conceal their carnal goings on to any casual passers-by in the hallway. By the time she left the building, however, the effect of Hazel's amorous distraction had faded, leaving her to face her dilemma as Minister for Health and Wellbeing. How best to put a positive spin on the latest fiscal measures?

Or, in the light of her lover's advice, was there any need to even try?

CHAPTER 5: LIFE AFTER LIFE OR
LAUGH AFTER LAUGH?

The last two schooldays of the week were something of an anti-climax for John. He and Mandy started sitting next to each other in English lessons and John felt a little deflated that this drew no particular attention to themselves either from their classmates or their teachers. When he remarked on this to Mandy, she suggested it might be a lesson to him as a teenager to be less self-absorbed and not to imagine himself at the centre of the universe. She eased his hurt ego, however, by confirming that her parents would be happy for him to come round to theirs for a joint homework study on Wednesday next week.

'Things *are* looking up', he joked. 'Perhaps one day they'll allow us to go out together somewhere purely for fun!'

Mike had a busy day at the community repair shop. Perhaps the extra demand for his services came from anticipation of the weekend ahead. Despite being like any other days for most adults no longer in work, no doubt for some Saturday and Sunday still retained a little residual charm as something to look forward to.

With Christmas approaching, it was the time when people rummaged through garages, cellars and attics to dig out their old gadgets and maybe consider passing them on to friends and family as gifts. Until, that is, they remembered the reason they'd been put away in the first place was that they were no longer needed or had stopped working. But since times had changed so much, who was to say these unloved items couldn't one day prove useful again?

Whatever the case, enough people turned up at the repair

shop to temporarily overwhelm Mike along with his fellow electricians, engineers and assorted craftspeople. On returning home in the late-afternoon, he proudly dropped nine pounds into his savings jar. He then excitedly tipped out all the coins and a single note to count a total of twenty-eight pounds. Surely, that would be halfway towards John's new shirt.

Fortified by his success, Mike summoned up the courage at last to ask Anne if she too had been able to put something aside out of her housekeeping allowance. He was delighted to learn that not only had she scrimped and saved to put away thirteen pounds since September, but that the shirt she had in mind for John retailed at exactly forty pounds. Pooling their funds would cover the expense with a pound to spare! With over an hour before the end of business and not wishing to risk a weekend price hike on non-essential goods – all too common these days - Anne jumped on a bus to town. She soon returned with the shirt which John had set his heart on two months ago when they last went shopping together.

Later that night with the others all in bed, Mike and Anne celebrated their parental triumph by cracking open a can of cider from their secret stash in the cellar. They shared their drink over the remaining pound in Mike's jar, declaring it as a deposit towards John's promised new trousers.

Meanwhile, Jenny, satisfied that this had been decreed at the family conference, applied herself to locating a suitable pet to keep gran company. She was painfully aware of her parents' lack of funds, but had heard from a school friend that strays or unwanted dogs could be still adopted without requiring a licence and that informal arrangements could be made without fear of persecution by officialdom. Provided, that is, the newfound canine friend was kept out of the public eye, preferably shut inside one's home or confined to a back garden.

Jenny followed Mary on Thursday evening to the bottom of

their garden and sat down with her in the customary spot by her husband's burial mound. She had assembled a collection of pictures of lapdog breeds from an old calendar in the hope of eliciting a preference from her grandmother. When Mary's face lit up at an image of a tiny Yorkshire terrier, Jenny asked her how she would fancy taking such a creature walks with her in the garden or just pampering it in her bedroom.

'That would be lovely, dear. What would we give it to eat, I wonder? I did own a proper dog many years ago as a child, but never had the job of feeding it. Mind you, that one's so tiny, I dare say it could live off a thimble-full of bread or biscuit crumbs....' Ironically, in the modern era marking a return to make-do-and-mend, the thimble imagery meant more to Jenny than to her gran for whom it merely represented a container with a very limited capacity. She'd never learnt to sew.

In the ensuing conversation, Jenny gained the assurance she needed that a tiny lapdog would be a real hit with her gran. All that remained was to put out the word at her school. It was Friday and by the end of the day, her prayers were answered. A Year 11 student known to her only by sight was waiting for her just outside the school gate. It was all arranged. Straight after lessons on Monday, Jenny was to accompany this girl home and collect the Yorkie together with a couple of cans of his favourite food. Little Jock, as he was called, though much loved, had suddenly become a major inconvenience to a family of just two. An elderly relative living some distance away had recently fallen gravely ill and so mother and daughter had too much on their hands to attend to Jock's needs.

It was half eight on Monday morning, 6th December. John was sitting with his registration group of Year 12s during the fifteen-minute form period with his tutor before going into whole-school assembly. These took place on two mornings a week.

Form tutor Mrs Hargreaves, though oppressed by the usual

Monday morning feeling, was sufficiently alert to realise that the study module designated for Autumn term week 12 could not be shrugged off as lightly as last week's one on peer pressure. Not unless she wanted her professionalism to be challenged by senior management who had eyes and ears everywhere.

Lower down the school, students were given a brief outline in Religious Education lessons of historical and current world faiths. Naturally, in Year 7 the treatment was fairly superficial, focusing on colourful rituals and symbols. Core religious practices and beliefs were gradually introduced from Year 8 as students' minds matured. The tiny minority of students opting for RE in Year 10 as an exam subject, delved into all the above in greater detail as befitted potential spiritual guides of future generations.

All students, however, were required to become well versed in modern English religious practices through various form study modules, twice weekly collective worship in whole-school assemblies and a compulsory weekly Religious Education lesson which continued into the sixth form. Many teachers secretly objected to this and genuinely struggled not to betray their scepticism or even cynicism to their students many of whom themselves became adept sceptics and cynics. Mrs Hargreaves fitted this category of teacher quite well, although she broadly agreed with the introductory part of the module.

'OK class, late in year 11, you'll recall, I hope, the module you did about the reasons for the rise of Christianity and its spread through much of the ancient world. Would anyone like to treat us all to a résumé?'

'To be fair, miss, it *was* a while ago,' carelessly remarked a bright but superficial girl called Sally with a low tolerance threshold for any discussion not connected to pithy popular music. RE was far too abstract to be worthy of her consideration.

John came to Mrs Hargreaves' rescue.

'The early Christian fathers believed this present life was merely a preparation for the eternal afterlife. Therefore, they were prepared to suffer persecution and even death in the belief that they would be rewarded in heaven for spreading the new creed. They also adopted distinctive doctrines to set themselves apart from other religions, particularly those that taught reincarnation like Hinduism, the world's oldest surviving religion. It was only in the third century, though, that the reincarnation doctrine was finally proscribed and all but a couple of references to it were removed from the bible.'

Mrs Hargreaves was impressed by John's correct usage of proscribed which he deliberately overstressed on the first syllable to avoid any confusion with its near antonym – prescribed.
'And why were Christians of almost all denominations ignorant of the beliefs of early Christianity?'

'Because records of it were destroyed or at least well concealed until just a few years ago.'

'Very good, John.'

He hadn't, she thought, explained the spread of Christianity very well, but Mrs Hargreaves only had five minutes left before assembly and needed to move on to the reasons for the revival of interest in Eastern religions in recent years. Although John was likely to know most if not all the answers, she wanted to bring in a couple of other students to complete the introductory module. This also covered apparent recent scientific evidence for survival after death and widely accepted proof of successive lives.

It was this evidence and proof part of the module that Mrs Hargreaves was uncomfortable with. As a trained science teacher herself, she couldn't square it all with her own atheistic belief system based on what she regarded as genuine scientific evidence. But then she could never understand why so many compatriots had for centuries gone along with an irrational religion such as Christianity with its inherent contradictions of tolerance versus exclusivity.

Anyway, Part One of the module was completed, which was just as well, as she had just caught a glimpse of the senior RE lead peering into her classroom. He could so easily have popped in for a spot check on the orthodoxy of her teaching methods.

Mr Warburton strutted out on to the assembly stage after the manner he had acquired during his first decade as a senior school leader. Just before reaching the headteacher's lectern, however, he switched into humble preacher mode and modified his gait accordingly. He still had to remind himself that for these twice-weekly whole-school briefings, he was expected to act more as a spiritual facilitator than a conventional authority figure.

The broad outline of his script had essentially been imposed by the Ministry for Education, Culture and Spirituality. It had been tweaked just once since collective spiritual attunement in schools had become compulsory eight years ago and replaced the vague but longstanding Christian devotions.

At least his authority as headteacher had not been usurped. The curriculum reform had left him a degree of freedom to adapt the language of the official script to harmonise with his own style of delivery. Similarly, he was at liberty under the act to insert discretionary elements to address the particular needs of his school community. Monday's message focused primarily on the collective meditative process, whereas Thursday's emphasis was more on applying the newly branded religion's teachings in practice.

'May the whole community of Summerfield School join together in quiet meditation while we reflect on our essential unity of spirit and purpose.' A single chime sounded to mark the beginning of the communion process. A second chime after two minutes marked the end of this first phase and was followed by: 'May an awareness of our common spiritual origin nurture us and make us ever more receptive to God's emanations and inspiration so that we may better understand our divine mission on this earth.'

There followed a few more abstract references to fulfilling said mission on earth in this lifetime to the best of our ability so that we might eventually go to our with a clear conscience and look forward to aspiring to ever loftier missions in future incarnations.

Then it was down to earth again with the remaining five minutes or so of assembly time dedicated to prosaic announcements. Today, these events on the school calendar, imminent parents' evenings, reminders and admonitions about frequently disregarded house rules around school uniform and behaviour in the corridors during break and the lunch hour.

This period of dead time dragged all the more for John given his eagerness to get to his English lesson with Mandy. Fortunately, Mr Warburton was in a relatively reticent mood and so the school community was dismissed early enough for most student groups to arrive and line up outside their classrooms just before a burst of jaunty jingles announced the start of period one. The music was carefully selected for its supposed psychological benefits of soothing the nervous system while making young brains more receptive to absorbing knowledge.

John ensured he was one of the first to enter the English room in order to make a beeline for the most remote pair of desks available. Within seconds, he and Mandy were sitting together tucked away at the back of the classroom in the right-hand corner, furthest away from their mutually favourite teacher. Mr Jacobs kicked off his lesson by reading out a selection of students' creative writing efforts from their most recent homework.

The task had been to project themselves into the most recent novel they had been studying for literature: *War of the Generations*. The plot was fairly straightforward and predictable in the modern literary context: a family was living through the dying days of consumerist society with all the intergenerational tensions that entailed. The principal characters were enlightened teenage children railing against their parents for denuding the planet of resources and upsetting its ecology with manifest lack of concern so long as the main victims of their environmental crime were populations inhabiting the global south. Most students had opted to invent a dialogue between a young and older protagonist of their choice.

John found the author's political agenda painfully unsubtle. Mandy broadly agreed on this point, but she enjoyed the novel for its stylistic merits and not entirely predictable plot. He and she had even dared to disagree with each other in a class discussion in which Mr Jacobs had amused everyone by playing Devil's Advocate to the extreme. In order to provoke his students into expressing opposing views, he took the stance of claiming that the novel was utter sentimental nonsense. John won admiration from his peers by pointing out the ambivalence around the treatment of digital technology. Had the author adequately identified and examined the impact of social media, for example, in contributing to the cultural barrier between children and their parents and undermining mental health?

Mandy teased John for claiming to have chosen English as the line of least resistance because his mother taught the subject. It was patently obvious to him that her real aim was to get him to admit that his main reason was to be in lessons with her. However, he was content to keep her guessing as a way of getting his own back for her teasing him and quite liked the idea that she might think him too proud to own up to his feelings for her.

In truth, he had opted for English as it required significantly less effort than his other subjects and his attraction to Mandy had come a while later.

It had been an unusually conventional lesson and the class were dismissed without the usual treat of a free-for-all end-of-lesson poetry session. This was promised for the second lesson of the week with Mr Jacobs on Thursday, though before then they would have to endure Mrs White, a rather less adventurous pedagogue who brought on more yawns than she inspired creative outpourings.

John's next class was History. The subject intrigued him and frustrated him in equal measure. He enjoyed listening to recordings of inspired lecturers and reading non-scholarly books which included contemporary accounts of people with lived experience. Where he fell down was on his inability to memorise key dates and the chronology of events. In the days when exam success required this skill, he would no doubt have scored lower grades. Such a chink in John's intellectual armour caused him grief in other areas of study too but it was probably this weakness, he told himself, which prevented him from becoming insufferably arrogant amongst his peers.

Meanwhile, Jenny was in her Year 10 Information Technology lesson. The classroom itself still bore the tell-tale scars of its former computer-populated glory from thirty-five years ago when it was refurbished as the dazzling new IT suite.

The headteacher at the time hadn't hesitated to convert the staffroom for the purpose. The third largest space in the school after the assembly and sports halls, it was ideal. This move caused a major inconvenience to the teaching collective, of course, who were dispersed and reaccommodated in the new *faculty hubs*. Simultaneously with the political controversy around contractual and curriculum changes which staff were also having to face, the timing of their enforced exile could not have been more fortuitous from the senior leadership team's perspective. With almost all the rebellious teacher elements now physically separated, there could hardly have been a more perfect microcosm of the divide and rule principle practised by the powers that be from time immemorial.

Mr Crosthwaite stood before his Year 10 class projecting his usual dejected but stern persona. He was in his late fifties – old enough to recall as a student the excitement engendered by the incursion of computers on both educational and domestic fronts. It pained him that no teacher under 40 in the school today had ever trained or taught using a computer and that it fell to him of all people, as the most senior of two remaining Information Technology teachers, to deliver the most excruciating part of the curriculum. A female student who had evidently just attained the age of contrariness appeared to have been reading his mind. It was Jenny.

'Mr Crosthwaite, this classroom is like a computer grave yard without any computers in it! Why and when were they all stripped out and where did they all go?'
These were essentially the very questions which Mr Crosthwaite was obliged to tackle with the class today. Had Jenny been secretly sneaking a peek at his lesson notes?

'Thank you, Jenny for the most perceptive and pertinent question I've heard from a student in weeks if not months!' Mr Crosthwaite delivered this in an indeterminate tone deliberately and skilfully employed to convey to his students an ambiguous mix of genuine admiration and sarcasm. The grave yard imagery was especially poignant for him, as he had attended this very school as a sixth former when the computers were installed only to return years later as a teacher to witness them being ripped out.

'It happened just ten years ago, Jenny, to answer your second question first. Why? Well, because the educationists decided they had got it wrong after all. The vision was that computers would make learning easier and more fun as well as give students greater autonomy – work at their own pace, do their own research and so on. That's why IT was meant to be embedded in every lesson. It turned out, though, that there were more downsides than positives.

'Too many technical failures slowed down the pace of lessons rather than making them more dynamic. More students were using computer monitors to hide behind and get up to mischief than those who actually used the new technology to good effect. And then there was the cost in money and environmental terms of manufacturing and running the computers. Energy costs and employing armies of support staff to maintain, reprogramme and upgrade them.'

Mr Crosthwaite went on to recite an almost interminable list of other drawbacks with computers which he was obliged to point out from the curriculum irrespective of his own opinions. Finishing on the point that psychological and empirical tests had shown that sitting at a computer, students were likely to spend less than twenty-five per cent of their lesson time on task – ten per cent less than in a conventional lesson. He dared to omit the more esoteric point with which he struggled to disagree – that any learning that actually took place behind a computer was more superficial, more about operating a computer itself and hence less meaningful as education for life. Unless, of course, a meaningful life was all about sitting at a computer!

'And that brings me to the point, Jenny – and the rest of the class, if you've not all fallen off your chairs asleep by now – where did all the computers go? I can't claim to know the precise destination of all our old computers, but I can tell you that across the country, many were donated or sold at rock bottom prices to developing countries. Older versions were taken apart, stripped and parts recycled or repurposed. But you'll be pleased to know that one or two computers were retained by the schools and not just as museum pieces, because, *in the right hands*, they are still useful for recording and processing data.'

Mr Crosthwaite paused for breath, as he had presented all this information at pace.

'Now you'll be pleased to know, class, that those answers to Jenny's questions cover nearly half of the module which by a strange coincidence happens to be programmed for today's lesson and is in my teaching notes!' He peered into Jenny's eyes in the hope they might betray an admission of guilt or highly evolved psychic powers.

Spurred on by Jenny's bold early intervention in the lesson and its informative outcome, Craig, another spirited pupil, attempted to tease out another detail of Mr Crosthwaite's module notes.
'So, sir, what's the point then of having IT classes in here? It's one of the biggest classrooms in the school and we're just a no-frills run-of-the-mill Year 10 group!'

Mr Crosthwaite didn't in fact know the answer to this question, but many years of dealing with students trying to catch him out left him prepared to tackle all comers.

'I suggest at break you have a word with Mrs Matthews about forging a career in school timetabling. They tell me it's so complicated that it defeats all algorithms and only a brilliant mathematical mind can manage it. To be serious, though, I'd hazard a guess that as the subject – my subject – still just about exists, the old computer suite is deemed the best location for IT lessons. And who knows, perhaps one day technology will advance to the point where students will be partly digitalised and can be plugged into the old computer terminals. This would work wonders for classroom discipline, I'm sure...' Once he got going, Mr Crosthwaite often surprised himself at the inventiveness of his own evil genius.

Jenny too was on form today as she continued her contributions to the discussion:

'I think timetabling all the IT classes in here is meant as a stark visual history lesson. Or perhaps more like a museum of information technology in education – past and present. Most of it past, not so much of it present! Apparently, there's also a huge pile of old mobile phones stored somewhere from when they set a legal limit of one phone per family.'

'I imagine half that pile goes back to when we teachers had to spend much of the lesson tracking down and confiscating mobile phones from students. Another blast from the recent past for which I thank you again, Jenny....'

The rest of the lesson was devoted to what Information Technology meant in these straitened times. Essentially, it boiled down to an effective means of transmitting factual knowledge and informed balanced opinions. This, according to the official Ministry for Education, Culture and Spirituality, was what it had originally been intended for. So, it was quite rightly divested of all the fun things like self-expression and self-assertion through social media whose overriding impact had been poor mental health for a whole generation. But it also meant a drastic curb on other bad things such as fake news platforms and damaging forms of exploitation through misleading advertising and financial fraud. All these themes featured in Mr Crosthwaite's seemingly interminable lesson notes.

Following her bold participation in Mr Crosthwaite's lesson, Jenny retained a buzz of excitement which lasted the rest of the school day. Moreover, her self-esteem and confidence had grown yet further from sensing the impact her comments had had upon her teacher and classmates alike.

The Year 11 Yorkshire Terrier owner detected Jenny's more assertive body language on meeting her outside the school gates at half three. It was only a five-minute walk to the girl's house. As promised, Jenny was presented with tiny Jock the Yorkie together with a copious supply of his favourite tinned food.

'You'll find him dead easy to get on with. He'll take to you instantly once you get him home and he'll soon be attached to all the family and you all to him....' her voice choked a little from emotion.

'Don't worry – you can always visit if you get the chance.' With that, Jenny handed Jock back to the girl for a moment while she snatched a piece of paper from her school bag and jotted down the Greenways' address. After exchanging the note paper for Jock, Jenny wished the girl and her mother all the best looking after their sick relative and set off home.

As Jenny walked through the door, she had a hunch something was awry. However, her mother emerged from the kitchen to greet her smilingly as usual to suggest what she might have for tea. She stopped in surprise at the sight and sound of Jock who had already begun to produce high-pitched barking noises on entering his new domain.

'I did say I'd be bringing him home after school today, mum,' Jenny justified herself.

'Oh, yes, of course dear, it's just I've been a bit distracted today for some reason. Can't quite put my finger on what's been bothering me, but anyway, it's great to see the little creature. Let's take him up to see gran right away!'

So, mum has been feeling odd too. Could we have picked up on the same vibe?

They went up together to Mary's room and Anne knocked lightly on the door. There was no answer so she knocked again a little louder. Still no reply, so the two entered.

'She's not here, so that explains it – she must have gone out into the garden a bit earlier than usual this evening,' Anne reassured her daughter.

It suddenly dawned on Jenny that her foreboding just before had been unconsciously connected to gran. Had she been hasty in acquiring a pet dog for her? Perhaps when she saw Jock in the garden, she would be shocked rather than pleasantly surprised and may have completely forgotten about her favourable reaction when Jenny showed her the pictures the other day!

But Mary wasn't in the garden visiting grandad's grave either. A degree of panic set in as they searched the rest of the house. They were almost certain that she wouldn't have gone out somewhere by herself, as she'd not done this independently for a long while even before grandad passed away. Unless... this was the latest stage in her dementia. Everyone had heard cases of elderly people forgetting where they were and wandering around the neighbourhood or trying to get back to where they had grown up as children.

They finally returned to Mary's room to hunt for any clues. Jenny immediately found a plain sheet of paper on her dressing table with the simple message: *Gone to hospital. Gran.*

'Why the hell didn't we look for a note at first?!' complained Jenny.

'We had no reason to think gran would have gone out anywhere. Anyway, at least we know now she knows what she's doing still and ...'

'...we can only hope she's safe.' Jenny finished her sentence. 'It could only be Wethersfield hospital where grandad died, so I suggest ringing there.'

Anne rang the hospital and got through right away. She gave her mother's details to the receptionist who couldn't offer any information except the ward number and that they could now see her as soon as convenient.

Relieved, mother and daughter hugged each other tightly. Minutes later, Mike and John had returned home, so the whole family except Jenny who had to look after Jock, set off for the hospital.

Wethersfield hospital was just a twenty minutes' bus ride away with a stop right outside reception, so, within an hour of Anne making the phone call, the three Greenways were in the lift and on their way up to the floor they'd been directed to by the receptionist. They stepped out of the lift immediately facing the sign *Geriatric Wards C to H*. Mary was in Ward H, the very last one down the long corridor.

As they passed the door leading off to each ward, John looked through the glass window and caught a glimpse of the first bay of four beds. It was hard to tell for sure, but it seemed that with each ward there were fewer people in sight – from about four or five, including nurses in ward C, decreasing to just one lonely figure in ward G. And no one to be seen in ward H.

Anne knocked at the door. No one came. Then Mike spotted and pressed a bell which after a minute or two summoned a nurse who at last opened up and allowed them to squeeze through into the ward.

'Who have you come for?', she enquired sympathetically with a subdued smile.
'Mrs Mary Garner.' Anne pronounced her own Maiden name which she'd neither spoken nor written down since she had discussed her father's death certificate nearly six months ago. It sounded strange too in the ears of her husband and son.

'Just one moment.'
The nurse disappeared into another room leaving them standing in the anteroom to the ward which John noticed led to a bay of just two beds unlike the four he'd glimpsed through the doors of

the other wards.

Anne, despite not having made the same observations as her son when walking down the corridor, felt by far the most uncomfortable as the nurse returned with a more senior-looking lady.

'Good evening. I'm Doctor Curtis. I presume you are Mrs Garner's family, the Greenways? I'll take you down to see her now, but would you mind first someone showing proof of identity?'

Mike presented his driving licence which, although he had become carless three years ago, had been useful in proving his identity on numerous occasions since then. Dr Curtis barely glanced at the document, as she'd clearly satisfied herself already that these anxious people before her were genuine. She motioned them to come through the first set of doors after the entrance to the ward and took them past the two unoccupied beds.

'Knowing you were on your way, we left her in the side room...' she stopped as Anne suddenly let out a suppressed cry of horror.

'But isn't that where you move people to be out of the way when...'
Dr Curtis looked puzzled as she ushered the incomplete family through another door past the bay of two beds. Mary lay on her back in a bed looking serenely at peace, but all three Greenways instinctively knew she was dead.

'What happened – when did she pass away? Suddenly, just after we called? When you said we could see her, we assumed she was OK...Why didn't you warn us?
Anne spluttered as the probable truth slowly dawned on her.

The doctor had also realised by now what had happened and resolved to tackle the situation with as much sang-froid as she could muster.
'I'm terribly sorry. There has obviously been a confusion. We had

no reason to believe that your mother hadn't informed you of her intention to request euthanasia and presumed that you were coming to claim, er... identify, her body...'

Anne's shock and grief gave way to anger.
'But my mother had dementia – she didn't have the capacity to make a request like that! How could you agree to euthanise an old woman in the space of just a few hours without doing all sorts of checks, talking to her family and giving her the chance to change her mind? It's murder! I've heard it rumoured this sort of thing happens in nursing homes, but never believed it could be done so casually in a hospital.

'I'm sorry Mrs Greenway, the law on voluntary termination of life did change quite recently. Our initial reaction was that it should have been more widely publicised. However, the Ministry for Health and Wellbeing instructed us it was too sensitive an issue to broadcast widely and would be better explained to individuals on a case-by-case basis.'

'Mrs Garner called the hospital on Thursday last week to arrange an appointment. She was put through to our department and we had quite a long chat with her to ensure she knew what she was requesting and all the implications. There was no suggestion at any point that she lacked capacity then nor was there today when she attended the unit. She was very sanguine about the whole matter. She explained her reasons for wanting to pass on very clearly and satisfied us that we should comply with her request. She said she'd talked it over with you and you were aware of her wishes. I must repeat: as Mrs Garner satisfied us that she had full capacity, we had to respect her wishes and it would have been an infringement of her rights to discuss the matter with a third party, even a family member.'

Anne felt a shiver go up her spine on hearing the words 'talked it over with you' and her outrage only intensified.

'Talked it over! She merely mentioned she'd like to join her husband who passed away in the summer. But she said this would be her New Year wish, so I didn't imagine there was any imminent danger and just thought she was in a low mood which would improve with a bit more time. I told her so and she didn't raise the matter again, so I thought I'd convinced her to see sense.'

Anne was painfully aware she had switched from blaming the hospital to justifying her own actions. Had she really been sure she'd succeeded in dissuading her mother or was it more a case of her not wanting to face the issue and just hoping it would go away? She had also begun to dread the reprobation of Jenny who would surely blame her mother for not taking her gran's threats of suicide more seriously.

This was the first voluntary euthanasia case Doctor Curtis had curated since the latest legislation had come into force only months ago. Understandably, she too was ill at ease and feared some adverse consequences arising from the misunderstanding, but she was confident she could handle these. She was also satisfied that she and the hospital had followed all procedures correctly in relation to Mrs Garner's voluntary suicide. When a patient or client presents as lucid and compos mentis there is no obligation to check for mental capacity in their medical records. And, as she had explained, consulting with the family would have been an infringement of Mrs Garner's rights in any case.

Emotionally exhausted, Anne at last calmed down and began to sob quietly. Doctor Curtis used the opportunity to suggest the family take their time to consider what they wanted to do with Mary's body. There were various options. The new legislation contained clauses referring to fees and charges related to disposal of the deceased. There was a clear nudge for citizens to leave their dear departed to be disposed of by the hospital if that was where they passed away. The fee for this was set at a minimal £20 which obviously and decorously came with an offer of a memorial plaque. This could be supplied by the state for a further moderate charge or provided at a higher cost by a range of private outlets.

The option of home burial was by no means discouraged provided that adequate rear garden accommodation was available. This was the natural choice of the Greenways. In this case, costs payable to the hospital were incurred for transportation of the body to the burial site and for the grave-digging service.

A bizarre negotiation took place owing to the fact that the Greenways' garden already contained one family member's body. However, it seemed that the government department responsible for revising relevant legislation had been meticulous in providing for almost every conceivable eventuality. The original legislation on garden burials had stipulated that bodies had to be buried at a minimum depth of 1.8 metres. However, in order to encourage such burials in smaller gardens where side-by-side graves were impracticable, this was revised to 1.5 metres. The grave-digging charge for this service was reduced proportionately owing to the lesser depth. The Greenways, led by Mike who had the best overall view of family finances, opted for laying Mary to rest above her husband in order to save £5 on the fee.

One final point had to be discussed when John volunteered to dig the grave himself with his father in the hope of reducing expenditure further. Unfortunately, the law did not provide for this option. Grave-digging was a legally protected occupation and only individuals licensed by the State could practise it.

The hospital admin officer who, like Doctor Curtis, was performing this aspect of his role for the first time since the new legislation, exercised his discretion in postponing one final discussion until two weeks after the burial. This was the option of opening up one's garden to other families who wished to bury their dead, but did not have adequate garden space. This could be arranged by the hospital, shave twenty per cent off the standard burial fee and provide the Greenways with potential extra income in future depending on how many plots they were able to accommodate.

The Minister for the Economy, Finance and Taxation, Sir John Beecham, was poring over the figures in a spreadsheet which the morning in-tray had brought him. It made for depressing reading. Over the third financial reporting quarter, consumer spending had remained almost stable despite his team's first quarter forecast that it would continue to decline by at least one per cent. Clearly, disposable income had not come down by as much as he'd been banking on and he knew he would be under pressure to agree to further intervention.

All he could do was present his boss with his best arguments to defer measures until the fourth quarter. Not being a financial wizard himself, the Prime Minister might just be persuaded by the 'blip syndrome' and that reduced consumer spending would be back on course very soon. He'd have to give his senior adviser, old Howard Morton, a metaphorical kick up the backside and pump him for a few more ideas. What a bore the whole situation was!

CHAPTER 6: BORN AGAIN!

It was Sunday, 19th December. Nearly two weeks had passed since the upsetting episode around gran's passing and her burial just five days later.

On that fateful day, Anne had returned home grief stricken and in dread of facing her daughter's wrath for her role in failing to prevent Mary's death. Jenny's reaction to the tragic news, however, was totally unexpected to all. She accepted her dear gran's passing with remarkable equanimity and without even a hint of wishing to blame either her mother or the hospital for what had happened. Instead, she was quite philosophical and talked about how her gran would be in a better place and almost certainly have been greeted by grandad in whatever dimension souls awaited their next incarnation. Anne was initially relieved, but soon suspected that her daughter had repressed her grief out of shock and that her true emotion was bound to emerge eventually.

John too exhibited few outward signs of distress and, seeing how perplexed his mother was, tried to explain as tactfully as he could, his own point of view. He himself had never felt particularly attached to his grandparents who had only moved in with the family a couple of years ago. He didn't see anything particularly sad about old people dying, especially when they could choose their time as in the case of gran. Even grandad had quickly reconciled himself to his terminal cancer diagnosis, saying: *You've got to die of something!*

He had more difficulty, however, trying to explain to his mother why he thought Jenny didn't appear particularly bereaved. His attempt ran thus: Jenny had been exposed to an awful lot of religious education at school. Legislation introduced even since his own Year 10 days had given more weight to this in the curriculum. Talk of death was well on the way to losing its taboo status - certainly in the case of the elderly and infirm. Why would aging people whose health and quality of life was steadily deteriorating want to put off their next incarnation into a new youthful body? And then there was Jenny's new responsibility of looking after Jock whom she was eager to integrate into family life and was busy acquainting with every corner of the back garden. Call it a distraction, if you like.

Mike had seen to most of the arrangements connected with Mary's burial. Anne had insisted he be present during the grave-digging and interment to ensure that the existing casket was not damaged in the process and that due decorum was observed. For example, there must be no skimping and the promised waterproof sheet had to be laid over grandad's casket before gran's was lowered onto it.

The grave diggers turned out to be most conscientious and accommodating souls. The older and more experienced of the two gave Mike a running commentary on the whole process, pointing out that the job would take less time than usual given that the earth had not fully compacted since it was last disturbed for the first grave. Once assured he was dealing with the son-in-law and not the son, he quipped, *'If only all old couples were as considerate in passing away so close together, it would make our job a lot easier!'*

Anne was present at the solemn moment when the sturdy impermeable sheet was folded in two and placed delicately over the first casket. This manoeuvre was carried out artfully and respectfully by the grave diggers so that no discernible noise was produced when the new casket was lowered onto it.

Moments after the grave had been refilled and the workmen had departed, Jenny came out into the garden with Jock who immediately claimed the fresh mound of earth as his territory by urinating on it. Fortunately, Anne was safely back indoors by this time and so was not witness to the act of canine desecration.

Since acquiring what was now tacitly her very own pet, Jenny had taken him out into the garden three or four times daily. It was, after all, the only place by law where his walking and toiletry needs could be satisfied. These sorties allowed Jenny to succumb to her grief in private and hide her tears from the others.

Once she had got used to Jock's ways, she felt confident enough to run to the bottom of the garden with him off lead. Following Mike's masterful job at plugging up the holes in the surrounding fence, he couldn't escape, though, sure enough, he'd tried more than once on the first day and nearly succeeded.

Jenny and John had helped their dad make the fresh earth mound secure against night-time animal raiders by covering it with a thick tarpaulin weighted at the edges by heavy stones borrowed from the rockery. Understandably, all surviving family members were more nervous than for the previous burial given gran's shallower grave. Anne had suggested levelling off the mound and permanently laying paving stones with a memorial plaque to mark the spot. However, this project would have to be shelved until they acquired more suitable stones. The memorial plaque would also have to wait until more urgent purchases such as John's trousers had been saved up for.

As promised by his former owner, Jock rapidly took to all the family and they to him. Although he refused to take a share of responsibility for the animal, John wasn't averse to playing ball with him occasionally in the garden and feeding him left-over food scraps after meal times. For Jenny's sake, Mike had made strenuous efforts to conceal his general dislike of dogs, but within twenty-four hours of Jock's being around, he had to confess to growing fond of the *little mut*, as he called it.

Each sight of Jock triggered a matrix of conflicting emotions and associations in Anne. However, feelings of regret, blame, guilt, love, finally morphed into compassion for the little creature itself. Occasionally Jock managed to slip into the kitchen and get under Anne's feet while she was cooking. Despite her irritation at the *little blighter*, as she took to calling him, she soon found herself stooping to pet its twitchy little frame.

As a result of the secularisation and de-commercialisation of Christmas in recent years, there was little to look forward to for John and Jenny except a welcome break from the drudgery of the school routine. At least virtually all members of Mike and Anne's generation had been able to enjoy some aspects of the festival. Whether this was the pious pleasure of remembering the baby Jesus' coming to earth to save humankind from the pains of hell, the stirring 19th century carols, the excitement of Father Christmas bearing gifts for the tiny tots, or the sheer greed fulfilment of teenagers. And then of course there was the exceptional licence to indulge shamelessly in copious fattening rich foods and excesses of intoxicating liquor.

Such joys were either gone altogether or reduced to a mere shadow of their former selves. The mere memory of them was a source of torment for Mike and Anne who suffered more as a result than their children who had never known such dubious pleasures. One day John asked his mum what Christmas used to be like. Observing her wistful faraway look and hearing out her artless attempt at conveying her feelings, he attempted to recall an old aphorism he'd picked up in an English lesson.

'What's that saying, mum: *What you don't know can't hurt you?*'
'Even better might be: *You don't miss what you've never had*, Anne suggested.

But there were still three days of school to go yet – Monday to Wednesday.
Jenny's school made the children study as normal right up to

period six on the last day, 22nd December. The only remnant of anything remotely connected with the bygone festive season was a special module taught in the weekly Religious Education lesson. This was reinforced by a form group tutorial and the headteacher's message in the final assembly of the Autumn Term.

In RE, Jenny and her Year 10 peers were subjected to a latter-day analysis of the Christmas story. Armed with the new progressive curriculum, Mr Hughes, the RE teacher, visibly relished the task of taking apart the nativity myth. He rubbished the notion of the immaculate conception and virgin birth and stressed the sheer historical improbability of everything surrounding these supposed events.

The core premise for debunking historical Christianity was constantly revisited in successive RE lessons. This was the recent discovery by scholars of texts which clearly illustrated how fluid and widely open to interpretation the earliest Christian records and teachings actually were. The official viewpoint was that this revelation only confirmed what had been long suspected by all critically thinking people when considering the vastly differing accounts of the four gospels. Accounts of Christ's life and teachings were more fiction than fact.

The various bodies of Christian dogma and doctrine had evolved over an extensive period of time and took widely differing directions among the different branches of the Christian church. This was inevitable because the Christian bible as a collection of scriptures did not prescribe a distinct theology. This had to be deduced by disparate brotherhoods of scholars who succeeded in devising sufficiently conflicting belief systems as to lead to religious armed conflicts between nations and often even bloodier civil wars.

An example of an age-old point of theological contention was that between the Trinitarians and the Unitarians as to whether God was one or three persons. Some sects even believed in a dualist god comprising the Father and the Son. Some theologians and atheists alike derided so-called unitarian Christians, calling them 'dualists' for believing in a secondary deity – *Satan* or the *Devil* – as God's adversary. How could a religion be true if it could not be grasped by ordinary folk, but needed to be explained by a priest or learned elite?

The primary goal of the early Christian fathers was to develop a creed which stood out as distinct from all contemporary religions. It also had to be as binary and simplistic as possible to appeal to the masses. Hence concepts of good versus evil, God versus Satan, the Father and the Mother of Christ, one and only one life followed by an ascent to Heaven or a descent into Hell with nothing in between. A passing mention of the Roman church's attempt to introduce Purgatory from the 12th century had to wait to join the curriculum until Year 11.

Jenny, like many of her more intelligent peers, had begun to ask questions about the fundamentals of life and so followed the concepts and arguments put forward in her RE lessons quite closely.

'Mr Hughes, I can see Christianity is just too illogical and childish to accept. But why should we be expected to believe a new religion just because the old one's no good?'

She'd not expressed her thoughts as well as she'd intended, but clearly enough, it seemed, to elicit a thoughtful reply from Mr Hughes who felt himself to be on an extremely firm footing.

'Well, of course we have to give a lot of credit to the most ancient widely practised world religion, Hinduism, which still predominates today in India. This religion predates Christianity by well over one thousand years and survived all attempts by imperialists to suppress it. Much the same can be said for Buddhism though this really emerged out of Hinduism at a later date and has similar core beliefs around reincarnation and karma. Our modern religion or 'new' religion, as it tends to be referred to, is founded on these beliefs which have stood the test of time.

'In your form tutor groups, you'll be discussing a bit more about why Christianity caught on so much in the West and how it was instrumental in creating the near godless society which evolved out of consumerism and the cult of the individual.'

John had already been exposed to the more sophisticated year 11 RE curriculum and had only occasionally been required to revisit key concepts in Year 12. The Ministry for Education, Culture and Spirituality, expected the up-and-coming generation of young adults to have fully assimilated all the key elements of the new religion by the sixth form.

John and Mandy had a few discussions about religion, usually outside school. They had different teachers for RE whose perspectives and approaches diverged considerably, despite the intended straightjacket of the statutory National Curriculum now in force in all schools.

Mandy's teacher stressed the apparent empirical proof of reincarnation as a universal supernatural phenomenon. What really swung the argument was when a number of senior establishment figures in developed countries 'came out', as it were, and confessed to memories of a past life. Had this been merely a passing trend, no doubt the public would have suspected the celebrities concerned of cynically using their revelations for self-promotion and boost to their waning popularity. However, interest generated in the media and scientific circles promoted research in the field which in turn rendered general discussion of reincarnation respectable.

Before long, serious research workers were funded to carry out numerous studies in communities across the world where this idea was taken for granted and where a remarkable body of evidence had built up over the years. Children from all cultures testified to past-life memories and gave detailed accounts of lives in distant communities which were well documented and verified. Accounts like these used to be dismissed by mainstream opinion in so-called developed countries purely out of prejudice and a desire to support the prevailing Christian religion.

It had been much harder to demonstrate the principle of karma to the public at large, but here too there was sufficient evidence to satisfy most reflective members of society. A vast number of near-death case studies appeared to provide convincing data, as unconnected people produced startlingly similar accounts of their experiences.

The most revealing factor was an almost universal involuntary review of one's life going backwards in time from their last living moment to their earliest memories. People interviewed generally sensed the purpose behind this was to face issues they had been unable or unwilling to face during their present life, but which they needed to deal with before reincarnating. How thoroughly they got through this process would determine the conditions they would be born into in their next incarnation. All very logical really, claimed Mandy's teacher.

It was this aspect of the new or rather 'old' beliefs which John's teacher stressed. He once made an interesting request of his students in a quiet and confidential tone. This indicated he was going beyond the remit of his official lesson plan and wished not to be overheard by the senior leadership team.

'I'd like you to consider carefully why you think the new religion with its karma and reincarnation teachings has become so popular in recent years to the point of driving out the long-established Christian beliefs. What are the implications for a society in which the notion of successive lives has become the accepted norm? In fact, if this were an exam class, I'd jolly well set you an essay on it!'

John brought this theme up with Mandy when she had at last managed to persuade her parents to let him come round to her place for a home study session.

Mandy set the ball rolling in the stimulating discussion which unfolded between them.

'First of all, I must say I don't trust people in public life, scientists and so-called experts when they claim they have experienced or proved something which no one has ever been able to prove before. What makes them so special? Most religions developed doctrines to serve the ruling classes and keep common folk under control. Like the idea of eternal punishment in Hell, for example. That was invented in the Middle Ages to frighten people and get them to donate to the church and buy redemption from priests. *Indulgences*, I think, it was called.'

John had heard arguments for talking down the old religion repeated in various ways and contexts throughout his school career. But the question was what drew people to the new religion and what its implications were. He needed to bring Mandy to the point.

'A belief that this life isn't the end can encourage different behaviour depending on the individual. People may be tempted not to make the most of this life and be complacent, believing they'll have another chance in the next. On the other hand, if they understand the idea of Karmic compensation for evil acts, they may try to improve their behaviour in order not to have to pay this debt. On the other hand, you'd think the Christian eternal bliss in Heaven versus eternal punishment in Hell would be a much stronger motivation to be good!

Mandy thought she saw the flaw in this argument:

'Yes, but the vast majority of people in Christian societies through the ages either didn't understand the church doctrines or didn't believe them even if they did. And little's changed today. Here we're assuming karma and reincarnation have actually been proven to exist, which I don't think many people are going to accept – even young people like us, no matter how much we get it rammed down our throats at school.'

'Well, here's what I'm inclined to believe. Before my gran got herself euthanised at the local hospital, mum had mentioned how she'd heard talk of euthanasia in nursing homes for people with no family connections. I think this new religion is being pedalled by the government to cut down the population. Talking of evidence: what about the upper limits the State will pay to treat people as they get older. In the old days, dad said, the NHS spent most of its taxpayers' money looking after people over 75, whereas now most of its resources go on younger people and hardly any on the old, so it's completely the other way round.'

'That makes sense, John. Filling the curriculum with these new religious ideas is obviously deliberate government policy. Belief in reincarnation takes away much of the fear of death and so it'll be easier to nudge older people towards ending their own lives given the promise of a fresh start in a younger body. Many will also feel under moral pressure to relieve relatives of the burden of caring for them as they get more infirm. But until you mentioned it, I'd no idea about the spending limits on people as they get older. That's shocking!'

The next day, John brought into school the chart his parents had discussed with him detailing maximum NHS expenditures for different age brackets:

Age bracket	Points (High is best)	Maximum annual State spend on an individual
1-12 mths	10	£10,000
1-7 yrs	9	£9,500
8-14 yrs	8	£9,000
15-21 yrs	7	£8,500
22-28 yrs	6	£8,000
29-35 yrs	5	£7,000
36-49 yrs	4	£6,000
50-63 yrs	3	£4,000
64-77 yrs	2	£2,000
78+ yrs	1	£1,000

On studying the chart, Mandy made two observations which hadn't occurred to John.

'I read somewhere that lots of people used to live well into their nineties and some still do, but only if they've been healthy most of their lives and extremely lucky in old age. But look how early old age starts according to the chart. I reckon all but the simplest operations would cost over £5,000, so if you needed that at 50, you'd be stuffed. That's around our parents' age for heaven's sake!'

'Also,' John continued the commentary, 'this is the maximum allowance in any one year and you don't, apparently, earn credits for each year you're not using the health service. So that would mean if you needed treatment for something every year costing, say £3,000 each time in your fifties you'd be covered. But if you needed an op just once costing £5,000, you'd be out of luck as the max is only £4,000! A health lottery if ever there was one!'

'And a wealth lottery too, as better-off folk would be able to top up, others not. I thought this endless anti-consumerism and green revolution drive was to achieve greater equality in society,' Mandy objected.

John continued, 'What was it Jesus is meant to have said: 'The poor will always be among us!' I suppose, to be fair, there are fewer desperately poor people nowadays with this universal wage business and the super stinking rich too have all but disappeared, but clever people with money will always find a way of hiding it if need be...'

'I suppose, John, as young people we shouldn't complain too much. In my grandparents' day, they used to say the older generation was stealing from the young – when more and more young people were coaxed into higher education only to amass huge debts and then not be able to find a decent job or buy a house like their parents could. Then there were the pandemics which the government brought in measures to tackle. These were supposed to protect the very old at the expense of children who lost out on their education and childhood by being stuck inside for months on end. It didn't stop a load of older people dying in the end anyway.'

John was impressed with Mandy's knowledge and analysis. However, he was growing increasingly impatient to get back to what his teacher had tasked him with:

'The more I think about reincarnation, though, the more implications come to mind – I mean apart from the obvious points we've already talked about: a temptation to be lazy and keep putting things off, not making the most of the here and now and fearing death less. What about how it ties in with karma – cause and effect arising from our actions. If a person's born or has an accident making them disabled does that mean it was their fault in this life or a previous one? And is being disabled a punishment or just meant to be a learning experience? And then there's the issue of how the government can use a simplistic interpretation of karma to justify all its policies."

'I'm not sure what you mean. Can you give an example?'

'Well let's do it together.' John instantly blushed on recognising his inadvertent double-entendre, but recovered quickly, 'Think of any policy or law the government might want to introduce and see if we can justify it in terms of karma and reincarnation.'

'Tougher prison sentences for environmental crime. That's one theme that keeps coming up in the news.'

'Okay, what would be the best karmic justification for that?'

Mandy began. 'I see how the severity of a penalty or length of a prison sentence can really be related to reincarnation and karma, but the purpose of the penalty could be. So, if karma is meant to be for learning rather than punishment, then logically the penalty should favour community service or restorative justice, for example.'

'But most laws are actually getting tougher so you could equally well justify the death penalty on the grounds that the condemned person would come back for a fresh start.' John at once realised his attempt at playing Devil's Advocate was unlikely to convince Mandy.

'Or you could put the opposite view that if life is for learning, then to execute someone would be to deprive them of an opportunity to acknowledge their guilt and make amends, ask forgiveness, etcetera. If they were executed, they'd not have this chance and be more likely to repeat the same behaviour in a future life and kill again....'

John couldn't fault Mandy's reasoning.

'But that at least shows the government can pick and choose its arguments to justify its policies.'

John had the last word on this topic, but the two went on to explore other scenarios and Mandy certainly proved herself as his intellectual equal. Before their joint home study period was over, they had considered how Christianity led to man's defiance of nature, provided a licence to exploit and kill other species as well as pursue limitless material wealth and economic growth with little or no regard for the finite resources of the planet.

CHAPTER 7: MERRY CHRISTMAS... EVERYONE?

John returned from his last day at school on Wednesday, 22nd December in the most downcast mood he could remember being in all term. Had Mr Warburton really needed to use his last address to the whole school exclusively to rant against the evils of Christmases past? John could understand why a Christian minister in days of old might want to remind their congregation of the 'true meaning of Christmas' and warn against succumbing to the temptations of a materialistic and consumerist world. But what was the point today when this world of plenty had largely disappeared?

Perhaps Warburton had hoped to offer some consolation to his impoverished audience by reviving the memory of the *evil filthy rich ruling class*, as he expressed it, and how they exploited the poor, owned second homes while others were homeless, consumed several times their fair share of the world's resources and produced a massive carbon footprint with all their fancy motorcars and long-haul flights to exotic resorts in all four corners of the planet.

But what, exactly, had happened to this iniquitous extractive elite in the aftermath of the environmental revolution? This wasn't taught in History or Society classes and there seemed to be no definitive official records giving an account of their fate.

John's parents had only talked of rumours along the lines that many of the privileged classes were imprisoned for social, economic and environmental crimes. Some perpetrators had apparently escaped to remote islands. These had been blockaded, forcing most escapees to surrender or starve, though an unknown resourceful number had remained in hiding and found a way to survive in their new environment à la Robinson

Crusoe.

Jenny had suggested that the cunning ones had probably come across primitive island tribes whom they came to dominate and exploit just like they had economically enslaved the populations who had banished them. Perhaps one day they would re-emerge to reassert their dominion.

But downbeat theological concerns and socio-economic upheavals of the recent past weren't the primary cause of John's dejectedness. For a start, his accursed new-fangled shoes, after barely three weeks, were already showing alarming signs of wear. The only question was whether dad's glue holding on the soles would fail before the cork they were made of completely disintegrated.

So much for dad's revived DIY skills! John reflected, perhaps if he had gone to the neighbourhood repair outfit, he might have got a better service from a retired cobbler! Come to think of it, he ought to have gone there in disguise to see whether his dad would have made more of an effort for a complete stranger than for his own flesh and blood. Still, he would have the whole of the two-week winter holiday to consider a new stratagem for obtaining shoes which were both legal and in once piece.

Then there was the disappointment that Mandy's parents wanted a 'quiet' family Christmas. In other words, John wasn't invited and Mandy, being part of this quiet family, wasn't allowed to come over to his place either. How on earth did Mandy's miserable mum and dad propose to fill the time in each other's company for two whole weeks? Surely, there was a limit to how many board games could be played before insanity set in. This gloomy thought brought to John's mind an amusing homophone which entertained him for a few moments: *When board becomes bored!*

But he was in for a pleasant surprise as he walked through the door to meet his mum, beaming in the hallway. Her expression briefly turned into a grimace as a sudden discordant screeching sound rang out from Jenny's room. The disturbance soon passed, however, and Anne's cheerful smile returned.

'You'll never guess what happened this afternoon! Mrs Watson from across the road came over to say she and her son have just been having an Xmas clear-out. She wondered if we'd be interested in a few items that they'd dug out of their roof space. One of these you've just heard now – a violin which Jenny has already laid claim to. You know she's always been passionate about music, though only time will tell whether she has any musical ability to match it.

'She also invited me round to have a look at some hardly worn clothes which belonged to her brother who used to live with them. He bought them before sadly passing away in the autumn from a stroke. Mrs Watson said she reckoned they'd fit you and I think they'd suit you down to the ground.'

With that, she ushered John into the lounge where she'd carefully spread out three shirts, two pairs of smart trousers and a jumper. John could just about picture himself wearing the jumper indoors if only to ward off the winter cold. However, though one of the shirts was too dark for his taste, the other two were perfect in colour, design and style. He immediately tried them on and was delighted at how well they fitted.

He was so eager to try on the trousers that, rather than run upstairs to the privacy of his room, he pulled off his school pants and measured up in these too, oblivious of his mother or anyone else who might pop into the lounge. There was a slight disappointment here, as the first pair was just a little too tight for comfort. But the second was perfect. Not quite suitable for school, but just the ticket for smart casual wear if such a notion still existed.

Anne explained that she'd considered putting all the clothes away till Christmas in just three days' time, but why put off the pleasure and, in any case, the family had always tried to exchange brand new gifts on special occasions. And what if none of them had fit or just not suited John? The same applied to Jenny's surprise gift of a violin too. 'Indeed,' John joked to his mum at his sister's expense, 'Why put off becoming a virtuoso performer any longer than necessary?'

There'd still be a couple of genuine Christmas presents too, Anne promised smugly!

Later that Wednesday evening, dad didn't disappoint either. He confessed to discreetly examining John's shoes twice over the past week and to hatching a new plan to restore them – this time more durably! He'd taken advice at the neighbourhood repair outfit and another volunteer had generously supplied free of charge a pair of completely new soles made out of leather. On animal rights grounds, this material had been outlawed in recent years for use in manufacturing new products. However, as yet the legislation hadn't been made retroactive and so there was no prohibition on repurposing leather used in manufacturing old clothing and footwear.

John's felt a renewed surge of faith in mankind and his conscience was pricked by remorse at having mentally castigated his father for supposed ineptitude and lack of parental concern. To make amends, he offered his father a hand next morning in securing the new soles to his uppers and, if necessary, trimming them around the edges once the glue had set. Dad's repair co-worker had deliberately cut the leather one size larger than John's normal shoe size to provide a generous margin for error.

Later that same evening, his sister resumed plucking and bowing away at her new musical toy. John wondered how long it would take her to produce anything resembling music. If only she'd acquired an instrument such as the saxophone on which, he'd been told, one could learn to play a simple tune within a matter of days. His thoughts then turned to the old piano in the living room which hadn't been tuned for years. A piano could blend so well with practically any musical instrument other than a poorly played violin. He had taught himself a few very elementary piano pieces just over a year ago and mentioned this to his mum who encouraged his interest:

'I'm sure we can look up a decent piano tuner in the area if you want to get back to that. Your sister could play that a bit too and give us a break from the violin. Given the government's encouragement to revive home entertainments these days, maybe we can get you a grant to buy a second-hand wind instrument. Then you could accompany Jenny on that.'

John was enthused. He opened the piano stool and pulled out an old theory book to remind him of the musical notation basics for sight reading. Within an hour, he was back to playing some simple arrangements of Christmas carols. And the piano wasn't desperately out of tune either, so retuning could wait till the New Year. After he'd laboriously sightread a simple arrangement of Silent Night for the third or fourth time, the tortured violin sounds emanating from Jenny's room suddenly ceased. Half a minute later she appeared by his side demanding her own turn on the black and white ivory keys. Her performance of Silent Night on the piano was far less tortured than the sounds she'd so far produced on the violin and perceptibly outshone his own. John's sense of sibling rivalry which had lain dormant for some time, was immediately reactivated.

Amateurish music-making was an entirely unplanned Yuletide treat for the Greenway family, but it did much to evoke something of the spirit of Christmases past. As promised, Anne managed to hire a piano tuner the very next day and so for the rest of the holidays John settled into his new role as page turner for Jenny whose talents by common consent were better employed at the piano than at the violin, at least for the festive period. His own musical ambitions were sustained by the vague promise of a grant application to the Ministry for Culture in the New Year.

John and Jenny also lavished several hours on piecing together and decorating a forty-year-old synthetic Christmas tree. This was only thanks to Mike's parents who passed it down when he and Anne married. Few of the original decorations remained sufficiently intact for display, however, but this just added to the excitement and challenge of creatively manufacturing new ones out of available materials hiding in draws and cupboards around the house.

The Greenways were painfully aware that they were one of only a handful of families in a position to adorn their homes in this way, because both new synthetic and real Christmas trees were no longer commercially available on environmental grounds. Last year, they knew of at least two residents in their road who had been fined for cutting down and decorating trees in their own garden. And since then, it was rumoured that penalties for such wanton acts of environmental vandalism had become even more severe.

Everyone in the family enjoyed old-fashioned board games apart from Anne. Feeling duty-bound to be a good sport, however, she joined in where an even number of players were required. This act of self-sacrifice reminded her of how she used to play along to please her father who had also been a great board games fan.

It was actually Mike's parents who had passed down all the games which he and his siblings had enjoyed as children. There was also a book outlining a treasure trove of ideas for games which could be crafted out of bits of cardboard with the help of coloured pens and pencils. A fairly abundant supply of these could be found in various drawers and cupboards of the Greenway's house, which was fortunate, as few shops now supplied them.

Mike succeeded in reconstructing the rules of an exciting detective game which he'd been passionate about as a teenager.

It involved solving a murder and determining where it took place and by what means. He set Jenny to work designing the board out of card cut from cereal boxes while John crafted the required three-dimensional playing pieces from the off-cuts. Amusement derived from attempts to sketch and construct the figures and objects required rivalled the fun of playing the game itself.

There were at least four conspicuous elements missing from the celebrations on Christmas day itself, if only from the perspective of the parents' childhood memories. One of these was the dearth of gifts. Mike and Anne had grown up accustomed to receiving at least a dozen brand new toys and other exciting presents well into their teens. Also, there had been the new and old Christmas Special shows on the television to look forward to and super-abundant meals with highly indulgent foods and drinks which were traditionally associated with the festive period. Very little of all this remained.

And then, of course, there was the absence of the two senior members of the family, both of whom only last Christmas had appeared to be in good physical and mental health, but who had sadly and, in gran's case, tragically, passed away within six months of each other.

Anne made a difficult choice just before Christmas Day. This was to seize the opportunity of her mother's passing to convert all her saleable possessions into cash. On Sunday, she gathered up all her mother's clothes. She washed and dried those which were suitable and binned the rest, though not before she'd considered giving these to Mike to store in the garage as rags. But that wouldn't have seemed right.

On Monday, she packed the clothes into two suitcases along with everything else – from trinkets to unused toiletries – and travelled by bus to a small neighbouring town which had an outlet selling second-hand goods.

Not so many years ago, Anne would have automatically donated all such unwanted items to a charity. However, on this special occasion she felt she had to put her own family first and try to fund at least one half-decent present each for her husband and two children. Maybe this time even a small toy for Jock. In the event, she returned home delighted with her purchases made from the proceeds of the sale. There was even a small surplus which she resolved to donate to a charity chosen by her family.

Anne felt a renewed gratitude to the neighbour for the kind gift of second-hand clothes. Even though these could only be regarded as pre-Christmas gifts, they had reduced the pressure on her to meet everyone's tacit expectations.

It also fell to Anne to provide at least some semblance of a Christmas dinner for her clan. The obvious strategy was to bake the remainder of her store of sugar, salt, butter and flour into fancy pastries and cakes. Using up all these ingredients now would remove the temptation to break the family promise, particularly Jenny's, to do without most of these when the New Year began.

Fortunately, there were still a few apples and plums left from the two fruit-bearing trees in the back garden which could also be used in baking. It was Mike's job to store these safely in the garage, allowing the family to indulge once or twice a week up to about February when supplies tended to be exhausted. The only way she could think to enhance main courses was to add a little gravy and spices to otherwise very run-of-the-mill staple foods.

That was pretty well it. Of course, it would have been so nice to have a few electric-powered illuminations and slow-burning scented candles strategically placed in the hallway and rooms to create a cosy Winter ambiance about the house. Anne couldn't remember exactly how long ago these were prohibited, but following the ban, she had kept a secret box of unused and half-consumed candles and incense sticks tucked away in the attic in the forlorn hope that one fine day the prohibition would be lifted.

So, Christmas day began with the present-opening ritual. All eyes were on John as he opened the first of his two gifts. He was, after all, the main stakeholder given his imminent entitlement to brand new school clothes. The others sensed that their own enjoyment of the occasion would depend to a degree on John's reaction. Thankfully, he was absolutely delighted with the shirt his mother and father had bought after pooling their meagre savings and earnings. The sale of gran's possessions had enabled Anne to buy her son new trousers suitable for school to go with the splendid shirt. She had ensured the size was right by measuring them up against the second-hand trousers which had fit him perfectly the other day.

Jenny too gratefully received her gifts – a much-prized toiletries set which she'd requested in an unsubtle bid in her battle against body odour. But to her delight and genuine surprise, she also received a maintenance kit and splendid case for her violin. These were clearly more modest presents than her brother's, but her turn to enjoy favoured sibling status would come once she entered the sixth form in under three years' time.

Mike presented Anne with an exotic bunch of flowers grown in a repair shop colleague's garden. Anne had bought her husband a fine set of drill bits for his repair shop work. John and Jenny had pooled their limited resources saved from at least two months' 'spends' to buy their parents a box of chocolates and tin of assorted biscuits. Both gifts were a genuine luxury way out of reach for the majority of austerity-stricken households.

The family meal all went to plan. The festive mood was jeopardised momentarily when Jenny, while helping her mother in the kitchen, expressed surprise at how they'd been able to afford all the little extras this year. Fortunately for Anne, however, her daughter readily accepted a matter-of-fact explanation of where the funds had come from. Anne was moved at this further proof of Jenny's growing maturity and forgiveness, if such were required, for what had happened to gran.

In contrast with the many little deprivations, some of the self-styled entertainments of the Greenway family's Christmas celebrations rivalled those of previous years. The biggest hit of all was a game which had been particularly popular with Mike's parents' generation and required no more than a few sheets of paper and pens. This was called *Consequences* and involved writing a line of a short story, then passing it on to the next person who would write the next line without looking at what had gone before. When finally read aloud, the resulting non-sequiturs and coincidental links between the stories generated much laughter.

Mike and Anne became restless by mid-afternoon, conditioned as they were from childhood to tune in to the Queen's speech. John obliged his parents by turning on the television which had stood silently in the lounge until just two minutes to three. Since the abolition of the monarchy five years ago, the Christmas Day speech tradition had been usurped by the Prime Minister who had stubbornly insisted on keeping to the same time and date. This was despite strong feeling among many anti-Christians that the occasion should be completely secularised and moved to New Year's Day. Just as Anne was arguing this point, the PM officially announced that this would happen as of next year!

The speech itself was broadly predictable in avoiding references to authoritarian and contentious decisions taken by the government over the past year. The PM thanked his fellow countrymen and women for their forbearance and assured them that he and his team appreciated all the sacrifices they were making. He did, however, venture to suggest that, over time, many would come to realise that giving up or cutting down on certain things had actually done them good. Over consumption of food and other excesses had not just caused a climate crisis for mankind as a whole, but had also brought grief rather than happiness to many individuals.

The moment the three-minute speech was over, Jenny switched the television off again. The two remaining TV channels could only offer rival film versions of the 19th century story by Charles Dickens: A Christmas Carol which they had all seen multiple times. John commented sarcastically that it was time the Christian 'Goodwill to all mankind' element of this narrative was re-written to reflect and glorify the new religion.

'I suppose the moral of the story is the same. What does our new religion have to say about what happens when we're at the point of death? Aren't we told we'll be met by departed spirits who will force us to review how we've lived our lives and then help us on our way into the next world?' Jenny's enigmatic tone left it unclear as to whether she was being rhetorical or challenging the others to a family debate.

John was curious: 'Are they teaching you that now in Year 10? If so, they've certainly moved the curriculum on since I was at that stage.'

'No, it's just I have a few mates at school who are interested in that sort of thing and we have lots of discussions.' She continued poignantly, 'It started when all our grandparents kept dying on us and we just wanted to have some idea about what happens next...'

'Happy Boxing Day!', Mike, who was first up to greet everyone in this manner, wondered what the relevance of this day would be in just a few years' time other than as a synonym for 'second holiday of the festive period'. Without anything in particular to celebrate at this depressing time of year, even the notion of festivity would probably be obsolete by then. He promptly set about putting the finishing touches to John's freshly repaired shoes which just need a sliver paring off the leather soles where these slightly protruded beyond the uppers onto which they were now, he prayed, securely glued.

Anne, who was tidying up in the hall, thought she heard a faint knock on the front door. She was about to dismiss this as a trick of the wintry weather when two more slightly louder knocks followed. Surprised that anyone should pay a visit so early on Boxing Day, she cautiously opened the door to find Mrs Watson standing there looking a very different version of herself than the one who had come round a few days ago bearing gifts. Her clothes were dishevelled and she was more agitated than Anne recalled ever having seen her before.

'What on earth's up Mrs Watson?' Anne's use of the surname seemed appropriate owing to the significant age difference between them, but then it occurred to her she didn't know her neighbour's first name in any case. Seeing the poor lady struggle to articulate what was troubling her, Anne invited her into the hallway.

'It's just my husband and I don't quite know where to turn. Our energy and water supply has just been cut off. You see, the other week we had a call from the utilities people. They told us that we'd been consuming an excessive amount of energy and water over the past couple of months and insisted on questioning us. They virtually forced their way into our house and started interrogating us about our energy use – which rooms we used, how long we heated them for, how often we washed our clothes, showered, etcetera. It was most unpleasant.'

Anne could hardly forget hearing the van pull up in the neighbourhood and how, fearing that she might well be the crew's target, had cut short her guilty self-indulgent extended shower. Chaffing marks were still visible where she had frantically rubbed herself dry with a coarse towel and hastily pulled on her clothes, expecting to have to rush to the door any second.

'I got a nasty shock that day too when I heard the racket that van made. I imagine all the neighbours did,' Anne empathised.

Mike and John, who had overheard snippets of the conversation from the lounge, joined the two ladies in the hallway. Anne quickly summarised what had been said so far. Mike invited everyone into the lounge where Mrs Watson continued her account. The elderly couple had been asked by the utilities van rogues whether either of them had any relevant health condition or conditions which entitled them to extra energy or water use. Neither she nor her husband was even aware such allowances existed or could be applied for.

'So, what happened after that? Did they give you any warnings or make threats?' Anne asked.

'That's just it. They said our water and energy use would be monitored over the next week to ten days and if it didn't significantly reduce, our supply could be temporarily suspended. We did make an effort to use less water and turned the heating down, but obviously not sufficiently to satisfy them.'

She had not been given any precise indication as to how much less energy and water she and her husband were expected to use and for how long their supply might be cut off if they failed to appease the authorities.

'Being vague is probably a deliberate tactic to get you to cut down as much as you can for fear of having your supply stopped. If they gave people an exact target, they'd just stick to that. Clever psychology!' John suggested.

But it was hard to see how the Greenways could help. Yes, they could decant some of their water into a large pan in much the same way as people in the old days used to call on a neighbour for a cup of sugar or flour when they ran out. But they could hardly share their energy supply: even the longest extension power cable wouldn't stretch to the other side of the road!

Anne felt a little ashamed at not having had the presence of mind to invite her distressed neighbour properly into the house and that her usually timid and indecisive husband had beaten her to it! But this emotion triggered a more appropriate response as a possible solution dawned on her.

'I can't imagine they'd be allowed to cut off your power and water supply for more than a day or two without giving sufficient notice so you could at least fill up a few bottles and pans for drinking water. I suspect there's been an admin error and you should have received a phone call or letter - or perhaps another visit. But we won't be able to even enquire about what's gone wrong until tomorrow, as it's a public holiday. Meanwhile, you and your husband should stay with us. We have a spare room which we can make up for two.'

A few moments later, Mrs Watson set off back to her house to gather a few things and bring along her husband. The Greenways took advantage of this time interval together to talk the situation through. At the risk of sounding churlish, given that he'd been joint beneficiary of the Watsons' generosity only days ago, John spoke first:

'It's very good of you to offer help, mum, but couldn't we end up in the same predicament as they are? If the Watsons stay more than a couple of days, we could also be assessed as having used excess energy and water and get cut off too...'

Anne had made this calculation at the same time as overcoming her resistance to offering up the room which until very recently had been her mother's.

'I don't think so, not without a warning anyway, and that would give us a chance to ask the relevant questions the poor Watsons didn't have the presence of mind to ask. Actually, I'm fairly sure we won't get into trouble. I doubt whether the bureaucrats will have cottoned on yet to the fact my mother died so recently, so our water and power allowance won't have been reduced. What's more, it wouldn't kill us to implement our New Year's Resolution to shower and wash less a few days early.'

'Yeah, no one's more anxious than I am about water rationing, but it might actually hurt less to reduce what we use gradually over the last six days of the old year. Then it'll comes as less of a shock in January.'

Jenny had tried hard to sound matter of fact and avoid the slightest hint of resentment in her voice. She couldn't, however, entirely dismiss the thought that perhaps Mrs Watson's generosity a few days before might have been a calculated insurance policy against likely consequences of the unwelcome visit.

Mike didn't contribute to the short discussion, but nodded from time to time, signalling support for the family's altruistic consensus.

Mrs Watson returned half an hour later accompanied by her husband with small suitcases. They also brought a shopping bag filled with groceries – a natural contribution towards their board and lodging perhaps, but a pleasant surprise to the Greenways nevertheless. On Anne's suggestion, the couple at last introduced themselves as Joyce and Terry so that all were now on first name terms.

The ice was further broken when everyone joined in a hearty meal followed by a parlour game once made popular by a radio and then television show. The format was that each contestant in turn had to think up a job or occupation while the others asked 'yes' or 'no' questions in order work out what it was.

Joyce and Terry cheated somewhat by choosing their actual past occupations, though this worked fine, as the Greenways had known very little about them until today. Joyce had been a shop assistant until her shop had closed down in the austerity years and Terry was a retired accountant whose role had become virtually redundant like so many with the decline of the consumer-driven economy. He remained active by giving financial advice to friends and acquaintances. This allowed him to earn a little pocket money like Mike. He also put in a few hours of voluntary service giving debt counselling at the local citizens advice centre.

The minister for Economy, Finance and Taxation was in a far more relaxed mood than just days earlier when the worst financial news had hit the fan.

'Yes, renationalising the energy companies was probably the smartest thing the government ever did. It certainly helped that so many of them went belly up with the sharp gas and oil price increases in the twenties and had to be vacuumed up by the bigger established energy companies. Then, with the next wave of price hike,s we were able to heroically bail the survivors out too. And coming in at the point of financial collapse meant we didn't have to pay out billions in compensation to the private owners, which we'd have had to do if we'd taken them over as going concerns. It doesn't often happen, but sometimes economic crises benefit the taxpayer instead of the taxpayer having to foot the bill.'

Howard had long since learnt acquired the wisdom to concur with his political master's train of thought:

'And into the bargain, they gifted us the technological infrastructure to monitor citizens' energy use, and therewith the capacity to ration it.' As it passed his lips, Howard felt this sentence to be exquisitely elegant until he realised that probably no one had used the word 'therewith' outside legal circles since a hundred years before his birth. After mentally rebuking himself

I must stop reading early 19th century novels! he continued:

'The difficult question before us now, however, is whether simply fining people would be more effective in getting them to cut down energy consumption than our present policy of threatening them with power cuts.'

'Yes, and there have been too many cases where utility teams on home visits have run maintenance checks on local sub stations shortly afterwards and accidentally disrupted power supplies. Word is getting out that we're running around callously turning off power supplies to people whose lives may depend on it! Certainly, it would make more sense to either fine excessive users or charge a penalty rate for units consumed above an agreed maximum.'

Howard, ever mindful of the civil servant's duty to make policy pay, felt the opportune moment had come:

'Yes, and, of course, it's important that we get the message out as to what the maximum usage is. I personally prefer the higher charge rate, as it sounds less punitive than a fine. Also, it's proportionate to the excess used. However, in order to make this work both in terms of reducing energy use and financially benefiting the Treasury, I beg your pardon - Ministry for Economy, Finance and Taxation - I suggest the higher charge rate should apply to all energy use in that particular financial quarter.'

'You absolute Devil, Howard, that's pure evil genius!'

'And in terms of social justice and for simplicity's sake, we'll fix each property's energy quota based purely on the number of residents. So, in other words, those living in larger houses won't get a larger quota just because they have bigger rooms to heat. Only those with serious qualifying disabilities will be able to apply for a higher quota.'

'Yes, I love it. If you could get the modelling of how the new scheme would work to me within the next 72 hours, I'd appreciate it. We want this legislated and through to public Comms by mid-January at the latest. Then it can be implemented by early February to yield maximum returns before the winter weather's out!'

His anxiously anticipated conference with the minister at last over, Howard walked back to his office on a cushion of air. He settled into his chair breathing a deep a sigh relief. Now he could look forward to his first night of undisturbed sleep in at least two weeks. He fell asleep easily enough later that evening, but woke up in a sweat in the middle of the night. Unfortunately, he was plagued with a social conscience.

CHAPTER 8: DEATH BY A THOUSAND CUTS

It was the day after Boxing Day or, as it used to be called, the third day of Christmas.

Yesterday, Jenny had felt herself bonding with the unexpected family guests almost at once and made a point of joining them for breakfast. Had she been able to examine her own unconscious mind, she would have realised this bonding was conditioned more by pity and empathy than by genuine personal appeal. No sooner had polite conversation begun than, quite out of the blue, she asked Joyce about her age. Although a little taken aback by the question, Joyce wasn't at all offended. She stared fixedly at Jenny for a moment as if to test her and proudly announced that she was in her seventieth year.

Jenny wasn't to be deceived and just as proudly declared:

'That means you're actually sixty-nine, then! My gran used to tease mum, saying she was in her fortieth year when she was only thirty-nine. It was a bit cruel of her really, as it's a big deal for women to get to forty.'

'It can be quite a big deal to reach seventy too, dear!' Joyce laughed. 'Or, to be clear, seventy *also*!'

This gave Jenny the chance to modestly show off what she'd learned at school not so long ago in English. 'Wow, *two* and *too*, that's a great example of a homophone!' she declared.

With the ice broken, it was easy enough for Jenny to learn that Terry, Joyce's husband, was considerably older at seventy-seven. The reason for this line of questioning at last rose to the surface of her consciousness and Jenny visualised the appropriate column and row in the NHS chart she'd taken some pains to memorise. The couple both fell into the £2000 maximum annual expenditure bracket, though Terry was perilously close to the abyss, having entered his seventy-eighth year after which benefits dropped to a meagre £1000, as had happened with her gran.

With the initial panic now over and proper introductions having been made, there was less pressure on the Greenways to entertain the Watsons the following morning. After a good lie-in, the elderly couple were content to watch television in the lounge for most of the morning while everyone else went about their usual business.

It was Monday and so back off to the repair shop for Mike. Although he would ideally have spun out his winter break a few days longer, he knew from experience that demand for his services was surprisingly high between Christmas and New Year. He was also anxious to earn a few pounds and build up his savings again ready for the next extra expense which no doubt lay just around the corner.

Anne had plenty of washing up and cleaning to do as well as make an early start preparing what she hoped would be another tasty meal for the expanded family. The enhanced array of ingredients provided by the Watsons would be put to good use. Later that afternoon, she welcomed Joyce's offer to labour alongside her in the kitchen.

Aside from their usual habit of avid reading, John and Jenny spent much of the day practising on their various instruments and attempting to perform a few simple pieces together. The hymns had now given way to a more diverse range of compositions from sheet music which they'd taken it in turns to dig out of the old piano stool's storage compartment. The violin had come with only a rudimentary theory book which demonstrated finger positions for the various notes in the Treble Clef, but Jenny preferred to find the notes by ear, a process which at times proved stressful for other members of the household.

Terry and Joyce, unaware of the siblings' limited musical prowess and repertoire, made a number of impossible requests for songs from a bygone era. Nevertheless, even though it wasn't specifically intended as such, the elderly couple chose to regard the performance as a personal tribute. John and Jenny would have enjoyed making music together just the same, with or without an appreciative audience.

Life went on peacefully enough in the Greenway household with no hint of the upsetting and disruptive events in store for the second half of the day. Anne succeeded with Joyce's help in serving up a delicious and hearty lunch and the whole family helped cheerfully enough with the washing up in the kitchen afterwards. Anne, however, slightly spoilt the harmony by casting disapproving glances at John and Jenny and even criticising Mike out loud for being insufficiently economical in their water use, particularly when rinsing the pots.

Jenny would have so liked to take Joyce and Terry out for a tour of the rear garden with Jock, but she feared the inevitable conversation as they approached her gran's still fresh burial mound. That would be upsetting certainly for herself and maybe for Joyce too.

After the couple had watched the first TV programme of the afternoon, they decided to nip back home to pick up a few more items. However, they returned barely ten minutes later looking perplexed.

'What's up Joyce?' Anne had lingered in the hall waiting for the couple to return, sensing there might be some news.

'I can't understand it! As soon as we got inside the house Terry automatically pressed the switch in the hall, as it was already getting a bit dark, and the light came on. So, I rushed into the kitchen, turned on the taps and after a few gurgles the water came through as normal.'

'If it had been just the water or the power, you might imagine it was a temporary fault, but it's hard to see how both could go off at once as they aren't connected are they?' Anne theorised aloud.

'In the old days, someone would have posted a card to warn if something was being cut off and give you an idea how long it was going to be for. Or you'd hear something on the news later on about how many houses were affected and when they expected to get the supply back on. But times have changed and no one knows what to expect nowadays,' Terry reminisced.

Within an hour or so, the Watsons had checked out of the Greenway house with the assurance that they'd be welcome to return if the problem reoccurred. Anne insisted they took back the remainder of the groceries they'd brought over to spare them having to shop for their evening meal.

Meanwhile, Mike was spending a fulfilling afternoon at the repair outfit. As in the previous two years, there was plenty to do because even local residents who still had jobs hadn't returned to work yet and had found time to sort through their various mechanical and electrical contraptions. It was a rather unfortunate sign of the times that many items brought in for repair had actually been exchanged between members of the same household as second- or third-hand Christmas gifts without first checking they were in working order.

Mike was engrossed in disassembling a food mixer when there was a resounding bang on the metal security door at the front of the workshop. Two men dressed in official-looking suits unceremoniously entered the building and moved to a central position among the four men and two ladies who were currently at work.

'I'm Nigel Crawley from Neighbourhood Compliance. Who's in charge here?' the sternest-looking of the two bellowed.

No one immediately answered, as there was no leadership

hierarchy among the group. Various individuals led on different issues such as opening and locking up, paying the electric bill, health and safety issues, insurance and so forth.

Perhaps because he was standing closest to and facing the bellowing official, the others hesitatingly looked across at Mike. He took the cue and replied:

'We're all equals here. It's a community repair outfit. We're just volunteers who use our various skills to try and mend things people bring to us. How can we help you?'

'We've recorded high levels of energy use in this zone and need to check out what's going on,' explained the rather less aggressive looking partner introducing himself as Simon Jones.

'Also, we're pretty keen on health and safety and hope you are too. Otherwise, it'll be a hefty fine and you'll get closed down until you meet the required standards.' It was Nigel Crawley, the sterner member of the duo again.

This caused something of a commotion with almost everyone talking at once. As the hubbub died down, each volunteer eventually had the chance to speak on their own account.

Julie, one of the lady volunteers 'on duty' that day, objected that she had naught to do with the imposters' concerns, as she specialised in repairing and altering clothing by hand. An old-fashioned seamstress, as it were. Two of the men angrily defended their right not to have their work interrupted, as they worked on joinery-type jobs mostly using non-power tools such as saws and chisels. One of them, Frank, did have an old cordless drill which he justified on the grounds that he charged it at home. Extra domestic power use, argued the two men, so that too would have to be looked into.

The long and short of it was that the outfit would have to close down until an investigation had been carried out. Each member of the informal cooperative was required to provide their contact details and those of the other six members not present today. If they were found to be in breach of any one of several relevant regulations, fines would almost certainly be imposed. These could range from ten to one hundred pounds per individual. In that case, they could expect a home visit later tomorrow evening.

'Tomorrow evening?' exclaimed Duncan, another electrical goods repairer who often worked in tandem with Mike. 'How can you complete a thorough investigation within 24 hours?'

Jones was visibly about to attempt an answer, but was deterred by Crawley sweeping an arm across his colleague's chest.

'We've seen and heard plenty enough here. We'll interview your co-workers this evening or catch them sometime tomorrow. Rest assured: you'll get a visit tomorrow evening so make sure you're in.'

So that was it. Everyone was sent packing just before half two. Duncan, whose job it was, locked up the workshop with extra special care, as many items belonging to trusting service users remained in the volunteers' care. He posted a notice on the metal security door which had taken such a pounding less than half an hour ago: *Temporarily closed. Please call me or a colleague for further updates from Wednesday morning.* He included his own and Mike's phone numbers.

Mike left the workshop at about half three on a Monday as a rule, so he returned home nearly an hour before the usual time. Still in a state of shock, he couldn't at first bring himself to tell the others what had happened and agonised for a while as to how best to break the news. In a sense, he felt it was really just his own news, as his repair man role only affected the rest of his family directly through the modest donations which he was normally able to contribute to the household.

He finally decided to call a family meeting for dinner at six o'clock instead of the usual practice on weekdays when everyone tended to drift into the kitchen dining room at various times. This suited Anne too, who also had something to announce. John and Jenny, sensing something was awry, agreed obediently without questioning and ensured they both arrived at the dinner table at six on the dot.

Anne had prepared what she frankly admitted was a 'slimline' evening meal, but had nevertheless employed as much ingenuity as she could muster to ensure quality and palatability if not quantity from the meagre ingredients available. This helped distract her from the unpleasant news she too had to announce to her family.

Everyone sat down in almost synchronised fashion. Even Jock was already waiting expectantly under the table for his intended and accidental treats. Husband and wife exchanged anxious glances with Anne nodding at Mike to go first.

Mike wasn't temperamentally the sort to overdramatise matters on his own account. He therefore rather played down the sheer shock and anguish he and his colleagues had experienced at the workshop. If anything, the others were relieved that least the unpleasant encounter with officialdom hadn't led to a serious and irrevocable outcome. Not yet, anyway.

Anne paradoxically felt the worse for having to follow Mike's narrative, as her news was surely more impactful and disturbing.

'I'm afraid no one's going to like this. I got a letter today from Inland Revenue. It concerns grandad and gran's estates.'

Mike looked puzzled:

'Estates? But they didn't have any, did they? Isn't that property, investments and savings and the like? All the money they got from selling their little house went to paying off our mortgage a few years ago when they came to live with us. Their pensions were pretty damned modest...'

'Well, that's just it. Although pretty damned modest, like you say, dad did have some savings – a matter of a few hundred pounds which eventually came to me. I've used them to supplement our citizens' income over the past four or five months and only £200 or so is left out of about £400. And now this!'

Anne passed round the table an inheritance tax demand for £208. The explanatory note was brief and to the point. A new law meant that the Ministry for Economy, Finance and Taxation was entitled to half of all deceased persons' assets.

'So, it's a ruddy good job I'd not had to spend all the money left over yet!'

'But surely, inheritance tax is just for people who are stinking rich and have hundreds of thousands in property and other assets!' exclaimed John indignantly.

Jenny had benefited from a rudimentary financial education in year 8 and understood the gist of the conversation, but was not yet able to fully grasp the implications of the situation for the family. She asked ingenuously:

'But doesn't that mean we won't actually have to pay anything back if mum hasn't spent it all yet?'

'Well, I'll have to check our account, but I guess we'll probably only have to find about ten pounds on top of what's left.'

John had a better understanding of the situation, however.

'What you're really saying mum, is that the main reason we've not been as destitute as we might have been since grandad died is because you've been topping up our household expenditure with an extra thirty or forty quid a month since the summer.'

'You've got it in one,' Anne sighed.

'But then it gets worse and better at the same time. Gran also had nearly £300 pounds savings from her pension, as she had a separate account from grandad's bless her. The letter from the Ministry for Economy, Finance and Taxation was really triggered by her death last month. So, when we inherit that money, hopefully in a few months' time, half of that will go to the Treasury, as it used to be called, too.'

Mike attempted to assess their predicament as it had emerged so far:

'So how long have we got to pay the death duty, or whatever it's called, on grandad's money? If we have a few months' grace, we'll be able to pay most of that off with gran's money along with what's due on her savings, won't we?'

Anne smiled: 'Creative accounting indeed. The letter simply states the money's due, so it's not clear how long we have. I'd best give them a call tomorrow, if I can get through, of course.'

There was another loud knock at the door. With the Watsons' recent comings and goings, no one was especially startled this time, although Mike's heart sank momentarily until he recalled that his next encounter with the official storm troopers wasn't meant to be until tomorrow. It was Joyce, this time without her husband.

'You'll never believe this, but just as we thought everything was back to normal, these two obnoxious men from some government ministry descended on us. They said we were being fined after all for overuse of water and energy. Twenty pounds for a first offence. When I explained our water and power had been cut off for nearly a whole day and night, they said they didn't know anything about it, but that their meter readings only covered from when they first came round until up to two days ago. They claimed to know nothing about the supply being cut off, saying it must have been a coincidence.'

'How long did they give you to pay?' Anne enquired.

'We could either pay in cash today, which was out of the question, or have the money docked from our Citizen's Basic Income due at the end of next month. There's a fiddly process whereby you can pay over three months, but there's loads of paperwork and a ten percent arrangement fee, so we opted for paying in January.'

'That's bloody lousy. I've never heard of fines for using too much energy or water before. Surely, we should have heard about it on the news!' objected John.

'We'll at least have time to raise a bit of cash before then so we won't feel the pinch so much. We've a couple of things we could sell,' Joyce mused.

Anne more than the rest of the Greenways was feeling uncomfortable for accepting such a generous bag of riches from the Watsons only days ago. She knew Joyce wouldn't accept payment now, but was already thinking hard to come up with a plan to help out the old couple when the day of reckoning came. Yes, at least there was time before the end of January with a few days still left of December.

Nigel Crawley and Simon Jones had come to the end of a long evening making surprise calls on half a dozen residents in the Greenways' area. The content of each discussion was essentially the same. Householders had been advised a few weeks before that they had been overconsuming water and energy, had experienced a temporary loss of supply and then been confronted by Crawley and Jones with a penalty notice.

Crawley knew through corrupt contacts in the Ministry that the actual legislation to impose fines for overconsumption would not come into effect until late January at the earliest. However, he'd been assured that there was no problem in issuing the fines in advance provided that the payments were suitably post-dated. This would provide him and his partner with an extra little bonus of roughly £28 between them which equated to twenty-five per cent of the seven premature fines issued. A masterstroke!

He hadn't felt it expedient to impart this good news yet to Jones who, owing to his fainthearted temperament, might have chickened out of the scheme. Crawley had already employed all his native cunning to convince his inexperienced colleague that running around the neighbourhood turning off energy and water supplies was officially sanctioned as a heavy-handed way of getting people used to managing with less power and water. It was for their own good in the long run, he argued, and there was no harm in the fact that they would earn a small bonus linked to their *customers'* reduced consumption. Jones, being somewhat gullible and naïve, trusted Crawley implicitly.

On Tuesday, *the day after the day after what used to be called Boxing Day*, as John joked, Anne called the HMRC enquiries line to query the letter they'd received about inheritance tax. She received a curt response or, in her own words, 'short shrift' from the voice at the other end. The days when children could expect to be provided for by 'intergenerational inheritance' were over. When Anne mentioned the paltry sum involved, the HMRC worker paused slightly in possible embarrassment before addressing her second question regarding how long payment could be deferred. 'Settlement to be made within a month of the date of the letter, 'came the reply. 'Thanks a million!' Anne replied, somewhat relieved if not exactly grateful.

Wednesday, 29th December, Jenny wrote in her journal which she'd promised herself to keep in earnest from the New Year. She was just getting into practice a couple of days early.

What mayhem we've had to put up with these past few weeks. Gran's passing – or rather virtual murder. Her burial and whole rigamarole over that. John's damned shoes. The Watsons' saga. As if they could have 'overconsumed' water and energy, an old couple like that! And the two nasty men. I wonder if they were the same ones who called on dad at the workshop and then again last night to demand yet another FINE! Thank God it was only £25, but nearly everyone at the workshop has been fined varying sums. It's great they've all agreed to club together with those who can afford to pay covering the couple who can't. Only trouble is it means dad has to pay £29 now. He looks really depressed over it and I can't help feeling it's more than just the fine. Is there something he's not telling us? I'm wracking my brains to see what I could do to bring in a bit of money.

There was, in fact, something Mike wasn't telling the children, though he quietly broke the news to Anne later that evening. When Crawley and Jones called as promised, they'd not only imposed the fine, but said from now on electrical repairs at the workshop were prohibited owing to health and safety concerns as well as energy consumption issues.

This effectively robbed Mike of his one remaining independent, albeit paltry, source of income, not to mention a sense of self-worth from serving the community and his only social outlet outside the home.

'What were the authorities trying to do, for heaven's sake?' Anne almost screamed in indignation. 'I thought the government was meant to be encouraging us to do more recycling, repairing and making do as well creative projects to bring back life in the community. Your repair outfit ticked all the boxes! And then there's all the rhetoric about the need to promote good mental health, as this will reduce the cost of treating people's physical illnesses in the longer term.'

'True', Mike agreed, 'and given how they've driven down spending on the NHS in recent years, you'd think they'd be investing more in that side of things now *in order to build a better, happier future for all*, as government narrative goes.'

Mike felt confident he'd quickly get over the initial shock and downheartedness engendered by the bad news and was already wracking his brains to find a way round the sanctions. He could turn up to the workshop anyway and try to help the others, but in some cases that would involve learning new skills which could actually mean placing a burden on his co-workers.

Or he could offer home visits to people who turned up with electrical goods for repair.... But then, damn! He recalled they'd been ordered to display a notice by the entrance: *No electrical goods!* Eventually, that would stop people coming and break the communication link with people seeking his kind of service.

Anne turned on the TV in the late afternoon on Wednesday to catch the news and weather report. Again, extreme weather was causing havoc in parts of the South. This had hardly let up in some regions since mid-Autumn. The Greenways were fortunate enough to live a long way inland in the North where they had so far been fairly well protected from the worst effects of storms. However, much more destructive weather virtually all over the British Isles was forecast for mid-January.

Only twenty years or so ago, various government grants had been made available to local authorities to alleviate the effects of flooding around coastal areas. Public money was even still being invested in defences to prevent further attrition to the coastline in some locations and a few sea walls were built in high-profile resorts popular both with locals and tourists.

However, in recent years, so many new areas had become threatened by the raging elements that this was placing too great a financial burden on the public purse. Compensation schemes for relocating residents with properties about to fall into the sea were discontinued so that unfortunate individuals facing this prospect had stark choices to make. Even more unfortunates whose houses had already been washing into the sea were faced with moving in with relatives, renting far inferior private flats or, as a last resort, being placed by cash-strapped councils in sub-standard bed and breakfast accommodation.

As if by synchronicity, just as the weather report homed in on the area in East Anglia most affected by the latest freak storms, Anne heard a loud thunderbolt signalling a sudden downpour closer to home. She cast her mind back to her childhood when, as if by magic, her warm house, filled with seasonal cheer, seemed to protect the whole family from the inclement elements outside. This sense of magical protection, like all childish fancies, naturally faded as she grew up, but the experience of recent years had eroded it away altogether. Now, she found herself forlornly praying for anything which might bring back just a little of that long-lost feeling of safety within the family home.

Anne's musings over these concerns brought to mind others of a more pragmatic nature. Most pressing was the need to restore her family's finances in the face of the latest catalogue of misfortunes. She had already made one painful decision by offering to the Watsons her mother's room so soon after her death. So why not, in the wake of this, steel herself to make another sacrifice, this time, for her immediate family's benefit? She discussed her idea with Mike who readily assented. Together, they then broached the issue with Jenny and John.

'... and so, if we agree to this grave hosting scheme within the next week before payment is due, we can get a considerable discount off gran's burial as well as being paid a tidy sum for agreeing to have a few other people buried in our garden.' Anne had decided to get straight to the point with her children.

'How does that work, then?' John questioned. 'Does that also mean that we have to open up our garden like an old-fashioned cemetery and let people just walk in whenever they want to pay their respects to their dearly departed?'

Jenny's initial response was even more bitter and resentful, but she did her utmost to conceal her negative emotions:

'Why not make them arrange with us when they're allowed to visit our graveyard and pay a small fee each time?'

Anne's heart ached for her daughter who she knew was still struggling to come to terms with her gran's death more than anyone else in the family even if she was putting on a brave face.

'You're not entirely wrong, Jenny. There are three packages, as they call them, based on how often they intend to visit, though it would clearly be impossible to police if someone overstepped the quota they'd paid for.'

'How the hell would they access our garden? We ourselves can only get in through the back door.' John attempted to visualise all possible scenarios.

Anne did her best to reassure him. 'It would either mean us letting them in through the front door or installing a gate at the bottom of the garden so people could access whenever. The gate's the only realistic option, though it would be at our own expense. The idea is that they would contact us by phoning first in case we were planning a family event in the garden. Or they could agree in advance to visit only on certain days between fixed times.'

It was time for Mike to enter the conversation.

'We've measured up the space available and reckon that without drastically reducing the area of the garden, we could comfortably fit in two more graves initially. One would fit either side of gran and grandad's about two metres away with possibly later on up to three more graves coming closer to the house. In a way, the symmetry of it all would be more aesthetic than having just an extra grave in one corner.'

Mike generally wasn't the most adept at putting a positive spin on dire situations, but this wasn't his worst attempt by any means.

Jenny almost immediately warmed to the financial rescue plan. John, however, needed a few moments while the altruistic side of his nature wrestled with the instinctive territorial aspect of his psyche. The inner combat over, he nodded assent.

And so, the Greenway family Diet decreed that their garden would become a public – or, in the old sense, private – cemetery. Anne felt it wise to specify that the extra income would go to pay off fines, plug anticipated holes in household finances and any surplus would be put away for a rainy day. In using the hackneyed phrase *rainy day*, she couldn't help feeling a better modern equivalent might be *stormy weather*. She laughed about this later with Mike who commented that *Here's that Rainy Day* and *Stormy Weather* were popular songs last century. Who nowadays would regard *rainy day* a sufficiently powerful metaphor for the severity of the problems facing the world, even setting aside the living reality of a climate breakdown?

It was Jenny's turn in the shower for the first time since Christmas day. How could it have been normal to have just two baths or showers a week when gran and grandad's parents were young?

She recalled grandad say: 'Families didn't all have running water when my parents were children, so it was quite common for several members of the family to wash once a week in the same bath tub of water heated up over the fire. They might get a jug of warm water to rinse a bit before they climbed out. A damned sight more economical, it has to be said. So even in the seventies of the last century, most people just bathed once or twice a week out of habit. It was only when showers became more common that people got soft and started showering once or even twice a day.

No one seemed to talk about what women or girls were meant to do when they started their periods, though her mum, bless her, had at least braved a mutually embarrassing chat with her about it. Jenny had come to the conclusion that *all over* showers would be a luxury to be enjoyed no more than once a month. She'd have to settle for washing just the relevant bits the rest of the time, as more or less agreed by the family collective.

The newly appointed Minister for Legal Affairs, Verity Shillaker, had spent the morning poring over various options for dealing with retroactive penalties against the most resource-wasting citizens. She had approached her research team in the vain hope that it might be possible to subject people suspected of historical profligacy to some form of carbon footprint test. Their left-brained reply was that science and technology had not yet progressed quite that far.

She was nevertheless convinced that there must be a way of arriving at reasonably accurate assessments of people's historic consumption levels, if only by analysing their current material status and projecting backwards. For instance, their present living accommodation provided a clue as to their general wealth. How long they owned this property was on public record, what they paid for it, etcetera. Then the tax office held records of virtually all citizens' earnings, at least over the past few decades. Banks and credit card companies, among the institutions still legally allowed to use computers, held digital records of customers' statements and these provided more than a clue as to their pattern of expenditure and how much disposable income went on non-essential items.

Foreign travel should prove a gold mine. For well over a generation up to about twenty-five years ago, nearly half commercial flights were for leisure trips. Cruises, by definition non-essential luxuries of the most egregious and ecologically damaging sort, were another easy target, as they were extremely easy to trace back to indulgers' bank accounts.

The minister smiled to herself as she considered how quickly public opinion grew accustomed to condemning privileged people for acts which, at the time they were committed, rarely raised an eyebrow. Venerated statesmen and adventurers of earlier centuries had statues of themselves toppled for crimes against humanity which were hardly recognised as such in their day. Actions and attitudes once taken for granted, but which subsequently came to be viewed as 'racist', were a case in point.

And then there was the whole catalogue of sexual assaults criminalised in the early twenty-first century which had been merely regarded as saucy banter or flirting when they were fashionable at the time.

So, why would pursuing, persecuting and even prosecuting wealthy individuals for past lavish lifestyles be any different? Especially in an era where world resources were universally known to be scarce and overconsumption recognised as the primary cause environmental degradation. Why should the perpetrators escape punishment any more than common criminals when people were dying in their droves as a result of their past and present actions? And the social justice side was so easy to spin with the most affected victims being those who contributed least to the climate crisis in the first place.

By the early afternoon, Shillaker felt she and her Civil Servant team had carried out sufficient research to be prepared for a joint workshop with the Minister for Economy, Finance and Taxation. The two then drafted a bill to present to Parliament which they hoped would cover all the bases and meet with near universal approval. With their collaboration complete, Shillaker confided her feelings to her ministerial colleague:

'Apart from the criminals themselves, few objected when parliament passed a law half a century ago enabling the authorities to confiscate ill-gotten gains or misappropriated assets from known criminals. All that has changed over time is the perception of who society's criminals really are. We are arriving today at a new concept that anyone who can be identified as consuming more than their fair share of the world's resources and/or producing an outsize carbon footprint - whether in the present or the past – is a legitimate person of interest to the law enforcement authorities and criminal justice system.'

Mike suffered from intermittent bouts of depression during the days following the incident at the workshop and its aftermath. The inspectors had come again on Tuesday evening, this time reinforced by the same policewoman who had tackled John over his shoe soles. The episode dealt a terrible blow to his self-esteem and morale. On Wednesday morning he really struggled to motivate himself to get up out of bed and face the world which had suddenly become so much more hostile.

He tried in vain to visualise himself returning to the workshop as if nothing had changed, but was defeated by the stark reality that he had effectively been banned from resuming his habitual role. His uncomfortable presence would merely cause others embarrassment. Everyone was on edge as it was, worrying about how to deal with people turning up with appliances needing electrical repairs. True, a sign had been posted outside explaining the situation, but how many people would notice and read this carefully?

Then there would be the added awkwardness of ensuring the money for the fine was collected from all those who had pledged their contribution. But if he didn't steel himself to go into the workshop today or at least tomorrow, he'd be chickening out and merely leaving others to have the difficult conversations. This would just add guilt to his depression.

Anne was a pillar of support, however. She had lived with Mike long enough to intuit what he must be going through and helped him give vent to the negative emotions he was experiencing – from extreme anger to acute self-pity. Then, for moral support, she insisted on accompanying him to work on Thursday. Mike took up the offer gratefully and so was able to steel himself to attend the workshop that day. Anne was quite successful in helping smooth things over by reassuring customers and his co-workers and offering to collect contributions towards the fine.

In fact, Mike's return to work was quite cathartic. Appearing with his wife gave him an alternative source of much-needed self-worth and status. He was able to talk to various colleagues about pragmatic steps they could take to strengthen the workshop collective. The very act of standing together, dealing with the unjust fine and talking through all the challenges they faced together meant that by the end of the week, relationships between most members of the group were stronger than ever.

This provided temporary relief for Mike, but he was still unable to envision a meaningful long-term future for himself at the repair shop. Despite joining in with the muted New Year's Eve celebrations with the collective on Friday, his low mood was back by the evening. It didn't help that two of his colleagues apparently reneged on their pledge to chip in with the fine. Duncan had been unable to contact them and they conveniently absented themselves on both Thursday and Friday.

Mike catastrophised the situation to himself. He imagined the worst-case scenario that this would not simply mean that everyone else would have to increase their contributions to the fine, but that a domino effect of disaffection would run through the ranks, destroying the newfound collective spirit and lead to closure of the workshop altogether.

Anne saw her husband's salvation partly in getting him to refocus his efforts on repairing the family home. His attempts to fortify more than one room against the elements earlier in the month had only been partially successful. She frequently had to brace herself against multidirectional drafts while working in the kitchen and this was only likely to get worse as winter temperatures dropped and the family's energy saving drive intensified.

As much as Anne appreciated the need for biodiversity, she

found it hard to be overjoyed at the sheer volume of visitations by the local slug population squeezing through incredibly narrow gaps around the door and window frames, possibly even through the brickwork in places. Coming down one night in the dark for a midnight snack, she had managed to squish a nocturnal visitor between the toes of her bare left foot before finding the light switch in the kitchen. Fortunately, she cottoned on to what had happened just as she was about to go back up to bed and thus avoided spreading its insides up the stairs.

All this notwithstanding, Anne was patient and wise enough not to mither her husband into addressing all the outstanding DIY jobs at once. She aimed to nurture him gently over the first few weeks of January, giving him time to lick the wounds to his pride and reappraise his situation. Then, little by little, she would subtly hint at one or two things he might do here and there to keep himself meaningfully occupied.

The Greenways' celebrations to usher in the New Year were remarkably cheerful in view of the outgoing year's sorrows and setbacks with so many anticipated and imminent hardships yet to come.

Given the narrowing of televiewing options in recent years, there were only three broadcasts across the two remaining channels which could cater for everyone's tastes and bring the whole family together. The first was the inevitable hour-long review of the past year beginning at 6pm. To their credit, the British Broadcasting Company team had worked hard to achieve a tolerably balanced diet for general public consumption. Every depressing item, broadly speaking, was matched by an upbeat *good news* or comic one.

If only to accommodate the government's need to justify recent and forthcoming stringent legislation, the BBC had been given clearance to include passing references to the increasingly dire environmental outlook which had come to light over the past year. Therefore, mention was made of melting polar icecaps, rising sea levels, worldwide flooding, storms and unseasonal droughts. It was acknowledged that all these phenomena were partly attributable to the international failure of eleventh-hour attempts to tackle the climate crisis and the causes and effects of global warming.

This bitter pill was sweetened by harking back to feel-good accounts reported throughout the year such as heroic acts performed by citizens from various walks of life, families being reunited with pets (though not dogs!) and the feats of rising musical and comedic stars. Even some tenuous statistical data was offered, suggesting possible improvements in certain sectors of the economy with associated employment opportunities.

'Better job prospects forecast for rogue government inspectors bullies!' John ventured his own commentary in the hope of amusing his family audience. 'And there'd be less flooding if dad and co hadn't been prohibited from repairing electrical goods like fridge freezers. All that thawed ice now just goes to raise sea levels.'

At least he managed to raise a snigger from his mother and sister.

The review over, Anne served up a purposely light rice-based evening meal in order to leave room for a further veg-based course at midnight. At eight, it was time for the second programme of sufficient interest to bring all the Greenway clan back to the TV again. This was a quiz show broadcast by one of the BBC's two rival channels and, given the celebrities billed to present it, promised to be frivolously entertaining.

The quiz master was once a leading stand-up comic who had retired into this formulaic role just as his creativity and originality began to wane. Nowadays, he derived most of his canned studio audience laughter by virtue of his branded facial expressions, script-writer-written jokes and a limited armoury of catchphrases.

The catchphrases appeared on the show in predictable order. The first was *Yer'll be glad yer stayed at home tonight when yer see what's in store for yer...* He had conceived this long-winded opener himself as the result of a wager with a friend that he could get away with using the same word more than three times. The second, *Now let's look at the ol' score board* was only approved following a brief lawsuit brought by the descendants of long-gone multi-talented variety performer and famous game show host. And finally: *As the music dies, yer pick yer prize* had been contributed by one of the camera crew.

The only salient feature distinguishing this New Year show from regular editions was that all the contestants were artless members of the public rather than the usual celebrities. Jenny and John enjoyed this the most, as some of the participants reminded them of classmates at school or even one or two of their teachers.

This show ended at nine leaving two hours for family entertainments before the late show ushering in the New Year. Jenny suggested calling on the Watsons in case they wanted to join them for the parlour games which they had enjoyed playing with the family a few days ago. That would make the gathering multi-generational, which was officially meant to be a good thing. Jenny mentioned this with a hint of sarcasm in her tone in an effort to emulate her brother. John, despite feeling a selfish impulse to resist the idea of having anyone intrude on their cosy family gathering, suggested phoning. They'd exchanged telephone numbers before the Watsons returned home.

Anne agreed. 'Yes, it'd be a nice gesture and they may be a little lonely with just the two of them. Joyce is quite lively and, well, let's be honest, Terry isn't the most enthralling company!' She ran off to find their number in the telephone book and make the call. Two minutes later, she returned looking concerned.

'Joyce thanked us for the invitation, but said Terry fell ill last night and she needs to stay in with him. He's got flu symptoms, so I said one of us would pop over later with some medicines. We built up quite a supply with all the bugs going around this year.'

Jenny obliged and was soon back to join in the family entertainments which included another hilarious round of *Consequences* and an interminable game of *Monopoly* which John had enhanced by inventing some amusing and often obscure additions to the *Chance* and *Community Chest Cards*. Among these were *New law requires all rented properties to retrofit state-of-the-art energy-saving insulation. Pay £100 to the bank for each house owned and £300 for each hotel.*

Jenny smartly pointed out that this must apply to all house and hotel owners, as the law could hardly apply to just the player who picked up the card. John had to concede. Mike suggested that the Free Parking square should be amended to *parking fine £50* to reflect the modern reality that nowadays free parking except on one's own drive was unheard of.

Finally, the still fully operational grandfather clock struck eleven and it was time for the TV show they'd all been waiting for signalling the countdown to midnight and the New Year. It was a surprisingly serious news-cum-documentary about the history of the Green or environmental movement and how this had become inextricably linked with government policy in recent times.

The narrative was clearly laced with strong government bias which the Greenway family members competed with each other to comment on during and after the broadcast. The most infuriating aspect of the spin was how the public at large were blamed for taking too long to get behind the government's environmental policies. Mike and Anne recalled numerous popular movements clamouring for ugent actions to tackle the climate emergency before the planet reached the point of no return. The electoral system discriminated against all but the two biggest political parties so the Green Party without proportional representation faced almost insurmountable hurdles in order to get anyone elected even at local level.

Anne pursued the commentary:

'When it suits them, governments are adept at hammering on at the public to accept the scientific evidence and criticise people for not heeding advice during epidemics and the like.' She paused so as not to distract the others from an informative part of the programme. 'But it was the government which ignored scientific advice about global warming and kept putting economic growth before climate action for short-term political gain.'

It was John's turn to show off his own knowledge of the tragically all-too-gradual progress of the Greens in elections. Even less forgiving than his mother, he went into lecture mode.

'The Greens warned that societies in developed countries had to be prepared to radically change their lifestyles, consume considerably less and drastically reduce their carbon footprints to avert disaster at home and abroad.' He checked eye contact around the room and, seeing that at least Jenny was listening, continued: 'If they kept putting off doing this through the democratic process, then governments would use climate crises to justify anti-democratic states of emergency, which is effectively what's happening now with a constant string of new laws being passed and going unchallenged by parliament.'

After the first half hour, the documentary's focus shifted onto the dire situation which prevailed in many of the less developed countries where floods and storms had wreaked havoc, often wiping away the flimsy infrastructure of State and resulting in civil disorder with high levels of unchecked crime and gang warfare. Better protected countries were no longer in a position to organise international aid and accept refugees owing to their own problems with internal migrations already being forced on many people living in coastal areas or on flood plains.

While viewing this part of the documentary, Anne's expression subtly and slowly morphed from indignation to one of perplexity. The subject matter seemed to foreshadow a thought beginning to form in her mind.

The programme-makers, however, had wisely ensured that the last ten minutes or so of their work ended on an upbeat note of optimism befitting the approach of a new year which promised something better than what many viewers had been forced to endure during the outgoing one.

Every conceivable bit of actual or hoped for good news was squeezed into this last little section: progress with onshore and offshore wind farms supplying ten percent more energy compared with the previous year and the prospect of even greater growth for the sector in the current year, an increase in domestic food production forecast to bring the country's self-sufficiency up to around seventy percent over the next two years and NHS improvements enabling people to live healthier into old age. The good news narrative wound up quoting encouraging stats in the education and leisure sectors.

A thirty-second interlude then featured a family playing a parlour game albeit much more animatedly than at the Greenways just an hour before. And, as if addressed directly at them, this was followed by what appeared to be a father and daughter making music together on a piano and cello respectively. The message, of course, was that the great English public would be well advised to settle for home entertainments as they are much more economical, environmentally sustainable and ultimately much more fun.

For the Greenways, the spell of the New Year celebrations was broken. In the space of less than five minutes, Mike and Anne had pronounced the customary toasts, a few more sips of the family's remaining stash of cider were swallowed by all, including Jenny as a special treat. Then a heated discussion around the points raised in the programme ensued.

'What a truck-load of complete and utter *shit* that programme was!' shouted John almost involuntarily and without referring to anything in particular, except perhaps his own pent-up anger and frustration at how divorced the government broadcast seemed to be from his family's situation through no fault of their own.

A year ago, his mother might have reprimanded her son for such profanities, but on this surreal occasion she was simultaneously amused and proud of him for displaying such intense emotion. At least he wasn't apathetic or boringly submissive like so many of his peers these days. Or even her own generation, for that matter.

'Not so sure about that, son! Nowadays, with freight all but gone from the roads, shouldn't it be 'train-load of excrement, to be both accurate and polite in mixed company?'

'The trouble is, most of what they said was true or at least hard to argue against,' offered Mike. 'In a way, that's the annoying thing!'

It was Anne's turn to be serious.

'The saddest thing is the way our so-called democracy broke down with the two big political parties wasting all their energy scoring points off each other instead of cooperating to tackle the climate crisis. So, when we got to crisis point, we went from failing democracy to no democracy. If we'd had proportional representation in the first place like most other civilised countries, we might be governed now by a coalition instead of a virtual dictatorship.'

John didn't agree. 'Yes, but most other developed European countries had proportional representation and coalition governments, yet few have managed the crisis better than we have in England. Or should I say, we haven't managed it worse than most.'

Jenny had been listening to the others intently and patiently and was now confident she knew what she was talking about.

'Yes, we discussed this at school in form period. The richest countries like France and Germany didn't do much better than us because populations there were too reluctant to give up their high living standards and drive for economic growth. The Germans are in a mess now because they depended on importing fossil fuels, gas and oil, despite their big Green political movement. The French thought they were alright *Jacques* because they had over seventy per cent nuclear power, but then they were stuck when some of the stations broke down or became too old to run safely. Also, when Russia refused to take any more of its nuclear waste – mainly spent uranium - it couldn't find anywhere to store it. It's a bloody mess.'

'But at least in Germany they've kept most of their democracy despite the climate crisis.' John commented.

'The Germans are so well trained to do what the authorities tell them, that they wouldn't know the difference anyway!' Mike couldn't resist an anti-German jibe.

Not to be outdone by her husband, Anne joined in the anti-European assault: 'The French seem content to pretend they have a democracy by directly electing a strong president in a two-round contest. They effortlessly flip from a highly centralised pseudo-democracy to revolution with regular street protests in between.'

'To be fair, there haven't been any revolutions since the mid-nineteenth century, but three proper revolutions and several near misses with lots of instability in between isn't bad going. And they've still ended up with more democracy than we have!' John concluded this strand of the discussion.

Anne would have liked to lament more about how everyday life had become much harder compared with when she was small, but she pitied her children who mercifully were unable to miss what they hadn't had: frequent holidays around the country and sometimes abroad, a growing wardrobe of clothes for nearly all occasions, fast and convenient car travel around town instead of slow, overcrowded and unreliable buses and railway journeys with ancient rolling stock. Most of the present generation couldn't even expect one daily nutritious and appetising meal. Even her own family couldn't take this for granted.

As New Year's Day was a Saturday, there was a long weekend ahead. Fortunately, the authorities hadn't yet found an excuse to do away with the bank holiday. John and Jenny used the extended leisure time to further hone their respective skills on piano and violin. Jenny wisely alternated practicing on the violin with the occasional short spell on the piano. This was not only to spare her own and other family members' nerves and eardrums, but just as importantly to avoid repetitive stress injury to her fingers through too much pinching and plucking. This motion was required in order to get to grips with her violin technique.

Meanwhile, John was content for his own progress on just the one instrument to be comfortably outpacing his sister's. He came to the considered view that there naturally had to be at least one legitimate arena for sibling rivalry and as he could never aspire to play the violin as excruciatingly badly as Jenny, he may as well aim to play the piano a little better.

The rivalry, however, wasn't shared by Jenny and even John's competitiveness was transformed into sheer collaborative spirit whenever they attempted to perform together for their own and sometimes their parents' entertainment too. Jenny soon learnt to recognise the essentials of musical notation from her theory book, but continued to follow her instinct and play mostly by ear. John, however, was only confident sight reading from the old sheet music in the piano stool. Brother and sister initially tried to convert the other to their own way of thinking, but eventually came to appreciate the advantages of both approaches.

On Tuesday, 4th January, the first normal day, Anne was quietly relieved to receive in the post an official-looking envelope containing the application form to accommodate *graves for strangers*, as she had taken to referring it. She wasn't sure whether she'd personally coined the phrase or whether she'd heard someone else use it, but it struck her as both euphonic and rhythmic, at least compared with the bureaucratic term: *application to host supplemental burial grounds*. Like most aspiring literate citizens, she had endured many a perplexed moment trying to distinguish between the use of *supplementary* and *complementary* and not to confuse the latter with *complimentary* and now, yet another tricky and surely unnecessary variant had entered her life – *supplemental*!

However, In the introductory address to the applicant, there was an attempt by the form designer to break away from the standard officialese. It opened: *Dear householder, the Department for Social Protection wishes to thank you for applying to your local authority to offer up space in your garden for the burial of deceased persons other than members of your own family.* Anne had done her best so far to visualise the author sympathetically, but couldn't suppress a giggle. 'It sounds like you'd be entitled to bury members of your own family whether or not they're deceased!' she muttered to herself just loud enough for Mike to overhear.

She explained the source of the humour to her husband and the two of them then spent the next half hour carefully reading through all the technical details, clauses and exclusions in the terms of the contract, then filled in the form together as confidently as they were able. They could expect a guest cadaver to be dispatched to them with the next two weeks or so. All the actual burial arrangements would be made and carried out by an appointed undertaker and payment of £30 per grave would be paid within two weeks of completion. They would be consulted on the precise siting of graves albeit within strict guidelines governing statutory minimum distances from existing graves and borders.

Anne had another amusing thought. 'Can you imagine if someone dug a grave so it just overlapped a neighbour's garden, over some disputed border, for instance?'

'Yes,' agreed Mike, 'it'd be damned hard to redress that after the event. I suppose you could try to settle the dispute by offering the neighbour payment for the portion of the grave which encroached onto their territory...'

'It's a pity they don't send a small deposit as a goodwill gesture or include in the fee a bit of disturbance allowance,' mused Anne. 'Though I suppose it's all factored in implicitly. We'll have to study the section on future maintenance liability and who's responsible for what – the host or the... tenant.'

Anne was also amused by the potential ambiguity around who was meant by the *tenant* – the occupant of the grave or the relative visiting the grave.

'I hope it's the surviving relative who has to look after the memorial stone itself and not the deceased. The contract mentions that any grey areas should be resolved by discussion between the host and tenant. I don't fancy having to hold a garden séance to conjure up the dead!'

Mike appreciated Anne's efforts to make him laugh. This also signalled that she had dealt with her mother's tragic passing sufficiently well to be at ease with the graves-for-strangers concept.

As a final step, Anne and Mike checked over the form multiple times before getting John to run down to the local post office and ensure it caught the van to the sorting depot on the same day.

It was Wednesday. Now, over a week since his pseudo professional crisis, Mike was still experiencing bouts of depression as he grappled with the reality that his role at the repair shop could never be the same again. In the morning, well before he was accustomed to setting off to work, he summoned the courage and motivation to give Duncan call.

Duncan, the de facto collective chief, lamented about the downcast mood among some of the team. But on the plus side, one of the two absentees on Thursday and Friday last week had got back in touch and stumped up the agreed contribution towards the fine. The gentleman concerned explained that his mother had fallen ill just before the New Year and everything went temporarily to pot. No such luck with the other chap, though, but at least there was a little less extra cost for the others to absorb than at first feared.

Much of the shop's appeal for Mike was that it had provided a change of scene and the chance to socialise outside his family circle. Therefore, switching his energies to home repairs wasn't an easy transition to make. It was, however, appropriate and timely given the visible and palpable collapse of so many interior fixtures and fittings, not to mention the house's exterior.

Anne was greatly relieved when Mike asked her to suggest where he might start on the DIY tasks, as this meant she didn't need to adopt her subtle hint-dropping strategy which she'd planned over the coming weeks. She wrote a list of chores in order of priority and also attempted to assess them for difficulty until it dawned on her that her DIY husband himself was the best person to do this.

Mike decided to get back into the groove by tightening screws on various cupboards, adjusting doorknobs, closures and doing similar little jobs. His confidence somewhat restored, he moved on to pointing the brickwork around the kitchen where the slugs and other creepy-crawlies were most obviously gaining entry of a night time. From this, he graduated to replacing the roof felt over the kitchen extension which had been showing signs of damp for several months.

Anne took pleasure noting Mike's progress and in crossing tasks off the list, occasionally new ones as they occurred to her. She began to consider enlisting the children to help their father with one or two gardening jobs, although she was wary of upsetting Jenny given the garden's association with her grandparents' passing. However, a condition of being granted permission to host graves was a commitment to maintain a tidy garden, therefore seeing to this had to be prioritised given how soon their territory would be entering the public realm.

Cutting the grass was naturally the first task which came to Mike's mind as he approached the decrepit garden shed. His heart sank as it dawned on him that his petrol-fuelled lawn mower had not been used since mid-summer when Anne's father had been taken seriously ill and non-essential routine jobs had shuffled off the family's agenda. A quick inspection confirmed his fears: the tank was almost empty and the petrol can was lying on its side on the shelf above with the lid by its side. No longer a car owner, he wouldn't be entitled to purchase any more.

After a moment's reflection, Mike reassured himself that people didn't generally mow lawns in mid-winter anyway, especially somewhat overgrown ones. The only thing to do was to exploit the available domestic labour force, meaning John and Jenny, Even Anne might lend a hand. If they could just tidy the bottom half of the garden where the new graves were planned, that would probably suffice for now.

With just two pairs of shears, the family of four worked in alternating two-hour shifts for almost the whole of Friday until the whole area around the existing graves was fit for its future purpose.

Verity Shillaker, Minister for Legal Affairs, attributed the success of her political career to forward planning and this occasion was no exception. With the retroactive bill on excessive energy and water poised to go before parliament, she immediately planned the next logical legislative step. A relatively short meeting with her colleague, Minister for the Economy, Finance and Taxation, had given her a clear brief.

The brief was to consider other punitive actions besides monetary fines for breaches of environmental laws both by private individuals and organisations of all types. Allied to this step was that of widening the criminality net, which was her favourite term for expressing the principle of increasing the range of actions which could become criminal offences as well as converting civil offences into criminal ones wherever possible.

She adhered to the tried and tested principal of incrementally ratcheting up the severity of the penalties in order to give the communications team time to soften up public opinion. *Severity, not Verity, is my real name.* Her recently inspired pun worked rather well. The prefix or reflexive pronoun *se* referred to the most important person in her world - herself.

CHAPTER 10: JOHN'S NEW CLOTHES

Meanwhile, Jenny was persevering with her new journal in which she was recording the events of her family's daily life. Within three or four days, she realised that she was falling into the trap of noting all the details of various repetitive routines. These were unduly time consuming to write down as well as tedious to read back so she resolved to make her journal primarily reflective, expressing her thoughts and feelings.

New Year's Eve was rather sad in some ways. You could tell, reading between the lines, as mum likes to say, that all the programmes on TV were trying to put a brave face on how much harder life has got over the past year and how it's going to get even worse this year. Mum and dad seemed to be more affected than me and John.

So many of the things that the adults complain about don't mean anything to us young ones. Mum keeps talking about types of fruit she used to enjoy from abroad, but I can't see why anyone would want more than we have now – different types of apples, pears, grapes and lots of berries. We even have quite a few growing in our garden. I hope the visitors to the graves won't swipe them all!

In some ways, I think we're lucky that we're having to focus on things that really matter like spending time as a family even if this usually means tackling seemingly endless problems together.

I still miss gran. The way she went was sad, but not really a tragedy. I can't help seeing the bright side, though that's not the right expression and I feel guilty even thinking that. Still, her death was painless. She would never have been happy without grandad. We keep forgetting she had the beginnings of dementia and would have soon got more confused and that would have been more stressful for her and all of us. She wanted to end her life in the hope of joining grandad. That may be possible and, if not, she may meet him again in a future life.

I find it hard to believe everything we're taught in school about reincarnation and sometimes suspect it's just to control us and make us put up with more. But there's no denying that the world's oldest religions have always taught this. John says just because ideas are used for the wrong reason – usually to manipulate people - doesn't mean they're wrong in themselves. Someone said, if you want to discredit a good idea, the best way is to ensure the wrong people get hold of it and promote it. Going back to gran again, if there's no such thing as an afterlife, it won't matter. When we go to sleep each night, we go completely unconscious, at least till we dream, and we wouldn't know anything if we never woke up again!

Jenny re-read her journal, made a few improvements to spelling and punctuation, then relaxed, satisfied that this was the way she intended to continue. She hoped the standard of her English would be awarded a top grade if assessed by her most exacting language teacher and was confident it was better than that of her least favourite teachers.

She mentioned her journal to John and suggested he keep one. But her brother said he'd be frightened someone would find it and not be able to resist the temptation to read it. Then he'd be mortified. She thought about this drawback more than once before committing fully to the project.

At length, she decided she'd either censor herself or invent a code for any really embarrassing personal bits. Rather like the famous Samuel Pepys who wrote his rudest and most shameful entries either in an early form of shorthand or even a foreign language. Scholars did eventually decipher this, but not before he was long dead, which must have saved him some discomfiture. *Unless he's looking down from another dimension somewhere and even then, he'd only be embarrassed if his guardian angel was looking over his ethereal shoulder too.* Jenny was amused at her internal dialogue and smugly proud of knowing the word *ethereal.*

She reflected on how Pepys avoided expressing opinions on controversial matters in case his journal fell into the wrong political hands. In the 1660s, you could still get sent to the Tower of London for criticising someone in authority or advocating radical policies. And Pepys was writing only a generation after a revolution and bloody civil war whose effects were still felt after the restoration of the monarchy.

I wonder if it will ever come to revolution and civil war in this country? Mum says we're heading that way and she may well be right after that TV chat we had on New Year's Eve!

On this note, Jenny concluded her last entry for the first week of the New Year.

On Friday, John and Jenny decided to amuse their parents by telling them about the New Year's Resolutions which their teachers claimed to have signed up for.

John introduced the topic. 'It was obvious that Warburton, the head, had told all our teachers to share their resolutions with their classes, the idea being to encourage us to take our own more seriously and stick to them. They keep telling us how it's our job to do the right thing and influence our parents on environmental matters.'

'Funny how in pretty well everything else, it's the parents who are meant to be role models for their children!' Jenny remarked. 'And it's not as though this panic over the environment hasn't been going on for well over fifty years, so grandparents, let alone parents, should have absorbed the basics by now.'

'Yes, well the logic goes that because the climate disaster wasn't so blatantly obvious in their generation, their job was just to pass on their worry about it to our generation and leave us to tackle it. It's down to us, as we have more of our life left to suffer the impact. Trouble is, the same logic ruled our grand parents' and parents' generations.'

Jenny and John took turns at telling their anecdotes. There was the case of Jenny's Science teacher, despised by most of her class, who virtuously announced she was going to stay back for half an hour after classes every day to ensure all items used in experiments were disposed of correctly, recycled or even reused if possible. A Year 10 student claimed they had seen her at least twice during the first week back leaving the premises less than ten minutes after the end of the school day.

John recounted his Geography teacher being caught in an obvious lie. He had boasted to his class about cutting out warm drinks except at weekends. An enterprising Year 9 class had snuck into his classroom during the lunch hour and rummaged around. As a dare, one of the most adventurous had climbed into a large storage cupboard only to find a kettle containing still warm water and an old plastic lunch box half filled with tealeaves. Milk and sugar were also secreted behind various books and boxes.

The intruders considered calling out the teacher during the next lesson, but decided it would be safer and much more fun to pour the remaining warm water into the sandwich box with the tea leaves. They then poured in most of the sugar and milk before sealing up the box and affixing a sticky note with the message: *Sir's tea-making team were here. You ruddy great hypocrite!*

Not all teachers failed the sincerity test in the New Year's challenge, however. John and Mandy's favourite English teacher, Mr Jacobs, gave the most convincing and inspiring account of his creative endeavours. He had taken his motorcar off the road four years ago for the same multiple reasons which had led most other motorists to do the same: unbearable peer pressure had played a part, but it was mainly the financial impossibility of running a car with the massive road tax levy coupled with the soaring cost of petrol.

For the first couple of years, he had kept the disused car on his drive in the faint hope that conditions would change and one day he'd be able to return to motoring. Then, when this clearly wasn't going to happen, he locked it away in his old garage, but had never got round to disposing of it altogether. Now with two children aged four and six, he decided to turn vice into virtue by converting the car into an exciting miniature adventure playground.

Mr Jacob amazingly got this project past the Ministry for the Environment as a qualifying New Year's Resolution by demonstrating how much energy and carbon footprint had been saved by not transporting it for scrap He also successfully argued that the children were causing less environmental damage by spending their leisure time in the adapted car.

The enterprising family man and popular teacher had first of all siphoned off the residual petrol and drained the oil for safety. He stored these substances in air tight containers for a possible future use. He rendered the car safe still by filing down any sharp or rough surfaces both inside the vehicle and on the external bodywork. He and his wife filled the car with educational games and small toys to keep the kids out of trouble.

Their only misjudgement was to lock the boot, thinking it would be a sensible safety precaution. However, their six-year-old soon discovered how to fold the rear seats forward, entice his younger sibling to climb into the boot and trap him in there by folding the seats back. So, the boot-locking policy had to be reversed.

Largely through their own fault, John and Mandy had been completely incommunicado during the winter break. More than once, John kicked himself for not prearranging a meeting on neutral ground before they broke up. Once at home, it wasn't feasible to chat over the phone. John's parents' would have been fine with it, but Mandy's parents who would have resented any intrusion on their family's privacy and sanctity over the festive season.

Although a postal service of sorts still existed and the two young people were both adept at putting pen to paper in their lessons, they weren't members of an earlier generation for whom letter writing was second nature. When finally meeting back at school, Mandy confessed that the idea of posting a note to John had once occurred to her, but she dismissed it as an eccentric fancy, as anything she might write would surely come out awkward and stilted.

If he were completely honest with himself, John would have had to admit that with Mandy, it was more a case of *out of sight out of mind* than *absence makes the heart grow fonder*. But what, after all, was this business of attraction and devotion to another person all about? And what was this love that his mother had once or twice talked about between her and dad? Such questions began to cross John's mind more frequently now that he was back at school, especially when around Mandy.

During the lunch hour of their first day back, John and Mandy had their first proper chat for nearly three weeks over a Kinder Juice in the canteen. John kicked off by relating the trials and tribulations of his own family in as engaging a manner as he could muster. Like young males the world over, he possessed in no small measure the instinctive drive to amuse a lady and impress her with his undoubted intelligence and wittiness.

As faithfully as she could, Mandy followed her own instinct to be an attentive listener and emoted appropriately at various points in John's narrative while awaiting her turn. However, when her turn came, she found herself at a loss for words, as virtually nothing of note had happened in her household for her to relate amusingly or otherwise.

'It was excruciatingly boring, to be honest. There was such a chronic lack of fun – no parlour games or deep philosophical chats like you lot had. Mum just looked more stressed than ever most of the time. First, she was worrying about what she'd be able to cook with such limited supplies, then she got irritable preparing what little we had. Dad was no help just sitting around watching TV or reading books about past sports personalities. He just kept saying 'It doesn't matter, love' whenever mum said anything. It could have been worse, I suppose. At least we didn't have great family rows and I was pretty much left to my own devices. They were both happy for me to spend most of my time in my room studying.'

John politely listened without interrupting, but couldn't help thinking: *Why were you happy to do that, is more to the point? And why didn't they let you go out once or twice and spend some time with me and my family? That would have brightened things up for us all, even if you'd dragged your dreary folks along with you!*

John was now sporting his new top and trousers. Following the intense build-up to receiving his coming-of-age gift, his main emotion on returning to school was an acute sense of anxiety. How to protect his brand-new garments from coming to harm? There were so many hazards which in the blinking of an eye could reduce them to second-hand worn and degraded status.

Avoiding a dirty seat on the bus was the first hurdle. Next was the danger of catching his trousers or jumper as he ran the gauntlet of disorderly exhibits in the art and crafts block. There was no way to avoid passing through this area on the way to his registration room. Needless to say, there were also the spillage risks in the school canteen. As nice as the Kinder Juice tasted, when spilled it didn't half leave a sticky mess on your clothes! He made sure his first lunch of the term contained no ingredients such as sauces which might be a cause for regret and adopted an extreme forward-leaning posture throughout lunch.

As the first day wore on without incident, John's anxiety gave way to a sense of anti-climax and disappointment. This was reinforced by the failure of any of his classmates, including Mandy, to comment on his new clothes. When John pointed this out to her, she tried to appear apologetic while trying to convince him that the true value of his new clothes wasn't their newness, but that they were his personal choice, allowing him to express his individuality in a rather bland and conformist world. She also suggested that he'd probably feel more comfortable in his new garments once they were a little worn.

In Jenny's school, sex education was still a moderately embarrassing process for teacher and student alike, but pedagogues generally agreed that recent tweaks to the curriculum had made lessons more relevant and appropriate than used to be the case. This consensus applied to recommended methodologies too.

Jenny's year 10 class of twenty-four contained a fairly representative mix of teenagers from different social backgrounds and an equal number of boys and girls. Sex education for this year group consisted of a six-part module with one session devoted to the subject each half term. Session one in the Autumn term had revisited the physiology and technical aspects of sex in a little more detail than in years 7 and 8. Session two covered sexual hygiene, sexually transmitted diseases and unplanned pregnancies were also introduced.

Today's session focused on the dangers of precocious sexual relationships and avoiding unwanted sexual encounters. The main focus was on discouraging what used to be known as flirtatious behaviour and inappropriate dressing by girls. Jenny began to feel uneasy as the lesson unfolded. Fifteen minutes had passed – nearly half the allotted time for the lesson – and so far, only her own gender had been directly alluded to. She put up her hand.

'Mrs Henderson, are we going to get on to the responsibility of boys and men folk in all of this before the lesson's over, or is that for next term?'

Representatives of both gender groups reacted with barely suppressed giggles.

Mrs Henderson took the intervention in her stride, as she was on the verge of shifting the narrative in exactly that direction. What a perceptive lass this Jenny was!

'A fair point, dear. We're just being realistic here. In most cultures, women have traditionally dressed in order to attract males. In our society, the temptation was much greater in the past when we used to import masses of cheap scanty sweat-shop produced clothes from poorer countries. In other modules, we've looked at the drive to stop society's obsession with fashion for reasons of environmental protection and social justice, but that's by the by. Home-made clothing nowadays is much more modest. The other thing which seems to be hard wired in nature is the female tendency to use body language and verbal language to entice her mate.'

'You mean, as my grandad would say, they waggle their arses to say 'Fancy a bit of that?' Coming from the most brazen young male in the class, the contribution was hardly unexpected.

When the laughter had died down, Mrs Henderson, struggling a little to retain her composure, resumed her. Yes, she explained, males had to recognise too that part of the price of living in a civilised society was suppressing their inappropriate and precocious sexual urges which tended to be stronger and more violent than those of females. The lesson ended with a stark summary of all the reasons why sexual relations really need to be out of the question during school years and ideally postponed beyond teenage years.

What would have intrigued a time traveller from fifty years ago was the fact that barely a couple of these fourteen- and fifteen-year-old adolescents had yet experienced any significant degree of sexual desire let alone indulged in intercourse.

The grave diggers arrived on Thursday afternoon, 13th January.

Remarkably, that same morning, just hours earlier, Anne had opened the letter from the local authority confirming that the Greenways had been accepted into the grave hosting scheme. It was as well that both she and Mike were at home and that the family had worked together just days before to get the garden in a respectable state to receive guests.

Anne signed the copious paperwork, while Mike examined the sketch plan of the garden just to be sure that the proposed plot was where he expected it to be. To his and Anne's considerable relief, everything was in order and by the end of the afternoon, three five-feet deep rectangular ditches had been dug at the bottom of the Greenway garden. One ditch was just two metres away, but parallel with Anne's parents' resting place with the second and third incipient graves almost perfectly and symmetrically positioned just in front.

Anne did the hospitable thing and twice offered cups of tea and biscuits to the workmen, but they politely refused on both occasions. Clearly, they were on a mission to get the job finished as briskly as possible and clock off for the day. Most professionally, however, before heading off home, they staked out the graves by placing a safety cordon around them and announced that the burial team would be arriving tomorrow.

Sure enough, at regular intervals throughout Friday, funeral parties arrived at the Greenways. Two of these entered the garden via the gate which Mike had installed at the bottom of the garden. It was as well they achieved this, as the first party consisted of quite a cortege with three vehicles including the hearse. The vehicles involved just managed to park in the rear access road with enough room for the mourners to slip out without being jammed against the doors. It was also a tight squeeze through the gate to say the least and at one point, two of the pallbearers had to perform quite a sophisticated choreographic manoeuvre in order not to trip and drop the coffin.

The last burial, however, unfortunately did not go entirely to plan from the Greenways' point of view. Unable to find the rear access road to the house and hence the gate into the garden, the funeral director came knocking at the front door. On hearing his plaintive patter about mounting delays, Anne was prevailed upon to admit the whole party, including the two sturdy men carrying the coffin, who then trekked through the family home. One of the men was particularly colossus-like and accidentally knocked over and smashed an antique vase in the hallway.

It was hardly the occasion to demand compensation for a broken vase and scattered dried flowers, so Anne suffered in silence until the last of the party had paraded through her home. Then, to add insult to injury, the rest of the damage was revealed. Someone had obviously trodden in a muddy puddle on the way in, as there were dirty black stains all along the hall carpet and halfway into the back room. Beyond that the trail ended, as, the filthy shoes had been wiped thoroughly clean on the family's best or rather *only* decent carpet.

'Don't worry – that's only the start of it,' muttered John. 'I'd like to bet we can look forward to a regular procession of bereaved relatives trekking through our house, wreaking havoc on their way to our garden. Perhaps we should just bulldoze a corridor from our front door through to the back garden!'

Admiring her brother's sarcastic prowess, Jenny attempted to upstage him:

'No, let's just put a note on the front door inviting visitors in and offering them refreshments for a variable fee depending on whether they want to stand in the hallway, sit down in the dining room or picnic out in the garden. A bit like how the poncey French used to charge in their fancy cafés – Monsieur, madame: dans le couloir c'est un euro, dans le salon – deux euros, dans notre jardin cinq euros!' She translated for everyone's benefit the varying prices in the hallway, lounge and garden. John knew just enough French to add: 'et dans la cimetière – dix euros.'

'I think I'd start with a polite notice not to pinch the family silver!' returned John.

'How about offering a twenty per cent refund on refreshments if they manage not to have broken anything by the time they get back to the porch ready to leave?' Jenny successfully vied with her brother for the last word of wit.

Mum and even dad joined in the laughter, but Anne couldn't help recalling the insightful saying: *Many a wise word said in jest*, or wasn't it actually *true word*? No matter, Jenny was content enough to have suggested yet another potential income stream which might be worth exploring.

In Bakeworth Prison, one hundred and seventy-five out of nearly two hundred inmates of the socio-economic criminal wing were variously occupied in the three recreation rooms. The prisoners had distributed themselves fairly evenly between the purpose-built areas. These comprised an active sports hall, a sedentary games room and the arts and drama studios. In total, twelve warders roamed freely in pairs round and between the different activity areas. In addition, the prison employed two sports trainers, a chess and crossword coach, three drama teachers and two music tutors. All bar two of the part-timers were at work today guiding their captive clientele towards self-fulfilment with varying, but encouraging degrees of success.

During the recreational recess, governor Maitland sat back in his swivel chair rocking gently smugly taking in the glowing report he and his staff had received earlier in the week. It was from His Majesty's Inspectorate of low security prisons for socio-economic offenders. He was discussing this now with his deputy.

'Why did it take so long for the service to act on what research had proved decades ago, namely that prisons only rehabilitate prisoners who actually quite enjoy being there?'

It was a rhetorical question which he'd put to countless inspectors, members of his own staff and even inmates during his five-year career at Bakeworth to date. His deputy was as ready as ever to oblige with a fashionable stock reply:

'I know, we'd been saying it for years – that locking people away in an unpleasant environment was because the public wanted criminals punished, not rehabilitated and retribution over reform was a political choice. But even when we got the message across that prison as retribution made people worse and more likely to commit more serious crimes, society reacted by just wanting to lock them away for longer. It's a pity that for so long politicians gave in to public pressure to demand that courts hand down ever tougher custodial sentences.'

There was more to it than that, of course. It had been amply demonstrated that occupational and talking therapy gave prisoners limitless scope for personal growth. Given their generally deprived social status, few of those winding up in the prison system had previously enjoyed such a wide range of leisure pursuits, including the chance to learn a musical instrument or dabble in amateur dramatics. Debating groups and literacy classes were placing so many former no-hopers on the ladder of opportunity to becoming confidently articulate and useful citizens.

Workers in the leisure department, however, tended to overlook the impact of other programmes operating within the prison. The nutritionists and canteen staff, for example, were proud of their input in providing wholesome menus which inmates looked forward to three times daily. Similarly, the medical staff responsible for giving every prisoner a full monthly medical, generally found their work at least as rewarding as colleagues outside the prison system. A captive patient population enabled them to work wonders with preventive medicine and intervene effectively in most cases where serious illness did arise.

As the deputy governor left his office, Maitland reflected on the failures of regressive interventions of the past such as inhumane and socially discriminatory use of the death penalty. This was regrettably still in force in the most repressive parts of the world such as the United States of America. Then there were the crude pseudo-scientific techniques used to treat mental disorders of the criminally insane or super aggressive. Perhaps the most extreme example of these were frontal lobotomies whose popularity had seen a resurgence in recent years.

Modern drugs administered to all inmates via their food and drink treated virtually all conditions including deviant social behaviour. It was largely a case of *a stitch in time saves nine*, Maitland had reassured everyone he encountered, from fellow professionals to the prisoners themselves. There were myriad cases of inmates now amicably sharing cells who on first arriving at the prison were deadly enemies from rival underworld gangs. There was no denying the transformation.

True, while in his current post at Bakeworth prison, there'd been five inmate deaths over eight years which were directly attributable to drugs regularly administered via inmates' food and drink. Two poor fellows developed an allergy and died of asphyxiation, another died of a blood clot and a third from sudden heart failure. Just one young man presented with a severe adverse psychological reaction leading to acute paranoid schizophrenia and ultimately suicide. However, these tragic cases had to be set against the previous eight years during which there had been several deaths by suicide alone and far worse rehabilitation and health outcomes for the prison population as a whole.

Maitland's training had also satisfied him that the present social and economic climate too had come to the aid of the prison service. Huge inequalities beget envy which in turn begets crime. Creating a more equal society primarily through the introduction of the Universal Citizen's Income had, in his view, been the single biggest factor in drastically reducing most forms of theft.

'These days, there aren't too many folks around in a position to go about flaunting their wealth. There's so little of anything to envy and be worth pinching, it's got to be good news for us who want to keep the prison population down!' Maitland thought out loud to his deputy who dutifully added:

'Well, if the present trend of early releases continues, soon we'll be able to transfer all inmates on the environmental wing to the new regional facility when it opens later this year.'

Upon release, inmates were now guaranteed comfortable accommodation with social support where necessary. Money worries were removed, as all were immediately entitled to the Universal Citizen's Income along with an advance payment known as an adjustment allowance.

In addition, it was normally possible to release prisoners in friendship groups of two or more, thus providing a peer support network in the same accommodation. This proved a practical solution for most ex-offenders unable to return to live with family members.

With their two children now a week into their spring term at school, Mike and Anne felt it was time to discharge their parental duty and enquire how they were getting on in their respective academic and social endeavours.

Anne was particularly anxious to talk to John about his feelings for Mandy seeing how much he had resented being barred from contacting her over the holiday. She had acquired the habit of catching John in the kitchen every day on his return from school and attempting to fish for clues as to how their relationship was evolving. However, to his mother's irritation, John talked about anything but Mandy, preferring to relate strange or amusing incidents occurring in the classroom or during his travels to and from school. At length, Anne lost patience and blurted out a string of uncoordinated sentences:

'You've not said anything about Mandy. You clearly missed her during the holiday. I thought you'd have invited her round again or you'd have gone back to hers after school. What's happened? Have you fallen out?'

'Mum, what business is it of yours? She's just a friend. I get to see her all the time at school and we have plenty of chats, but...'

'Isn't she your girlfriend, then?' Anne resumed her awkward interrogation.

'We don't do girl and boyfriend these days, mum, you should know that.'

'Yes,' she replied, despite knowing nothing of the sort, 'but don't you find her .... attractive at all?'

'She is.... good looking and all that, but what's the relevance of how attractive she is? People don't get married till they've left school and normally not till they're over twenty at least.'

The conversation which had faltered from the outset came to a grinding halt.

Anne was beginning to suspect something was awry with her son's hormones.

For his part, John was beginning to suspect something was awry with his mother and made a mental note of talking to his dad at the first opportunity. Perhaps he ought to explain to both his parents what they taught in Personal and Social Development classes at school these days. This seemed a classic case of the generation gap and wouldn't be so surprising given how often his teachers complained about constant revisions to the PSD curriculum.

At each review, they claimed, some modules were added while others were removed and the rest was often changed beyond recognition. John knew enough about human nature already to appreciate that people, his teachers being no exception, like to moan and in the process tend to exaggerate, but there must be something in all this. *I know*, he thought, *I'll ask mum and dad what they learnt at school about personal relationships. As mum's so obviously embarrassed by the subject, I'll start with dad.*

John was soon to discover that his dad was no better than his mum in this department. Still reeling from the shock and upset of the repair shop affair, Mike was ill-equipped to manage an excruciatingly embarrassing conversation with his son. At least it had shaken him temporarily out of his low-level depression which generally descended upon him once he had finished the day's DIY tasks. The latest of these was to fix leaking taps in both the kitchen and the bathroom.

As he retired for the evening, Mike found he coped better psychologically with a task in progress than with one which was completed. Initially, this seemed contradictory until he recalled a workmate who had been made redundant at the same time as himself.

This fellow claimed he had found solace for eighteen months by immersing himself in DIY jobs around the home. He redecorated and fitted new carpets in every room, resealed the bath and kitchen sink, rewired half the plugs, replaced all the light bulbs and completed every other conceivable upgrade.

Finally, with nothing left to do, he found himself at a loose end and, with the opportunity to ruminate at leisure, the true enormity of his job loss began to sink in with its attendant drop in income and loss of social status. Soon his sense of self-worth deserted him and he sank into a deep depression worsened by heavy drinking.

With only a few cans of cider left in the family drinks cabinet after the Christmas celebrations and no plans to replenish the family stock, Mike was hardly troubled by the spectre of alcoholism. He did, however, fear falling into John Bunyan's slough of despond and had spent many a moment since the workshop debacle trying to identify which particular sins were weighing down so heavily on his conscience.

Just now, he had attempted to give John an honest account of what he remembered about his sex and relationships lessons at school. But he was unable to bring himself to seize the chance of a frank father-to-son chat about all the issues around the subject and was left feeling guilty and inadequate. It was as if his sin of omission was serving both as a magnet and magnifying glass, bringing into sharp focus all his character flaws and defects.

Mike was a self-confessed moral coward, always leaving difficult decisions and conversations to Anne. Being made redundant, he had failed to provide adequately for his family. And now, having lost what little he'd been able to earn at the repair shop, he was again looking to his wife to be the only family breadwinner. Similarly, he had shirked much of his role in bringing up the children. He had made too little effort to welcome his parents-in-law when they moved into the family home. Having done little more than tolerate their presence while they were alive, he now felt an overwhelming sense of guilt for the passive role he may have played in their premature deaths.

While indulging in such self-deprecating musings, on another level, Mike knew that he was catastrophising and that his feeling of guilt far exceeded his actual culpability. It was a feature of his depression that simply knowing he was not really so bad was not sufficient to make him feel any better about himself.

If the abortive chat with his son just now had temporarily distracted Mike from the worst of his depression, then what happened next would have a much longer and more profound effect.

Anne had read somewhere in an old withdrawn library book that many events were connected not by cause and effect, but by a phenomenon known as *synchronicity* by certain philosophers, mystics and parapsychologists. The term essentially refers to two or more occurrences in time and space which are felt to be related in some way, but not in the sense of a chain of events in which one causes the other. For some, synchronicity also implies the notion of meaningful coincidences which may have a metaphysical origin intended to teach the observer a spiritual lesson.

Earlier that day, Mike had been running up and downstairs with various tools in his frantic attempts to tackle the dripping taps. These had followed a familiar pattern of beginning with a slow drip-drip about every thirty seconds. The frequency had imperceptibly increased over a few weeks to reach almost one drip per second, which, in these days of water shortages, could not be tolerated. Mike immediately ran into difficulty in trying to locate the stop tap behind the kitchen cupboards, then, when he'd at last found it, a supreme effort was required to open it. A build-up of corrosion over many years had caused the valve to seize up.

While Mike was engrossed in his tap assignment, Anne became inexplicably nervous and distracted. She was unable to settle down to her own usual routines inside and outside the house and finally consoled herself with serial cups of tea consumed in front of daytime TV programmes which she would not normally have considered worthy of her attention. It was as if her very autonomy was suspended and subject to a successful outcome of Mike's endeavours with the taps.

Having exceeded her normal daytime tea intake, Anne soon found she was needing to empty her bladder every hour or so. This caused the new anxiety of having to decide after how many uses to flush the toilet, which was further complicated by the fact that she was using both loos to minimise her embarrassment – the upstairs one when Mike was working downstairs and the downstairs one when he was working upstairs.

At last, by the early evening, Mike had adjusted the bathroom tap successfully and replaced the relevant parts of the kitchen taps. Anne resolutely flushed both loos and sat down, this time purposefully, in front of the television to catch the six o'clock news.

Nothing in the reports was genuinely 'new'. There were the usual updates on severe weather conditions wreaking mayhem in far-flung corners of the earth such as North America, South-East Asia and parts of Africa. However, even the major population migrations which these were causing within and between countries and continents had long since lost their power to shock or surprise.

Anne followed her usual practice of selectively tuning in to content which was likely to have an impact on her family and immediate environment, but dismissing everything else as frivolous distraction or voyeurism. According to these stringent criteria, on the evening of Saturday, 15th January, only the regional weather report qualified for her attention.

In January, it was natural to expect cold and windy conditions with frequent storms bringing down fences and uprooting trees which fell across roads, occasionally damaged property and caused the odd human fatality. However, as the rate of climate change accelerated, there always lurked the promise of something a little more sinister.

Given the unpredictability of weather systems these days, forecasts had largely given way to meteorologists merely doing their best to describe and keep up with prevailing conditions in a given region. This evening was no exception. An almighty wind and rain storm was causing untold destruction in neighbouring towns just a few miles to the North and West of their location. It was anyone's guess whether their town would be spared a similar fate or the next in line to suffer it.

The answer came moments later. A sudden torrent of rain, lifted by gale force winds, swirled around in the air before crashing down upon the house in waves. Within minutes, water was entering the building through every conceivable crack and crevice making a complete mockery of all Mike's efforts of the past ten days or so. The groundswell was sufficient to force a huge volume of water under the front and back doors while at the same time, gallons of muddy water broke into the cellar through the outside basement entrance, much of it pouring in through a loosely fitted window which immediately gave way just below ground level.

Fortunately for the Greenways and most of their neighbours, damage to their property was largely restricted to a flooded cellar and drenched downstairs carpets. The incident, however, despite being over within four or five minutes, left everyone in varying degrees of shock.

As soon as the influx of water into the ground floor had subsided somewhat and he felt it was safe to open the front door, Mike rushed outside the house and made a quick assessment of the situation. He relied as much on sound as sight, as it was already pitch dark. There was still a river of water running down the road, but its course seemed to be perceptibly slowing. In case this impression was the result of wishful thinking, Mike waited a few more minutes before running across the road to check on the Watsons.

Fortunately, houses on their side of the road were on slightly higher land than the Greenways' side and so very little of the flood water had entered their house and this appeared to be the case for the other houses on that side of the road. Mike returned following his modest act of spontaneous heroism to be met by Anne and John in the hallway. Anne too was instantly uplifted by her husband's alert facial expression and body language, both of which suggested a degree of renewed self-worth. How odd that she and her husband should both experience such positive emotions when moments before they'd feared for their lives.

Mike, who, until the storm had faced the prospect of terminal depression like his former colleague, quickly reappraised his situation. He would now certainly have his work cut out with all the repairs needed in the Greenway home, not to mention the task of pumping out thousands of gallons of water from the cellar.

Slowly recovering from the initial shock, Anne's musings prior to the flood resumed where they had left off. She recalled how she had felt ill at ease during much of the day while Mike had been running up and downstairs repairing the dripping taps, this somehow being linked to her sitting restively and unproductively in front of the TV drinking endless cups of tea which in turn led to frequent trips to the loo. Then, suddenly, the mystic significance dawned on her: tap water, too much tea, pee, loo water and finally flood water. The liquid connections appeared strangely meaningful.

Anne did not, however, share her mystic notions of synchronicity with other family members. In fact, she began to blush with embarrassment at the mere thought of how they'd be likely to react. Besides, who really needed to know her most recent urinary history? Just as she was about to bathe in a newfound sense of relief, Jenny burst out of the back room into the hall where the others were still standing.

'You've all been worried about the house getting flooded! What about the visitors' graves in the back garden?'

CHAPTER 11: AFTER THE DELUGE

On Monday morning, 18th January, Roger Mayhew, Minister for Education, Culture and Spirituality, was enjoying an all too rare opportunity to converse with his counterpart in the Ministry for Health and Wellbeing, Hazel Cruickshank. The initial reason for his pleasure was Hazel's attractiveness and reputation for being readily available to any presentable moderately powerful male in government service - a profile he believed he fitted. However, he would have to admit that the content of their discussion today was almost as bizarre as the contents of her blouse and knickers were enticing.

Hazel kicked off with a little prehistory to set the scene: 'We've come a long way since the days when we were struggling just to stop kids from getting tanked up on fizzy drinks.'

'Absolutely, I remember when the law was passed to ban schools from selling them just to plug their impossible budget deficits. It would have made more sense to simply ban sugary and fizzy drinks sales from all outlets.'

Hazel appreciated nothing more than being agreed with.

'Certainly, if the State's going to intervene proactively in engineering children's diet it ought to look at both sides of the story. That means prohibiting or strongly discouraging harmful food and drink products on the one hand and on the other – promoting healthy nutrition by all available means.'

'That goes without saying, of course. It's hard to believe how much utter trash cynical so-called food manufacturers used to market to children with a view to hooking them for life. Sugary sweets and drinks, salty breakfast cereals and fatty burgers, all just storing up future problems for the publicly-funded NHS.

All the while, irresponsible manufacturers and their greedy shareholders just ran off with the profits.' Roger was by now fully warmed up in his Yes Man mode.

Hazel was only half listening, but it didn't really matter as she had rehearsed carefully what she was about to say next and would say it anyway, with or without a segue from Roger.

'There are two fundamental things we need to decide today. The first is whether to step up promotion of school meals and drinks across the whole student population or focus our efforts on targeting those in the least privileged areas.

'As budgets get tighter even among the so-called middle classes, I imagine it wouldn't be too hard to encourage a whole-school ethos around enjoying school meals together. Better for social cohesion and equality in the long run. Easiest approach to sell to the public at large. Those ancient arguments about education being a great leveller up are actually beginning to mean something again.

'Trouble is, our demographers aren't sure yet whether population sustainability is best achieved by lowering the birth rate in just the socially deprived groups who tend to over procreate and be a burden on the State, or by lowering it across the board. The latter approach is easier to manage and sell to the public, but would risk fertility dropping to dangerously low levels in former middleclass families. And, whether we like to admit it or not, these still form the fabric of society.'

The two briefly returned to the ethical arguments for the State intervening in public catering. Roger casually compared the introduction of fertility-inhibiting additives to processed foods intended for consumption by young people with the controversial introduction of fluoride to drinking water many decades ago to prevent tooth decay.

Hazel resorted to a ploy frequently used by her ministerial colleagues and cited the *National Interest* in order to justify an ethically questionable policy.

'It's for the good of the individual and society as a whole, after all. Before long, I'm sure the climate will be right for us to speak openly about this practice. If, as is more likely, some smart Alec gets wind of it first, we'll cross that bridge when we come to it.'

Roger smirked as he picked up on Hazel's presumably inadvertent use of 'climate' and 'wind' metaphors in her last two sentences. *Too true*, he mused, *if the damned weather gets much worse, responsible adults will have far more urgent matters on their minds than railing at the government for feeding their spotty teenagers healthy food drugged to make them less randy!*

However, any explicit mention of the bonus side-effect of government-sanctioned additives in drastically reducing young people's sex drive was scrupulously avoided by both ministers.

The provisional agreement was to run a trial in the North where headteachers would be tasked to promote school meals among whole school populations while holding fire in regions south of Birmingham. Subsequent studies would then, it was hoped, reveal the best way forward for the country as a whole.

Obviously, for the purposes of getting these measures through parliament, the bill would be framed merely in terms of trialling free or low-cost school lunches throughout the North. The North meant North of Birmingham, as this definition still sufficed for Westminster and Whitehall.

The final issue discussed was the question of increasing the range of Kinder Juice flavours on offer in schools and general food stores. Surveys up and down the country had found that the original Kinder Juice launched just two years ago had become the drink of choice for at least seventy per cent of children when at school and even in many social venues outside the home.

Hazel and Roger agreed that in order to maintain the momentum generated thus far, it would be timely to introduce a new flavour, ensuring it was available in local food stores. Demand would be embedded in the public consciousness via an intensive TV advertising campaign backed up by suitable promotion in schools.

Jenny's stark declaration just minutes after the flash flooding had subsided sent a shiver down everyone's spine including her own. It was in giving voice to her fears that she realised the full force of their implications. Anne was first to begin to articulate what was also slowly dawning on Mike and John.

'There'll still be too much surface water on the grass to see properly in the dark, but surely the soil will just soak it all up and there can't be any danger of...'

'... of it washing up any dead bodies!' John, who still took childish pleasure in explicit gory details, completed his mum's sentence.

Mike's renewed sense of his role as lead householder and chief responsible adult impelled him come forward:

'I suggest the sensible thing to do is give it another half hour or so to be sure the storm's over. Then I'll arm myself with a torch and do a quick scan across the garden. Just to give us a bit of peace of mind....'

'...that no dead bodies have popped up ready to treat the neighbourhood wildlife to a midnight feast!' Observing the horror-stricken look on Jenny's face, John recognised he'd gone too far down the road of bad taste. It had escaped no one that gran could be among the human floaters.

The Greenways' immediate prayers were answered as there was no further rain that evening. Mike duly trotted out into the back garden with a mechanically powered torch charged up to full strength thanks to his son's biceps. He tentatively advanced halfway into the garden until he sank into the mud. The suction threatened to swallow up his loose-fitting wellingtons. He'd made enough ground, however, to be able to see the crosses marking the three new burial plots and ascertain that nothing untoward was poking up above ground level in the grave area.

Reassured, the Greenways retired for the night with the understanding that first light tomorrow morning would see everyone on their hands and knees carrying out a concerted ground floor clean-up operation.

As Anne's head hit her pillow, she had already conceived a new plan to give the family finances a further boost. She promptly drifted into a deep sleep, trusting her subconscious to do its work during the night so that on reawakening, her inspired plan would surface fully formed and ready to announce to her family.

Governor Maitland scanned down the current list of inmates housed on the environmental or *eco* criminals' wing. It was hardly surprising that their number had seen a huge surge in recent years. At last, the State was catching up with these shameless individuals – from the serial domestic energy squanderers to the serious corporate polluters who had got away for decades with fraudulently peddling their greenwash image while secretly disposing of their filthy waste in rivers or shipping it abroad.

Nearly all these characters had the outward appearance of respectability but their motives were no less reprehensible than common socio-economic criminals. If anything, Maitland considered, they were more so. True, the corporate criminals were worse given the scale of their premeditated deceptions, but the worst petty offenders were hardly less culpable, as they selfishly or lazily consumed more than their fair share of the planet's resources. All over consumption contributed to deadly climate change by pushing out millions of tons of CO_2 and other toxic gases into the atmosphere.

No citizen with half a brain these days could claim to have missed all the government public information films and documentaries presenting the incontrovertible scientific evidence of the complete mess humanity had made of the planet. Some individuals admittedly fell into both categories, combining environmental with socio-economic crime. Generally, these criminals were to be pitied on account of their severe social and educational deprivation or, in some cases, limited intelligence. Consequently, they were usually housed in the mainstream wing of the prison. This was where Maitland, who liked to see himself as a progressive, preferred to spend his strictly rationed time outside the office overseeing the rehabilitation work.

The focus in the eco wing was to force inmates to acknowledge the error of their ways and to make amends for the harm they had done to the environment. This was achieved, for example, by reducing their food rations for an initial period and heating their cells to the minimum temperature required to maintain health. Recreation consisted of restorative justice tasks such as tree planting and growing fruit and vegetables in the prison garden. Whether the inmates got to enjoy the fruits of their labour depended on a complex hierarchy of factors such as how near the end of their sentence they were and, needless to say, how egregious their original environmental crimes had been.

Although it still awaited final approval from the Home Office, there was also a scheme afoot to allow relatives, who may well have been complicit in environmental crimes, to reduce prisoners' sentences by committing to verifiable sacrifices themselves. Maitland found this initiative progressive in the extreme: what could be better than State sponsorship of whole-family rehabilitation?

Mike who in recent years had despaired at the countless unwanted cracks and crevices in the ageing structure of the Greenway family home, especially during his frantic attempts to plug them, now found that the situation was oddly reversed.

While everyone else was busily mopping and soaking up the moisture which had got into the ground floor mainly via the front door, he gingerly ventured half way down the cellar steps for the third time since daybreak and observed that the water level there was steadily dropping. On first inspection, at least five steps were invisible under the water, whereas now all but the last two or three had reappeared.

This was presumably because the brickwork and masonry in the foundations of the house was even less water tight than on the floors above ground, allowing the water to soak through into the earth. Mike wasn't entirely sure whether this was something to be grateful for or not. At least the electrics had not been affected which seemed a small miracle in itself. He returned upstairs to help the others in the mop-up operation being carried out primarily in the lounge and dining room.

The bold decision was made to roll up both carpets and leave them to drain outside, possibly with a view to cutting them up and eventually reinventing the salvageable sections as rugs. Amazingly, once this operation was complete, there appeared very little irreparable damage to anything else.

Jenny, John and Anne had been reassured first thing in regard to the back garden. Jenny had volunteered to advance to the grave area wearing her dad's boots which she'd made fit by putting on three pairs of thick socks. In broad daylight, she managed to avoid the muddiest parts of the lawn where there was the greatest risk of sinking knee deep. When she reached the bottom of the garden, it was immediately clear that the only visible damage to the burial sites was that one of the tomb stones had slightly tilted over. She was able to push this back to a more or less vertical position thanks to the earth still being softened by the moisture it had absorbed. Later, she would look around the garden to find a couple of suitably-sized stones to wedge firmly up against the grave stone to keep it in place.

While she was thus engaged, Anne confided to John that

although the hosted bodies were brought to their home in traditional wooden coffins, these had hinged bottoms. As they were lowered into the graves, a catch released the coffin bottoms so that the bodies were actually dropped into the grave with the coffins then being retained for future use. This aspect of the burial procedure had been outlined in the small print of the contract which only she and her husband had read, though Anne suspected that Mike had left her to check through these details by herself.

Had she thought there was any real danger of Jenny finding unearthed corpses, she wouldn't have dreamt of allowing her to volunteer for the present mission. Another detail of the burial was that a layer of tough wire gauze was fitted over the bodies to render it virtually impossible for them to be brought to the surface by even the most enterprising wildlife or, as it turned out, extreme weather events.

Anne, who was in charge of the overall clean-up operation, called a well-deserved mid-morning break. There was a homemade biscuit and half a cup of black coffee with a flat teaspoon of sugar for everyone. Even Jock got a couple of scraps left over from breakfast. This was also the moment Anne planned to announce her scheme to place the family finances on a secure footing, hopefully, once and for all. When everyone appeared to be sitting as comfortably as possible, she began.

'Thanks everyone for mucking in with the cleaning effort – and excuse the pun! At this rate, apart from the cellar, there'll barely be a sign of last night's flood left by late afternoon. I think we'll all agree that things could have been a lot worse and if they had been, I wouldn't be saying what I'm about to propose now.

'Down South, there've been almost weekly cases of extreme weather causing mayhem with people's lives. So far there've only been a few dozen actual tragic deaths, but hundreds of people have permanently lost their homes and are now having to live in shelters indefinitely, often far from home and denied many comforts and benefits of civilisation...'

John couldn't help himself: 'Come on mum! Great speech worthy of a true politician, but now you've proved to us you're fit to be Prime Minister, get to the point?'

Anne, now used to her son's ironic interruptions, wasn't to be knocked off her stride:

'Exactly what I was about to do, son. So, as weather conditions aren't yet nearly as bad here up North, I propose we open the second floor of our house to a less fortunate family...'

Here Anne paused and Jenny used this for her own interruption:

'When you say 'less fortunate family', do you mean we are relatively fortunate in having only two relatives die in six months, the chief breadwinner losing his job, being forced to give up our garden to other people's dead relatives and having only half of our house flooded as opposed to all of it?'

'I think that's a fair assessment!' smiled Anne unperturbed. She then proceeded to expound the details of her scheme. She had recently read somewhere that it was costing the government more to maintain refugee families in shelters, whether makeshift of purpose built, than to pay host families to look after them. There was, rather like the host grave scheme, a standard pro forma to make applications which she had already obtained and partially completed.

All Anne needed was the family's consent and they'd be well on their way to supplementing the household income by up to forty pounds a week. Obviously, this would have to include energy and water costs, but the guest family would still receive half their Universal Citizen's Income which would go towards food and other incidental expenses.

Her calculations also revolved around an assumption that they would host a family of three or four based on the number of rooms they could realistically free up. One room could go to a couple or possibly a single parent, the other could accommodate up to two children who would obviously have to be young enough to share. Another combination would be a couple sharing a room and a child with its own room.

They could also consider a single parent and child either sharing just one room or occupying a room each. The problem with that would be a very similar level of sacrifice in terms of space for the Greenways, not to mention inconvenience, for less financial gain, as payment was based simply on how many people were being hosted. There were just two pay rates – one for adults and a lower rate for children under sixteen.

There followed a somewhat uncomfortable discussion around whether anyone would have to move rooms. This was settled quickly by Anne who had already thought this through. The adult or adults would have her parents' old room and the child or children would have the so-called spare fourth bedroom which was barely bigger than a box room. At present this was filled with all manner of junk which had been stored there since they bought the house. It would be Jenny and John's task to sort all this for sale, recycling or relocating in the roof space with their parents adjudicating over disputed items.

Everything was amicably agreed within twenty minutes after which Anne called time on the mid-morning break. The family got back to their cleaning up work with a renewed zeal powered by a supreme sense of achievement. As Anne had predicted, allowing for one more short break for lunch, by the dusk the ground floor was restored almost to its former glory, albeit minus the two carpets. These were carefully cut into quarters for conversion into rugs and hung out to dry under the carport which had seen no better use since the disappearance of the Greenway car several years before.

Forty-nine-year-old Harold Jackson was settling down in front of the TV in anticipation of a peaceful evening if not an entirely comfortable one. The storm a few days ago had completely shattered his lounge window. Faced with an indefinite wait in the queue for a qualified glazer, his short-term solution had been to board up the gaping hole in his front room with three separate pieces of plywood which he'd providentially stored in his garage. Between them, these just about filled the gap, but despite his best efforts with miscellaneous nails and bits of tape, Harold had failed miserably to exclude multiple drafts.

Had Harold been a devotee of the new religion, he would have been at a loss to understand what possible karmic debt he could have incurred to deserve such destruction being visited on his property. His life to date had been morally impeccable in all important respects. He had honoured his parents, been faithful to his wife, brought up two fine children, worked hard at his job, paid his taxes and always striven to be a good citizen. His worst sins had surely been no more than occasional spells of laziness, bouts of overeating and other such pardonable indulgences.

And to think that it was a piece of vegetation from his own garden which had come flying through the front room window – a dead branch from his very own ash tree which he had noticed beginning to split just before the storm. He had even made a mental note to saw it off come the first day of half decent weather in February! Harold was sinking still further into self-pitying mode when there was a loud bang on the front door.

Nigel Crawley and Simon Jones had been commended for their Sterling work in 'cracking open' Mike's former workshop, as their equally corrupt line manager termed it when confirming their pay bonus. To provide them with an extra opportunity to add to their bonuses, he sent them back to the neighbourhood just two streets away from where the Greenways lived, but this time on a rather different mission - a surprise visit to Mr Jackson.

Nigel had lately been taking his mentoring role extremely seriously and his understudy had received several practical lessons in the art of what he alternately termed assertive officiousness or officious assertiveness. It was in this spirit that he had instructed Simon to hammer on Harold's door.

On opening up and viewing the two men before him, Harold experienced a sense of déjà vu. He hadn't personally encountered Crawley and Jones before, but accounts of two officials throwing their weight around in the neighbourhood had reached him via the grapevine just before the New Year. *Surely, they've got nothing on me?* The reflex thought was born of his native self-preservation instinct.

'Mr Harold Jackson, I presume? May we come in for a moment?' It was Simon Jones who uttered the opening gambit which by now Nigel Crawley was happy to entrust to his junior colleague.

After a barely perceptible hesitation on account of his broken window, Harold ushered Jones and Crawley into his living room. His split-second decision was that on observing his unfortunate circumstances, the official-looking characters might be inclined to pity him rather than take offence and that this could gain him favour in case it turned out that he had a case to answer after all. It didn't occur to him that they'd already had ample opportunity to study his boarded-up window from outside the house.

Initially, Harold was put at relative ease, as the men's questioning revolved exclusively around his energy and water use which was exemplary. Harold interpreted this approach either as a formality to break the ice, as they already had print-outs of the relevant data, or as way of testing his honesty. No doubt some people when questioned gave less than truthful accounts which then contradicted the data. However, the conversation then took a bizarre turn with Nigel leading off:

'Mr Jackson, the second part of our interview concerns your consumer habits and other aspects of your lifestyle. Now, we've examined your bank and credit card statements over the past ten years and this has enabled us to create a profile of your habitual spending patterns.'

Up to this point, Harold had been merely surprised rather than alarmed by the visit, as he had never wittingly purchased anything which he would be ashamed to admit to in mixed company. No sex toys, subscriptions to massage parlours or anything else which might compromise or embarrass a middle-aged man before his local community.

Had the interview taken place some twenty years earlier, he might have been indignant at the idea of someone, even an officer of the law, accessing his purchasing record without firm grounds for suspecting that an offence had been committed. But these were different times.

'Mr Jackson, several of your till receipts over recent years bear witness to frequent purchases of luxury items coming with excessive packaging. Examples of these are sweets and chocolates individually wrapped in non-recyclable plastic and foil. While we accept that manufacturers share responsibility for minimising and preferably eliminating superfluous packaging, we must recognise that consumers also have a role to play. If only people wouldn't buy such products, then producers would respond to the market and consider reducing unnecessary packaging.'

Harold was quick to defend himself on this point:

'Fair enough, but surely the government also has a role to play. It should have brought in laws forty years ago when it started preaching to Jo public about environmental degradation, not leave it till eighteen months ago!'

'Yes, Mr Jackson, but your till receipts clearly indicate that you have done little if anything to curb your predilection for such luxuries even since the legislation came into force...'

'And there was nothing illegal about continuing to consume such 'luxuries' as you call them until manufacturers' stocks ran out!'

'Yes, Mr Jackson, but I did mention the sweet and chocolates merely as a particularly egregious example of your habitual purchase of products with excessive packaging – an example which is indicative of your apparent general disregard for the collective national drive towards responsible consumption. So, let me cite other examples of your favourite products with unnecessary packing going back ten years or more such as plastic trays used for packaging various fruits and vegetables.'

Harold knew he had stated his case well, but saw that any further remonstrations with this awful Crawley character would serve no useful purpose. He would from now act the compliant and contrite citizen so that, if nothing else were achieved, he would at least shorten the interview's duration. He therefore assumed an air of dutiful attentiveness as Crawley resumed his virtual monologue during which he learned some interesting facts about changes to the law, enhanced technologies and more about his own consumerist behaviour going back up to twenty years.

His ownership of a pet cat up to its death eight years ago was on public record. The evidence for this was circumstantial and based on his purchases of tinned cat food up to ten years ago when manufacture of this was outlawed. His poor cat had survived quite happily for a further two years on kitchen scraps and mercifully passed away of natural causes just weeks before all cats had to be destroyed by law as parasitical vermin. He had been aware of a few cat owners who defied the new legislation by securing their homes or their external boundaries. Stray cats continued to be fed from door to door, though these gradually disappeared as they were rounded up and euthanised by local authority inspectors.

Harold still kept a pet hamster in his back room and prayed it would keep quiet until the men had gone.

The third phase of the interview was taken over by Simon Jones to whom his partner had entrusted the task of delving into Howard's carbon footprint. All conceivable elements were covered from his ownership and historic use of a private motorcar to foreign holidays involving air travel and going back to his mid-twenties. Here, Harold was even given a score which Simon claimed was just about average for a man of his age and social background. This was the first bit of good news imparted to him since the interview began!

Crawley then rounded off the interrogation by mopping up miscellaneous themes such as how often Harold flushed the toilet, cleaned the kitchen and bathroom and how much effort he made to minimise water use, etcetera. In this section, there was even a challenge to Harold's clothes buying habits and whether he purchased a substantial number of clothing items from second-hand shops. Harold was surprised that questions needed to be asked on this subject given the stunning technology which had determined virtually all his other purchases over the past quarter century.

'Unfortunately, it's only the supermarkets and department stores that have the technology to read that far back in time,' was Simon's answer expressed in an amicable tone and thereby earning him a reproachful look from Crawley. Harold was somewhat reassured by this and volunteered the fact that he often repaired his own clothes by sewing on the odd button or an elbow patch even occasionally sewing up a seam or replacing a zip. This was something he had undertaken to do more of as his New Year's Resolution.

'Oh, and you've pre-empted what was going to be my last question!' Simon smiled innocently.

'Well, I'm afraid it isn't *my* last question or rather statement!' Crawley couldn't bear the prospect of his partner lightening the atmosphere.

Harold, who had relaxed a little anticipating a final question to come from the milder-mannered Simon Jones, tensed up again as even this was usurped by Crawley:

'Yes, we have a record here, as you would expect, of your New Year's Resolution as submitted just two days before the deadline on 27th December. I am not going to question its authenticity, as clearly it met the ministry's criteria. However, it would be remiss of us not to take this opportunity to ask you to demonstrate how closely you've been adhering to your undertaking to reduce your evening TV viewing. Of course, the fact that you had the television on as we arrived at approximately quarter to six doesn't augur particularly well...'

Harold recalled that he had instinctively switched the TV off on hearing the banging on the door, so had the couple been eavesdropping outside the front room window for heaven's sake? He refrained from articulating the question aloud, but his facial expression betrayed his indignation.

Crawley, who had paused to observe his intended prey's reaction, continued:

'TV viewing data is also naturally recorded in much the same way as energy and water consumption, though regrettably we don't have this to hand. However, if you would be so good as to estimate for us by how much you have been able to cut down your evening viewing since January 1st it would greatly assist our investigation. We will certainly check the veracity of this when we get back to base and no doubt this will give us a greater insight into your moral makeup.'

Harold confidently estimated that he'd reduced his evening viewing by eight to twelve percent, so an average of ten per cent and meekly awaited Crawley's final question.

'The biggest elephant in the room, however, as I'm sure even you realise, Mr Jackson, is the fact that you are living alone in a three-bedroom house and have been doing so since your wife left you three years ago, just one year after the departure of your youngest offspring.'

Harold at this point could sense the growing heat of an internal fuse which was about to ignite the cumulative anger welling up within him.

'This house was built over one hundred years ago as a family home for a couple with at least one child on the way. In this day and age of devastating climatic degradation, I am sure you are fully and painfully aware that it is outrageously selfish for a single adult to be taking up so much living space when there are many families made homeless by extreme weather events and who are having to live in cramped and makeshift hostel accommodation.'

Crawley again paused in order to admire the psychological impact of his sententious lecture-cum-accusation. Indeed, Jackson was becoming quite flushed in the face.

'The evidence of your infrequent social life and outings to certain bars and clubs suggest that you possess dual sexuality, as it is nowadays commonly termed. In your position, therefore, I should have thought you would be in an ideal position to acquire a partner of either gender who could share your house, thereby contributing to solving the housing shortage.'

This brazen intrusion into Harold's social and personal life was the final straw. Verbally paralysed with rage, he suddenly stood up and lunged at Crawley, punching him twice hard in the chest. Crawley reeled back, stunned, but quickly regaining his senses enough to order his partner to call the police. Jones obligingly did so after overcoming a nervous fumbling fit in getting to grips with his phone's keypad. Fortunately for Crawley, Harold didn't follow up his offensive, but sank back down into his seat holding his head in his hands, his anger demon now sated.

Withing three minutes, community lady police officer, Margaret Warwick, walked briskly into Harold Jackson's lounge accompanied by a sterner looking male officer. The two handcuffed and bundled the forlorn gentleman into the police van parked directly outside the house. It already contained three other gents and one lady, each with their own story to tell of how they had fallen foul of the law that evening.

Courtesy of Harold Jackson's right fist, Nigel Crawley had suffered nothing more than a couple of bruised ribs followed by a mild dose of post traumatic shock. Once the initial pain had subsided, he drifted swiftly out of self-pitying mode and back into character. His mood even brightened as new vistas of opportunity opened up before his devious mind. The evening shift was now over and a few minutes after leaving Mr Jackson's house, Jones awkwardly ventured to initiate conversation.

'Rather more than we were bargaining for wouldn't you say, sir?' There was no contractual requirement for Jones to use an explicitly deferential form of address, but despite being somewhat old fashioned, *sir* seemed the most apt way of expressing his obsequious relationship with his line manager.

The pained expression on Crawley's face slowly morphed into a self-satisfied smirk.

'It was a bit hairy at the time, but I got the result we needed. Obviously, I needed to provoke him into raising his voice and even get verbally abusive to justify calling the police, but he seemed such a push over to start with I didn't expect him to get physical, the bastard.'

During previous home visits, Jones had learnt many a trick of the trade under Crawley's stewardship, but he was genuinely taken aback by this latest revelation. Usually, the police were summoned only when there was hard evidence that a significant environmental or other offence had been committed. The case against Jackson was the flimsiest he'd seen so far, so Crawley's latest departure struck him as a completely different ball game.

'But you know what it means, don't you Jonesy?'

'Well, I presume, sir, he'll get a stiffer sentence for common

assault on top of any environmental offences he's committed....'
Jones somehow knew he'd imperfectly read his boss's mind.

'He deserves everything the judge throws at him, but that wasn't what I meant. You were quite right when you said 'rather more than we were bargaining for'. For us, it means we'll get a hefty bonus for making a house available to a needy family who have lost theirs in the latest climate carnage down South. And for me, it means I'll get compensation for sustaining an injury in the line of duty and I reckon a tasty sum at that. Pretty damned good day's work, I'd say!'

CHAPTER 12: PROOF OF KARMIC JUSTICE

As Jenny awoke at seven o'clock on Monday morning, 24th January, she required more than the usual degree of willpower to extract herself from the relative warmth of her bed. This uncomfortable task accomplished, she threw on her dressing gown and immediately wrote up her account of the day before.

She knew from experience that this was the best possible discipline for ensuring she kept up with her journal. Her memories of the day gone by were not only still fresh, but they benefited from a night's sleep for processing by her subconscious mind. What's more, with a bus to catch and a full school day ahead, there was no time for dillydallying. She wrote:

Sunday was a distinctly uneventful day as compared with mid-week when we endured the terrible flooding episode. Now that's all subsided – and I mean literally with even the water in the cellar having disappeared through the cracks dad keeps talking about – we all seem to be in a state of anti-climax. The last of the damp in the lounge and dining room has all but dried out. I wish I could say the same for the kitchen where the musty smell is so off-putting when we're in there cooking.

Mum said how much worse it would have been only a few years ago, as the water would have brought in all the filth from the litter and dog mess strewn all over the roads and pavements, so the whole place would have stunk to high heaven. I know she was trying to look on the bright side, but I couldn't resist pointing out that in those days before the real climate breakdown, there probably wouldn't have been the storm to bring the flood water into the house in the first place. Having made this smart-Alice remark, I noticed John's envious look for not having got in there first!

It was quite nice playing the usual family parlour games after lunch which have now become something of a habit since Christmas time. During the round of consequences, dad got amusingly embarrassed. It was only after he'd read out his silly story right to the end that he caught on to the inadvertent innuendo. Everyone laughed and mum more than anyone. Here Jenny paused to admire her choice of the word inadvertent until she realised that this was not quite correct usage, as although innuendos were produced by chance, they were hardly inadvert, as this was largely the aim of the game.

Our peace was disturbed at about seven o'clock by the deafening racket of a police car tearing down our road before stopping a couple of streets away. John and I wondered if it'd been something exciting like a burglary or scandalous like a case of domestic violence. We were in the lounge about to turn on the TV for some news at the time and decided to get dad to go and find out, but we couldn't find him anywhere. It turned out he'd already set off down the road without needing to be asked. No doubt he was still charged up by the community spirit he rediscovered when we had the flood.

Ten minutes later, dad came back and told us a middle-aged bloke just two roads away had been arrested for no obvious reason. He'd asked a neighbour who had come out to see what was going on, but this chap couldn't enlighten him any further.

Jenny checked her watch and found she'd gone over her allotted journal writing time slot by about two minutes. She'd have to make that up by throwing on her clothes and guzzling her breakfast extra quick, while knowing it would be bad for her health. All the more reason to stick to her timings in future!

That evening, the Greenways were huddled together for warmth in front of the TV for what promised to be an intriguing documentary on channel 2. The programme was billed as providing proof of survival after death based on evidence gathered from two continents.

It started with a précis of what was taught concerning life and death by the world's oldest religion and which even today claimed the greatest number of followers. The next focus was on a teenage girl from the West Midlands who suffered from nightmares with a recurring theme. Her parents became concerned about how this was affecting her sleep and ultimately physical and mental health, so they sought medical advice. Their general practice doctor got her an appointment with a counsellor who was also a psychologist.

A therapist suggested she record the details of her nightmares and discuss them at her next counselling session. She came back two weeks later with an intricate account of how she had lived in a village in an Asian country whose name she attempted to write down phonetically. She did the same with names of her family members and an important building they seemed to live nearby. Although in the dream she thought in English, all speech was in a foreign language which she understood, but couldn't name. The nightmarish part of the dream was around a tidal wave which they all knew was about to crash down on their coastal village. The girl always woke up just as her house was about to be engulfed.

The next part of the documentary was predictable in the modern context and caused John and Jenny to almost groan out loud. It involved scholars working on the names the girl had written down which enabled them to trace her village, her own name and that of her family members to one which existed about eighty years ago on the flood plain of Bangladesh. The language was Bengali and official documents recorded the family as missing with their village now under two metres of sea water.

In an interview with the girl herself, the final part of the programme revealed that once the mystery had been solved, the nightmares ceased and any dreams the girl had about her former life were recollections of happier times, albeit in a much harsher environment than the one she enjoyed today in a provincial town in the West Midlands.

All the Greenways had been uncharacteristically self-disciplined in not shouting out disparaging comments during the programme, but confining themselves to the occasional tut or groan. However, once it was over, the inevitable family debate immediately followed.

Anne got in with the first review:

'I'm open minded about the whole reincarnation thing, but there's nothing new about the girl's story. In my grandparents' day, bookshops were awash with New Age literature and there was a whole section on reincarnation and karma. The only difference is that then it was still a minority interest which got you labelled as a fanciful crank. Nowadays it's become official and mainstream.'

'There are other explanations than reincarnation,' Jenny stated confidently.

'One is that the girl could have unconsciously picked up information from people around her. There are lots of Asian families in her town. She may have heard a story from someone which stuck in her subconscious memory. It then kept breaking through in her dreams so she'd have to deal with it, as it was obviously worrying her. Eventually she did just that with the help of the therapist.

'Then there's another supernatural or metaphysical explanation I've read about. It's the idea that we all have access to all knowledge if we attune to it. So, this girl, again perhaps because she was surrounded by people from that country, tuned into its culture and history. She then imagined herself as this person from a past age whose records she'd psychically attuned t.'

'I didn't think there could be a spookier explanation than reincarnation, but you've certainly hit upon it, siss!' John laughed. 'I just think if the government wants to push this new religion, they should be honest and admit they've lifted it virtually wholesale from an ancient culture. I think the reason they're not doing is because they're too proud to admit that this huge country which they formerly exploited under the British Empire actually had all the important questions around life and death worked out before them.'

Mike, true to character, left his comments till the end so as to complement what the others had said rather than risk coming in first and finding he was out on a limb:

'Thinking in terms of the law of averages too, it's quite possible that the girl used names for her family which she'd heard around her in the community and that there would be lots of villages with the same or a similar name to the one she dreamt about. They did say that she wrote down a rough phonetic spelling, so this could be widely interpreted. What I'm saying, is: get anyone to make up half a dozen random common Asian names for an imaginary family and village they come from...'

'But what about the important place nearby?' Jenny challenged her dad.

'Yes, well there may be lots of important places with the same name too, like the Empire Theatre or Royal Hotel in most cities in this country. Anyway, with this random basket of names, you're then bound to find that almost exact combination in several places around a place as big as Bangladesh.'

'Now, that *is* clever!' exclaimed Anne keen to encourage her husband in his newfound self-confidence despite her recent feminine intuitions that all was *not* right with her husband.

John decided he'd round off the discussion by interpreting the intent of the programme makers.

'But the real message they want you to take away is that however lousy life now seems here in England, it's much worse in other countries past and present, so be grateful. And if you're unlucky enough to be washed out of house and home, it's still probably better than living in a piss-poor historically exploited corner of our former British Empire - Bangladesh. But, at the end of the day, if you get drowned in the next flood, never fear – you'll be rewarded for all your forbearance and suffering by being reborn into a much cosier environment next time – just like the girl in the story!'

'So, in other words, the cunning government propaganda machine has all bases covered…' mused Jenny.

Anne rounded off the analysis for the family:

'And, although it wasn't acknowledged in the programme, there's a kind of karmic justice aspect to all this. The richer countries which, through unfair trading relations continued to exploit former colonies long after the British Empire collapsed, are now catching up with them in terms of climate chaos. *What goes round comes round* – as common folk still say, unless they've been unfortunate enough to have read the Bible, and may prefer: *As ye sow, so shall ye reap.*

Sixty-two-year-old Prime Minister, Sir Robert Wallace, entered the Cabinet meeting room where he had gathered a slightly larger than usual collection of his senior colleagues. Ever since he acceded to the top job, he had been longing for a suitable occasion to crack a witty joke referencing the similarity of his august-sounding name with that of Sir Robert Walpole – the first de facto British Prime Minister from 1725 to 1742. This would have been just such a suitable occasion had he not failed yet again to think up a witticism to go with it. *Never mind,* he consoled himself, *few of the present generation will have heard of Sir Robert Walpole, anyway.*

Although camouflaged to some degree by other themes, the matter in hand was essentially to discuss reform of the judicial and penal system which he deemed sufficiently important and pressing not to entrust solely to the present incumbent of the Ministry for Legal Affairs, Baroness Verity Shillaker. She had only been in post since the last shuffle six weeks ago, which was too little time to get on top of her ministerial brief. Two of the other cabinet ministers present had occupied that post for several months apiece as a stepping stone to more prestigious roles. Sir Robert hoped they had stayed in place just long enough to absorb the rudiments of the job sufficiently well to have an informed opinion on the forthcoming discussion topics.

'Ladies and gentlemen, thank you for making yourselves available at short notice for this highly important discussion. I know you are all up to your ears in work within your own departments.

'Never in my recollection has so much urgent legislation been required by an incumbent government over so short a time span. Environmental law has barely kept up with the rapid deterioration of the climate crisis, particularly along the southern coastline which is disappearing into the sea as we speak.

'Some of you will remember the day the government formally relinquished all coastal defence projects as futile. Ever since, it's been a case of adaptation and long-term mitigation of effects rather than a hopeless effort to eliminate them altogether.

Had our predecessors been bolder in taking timely action, no doubt we would not be facing the unpalatable yet necessary steps we are having to take today. We've all been complicit in drafting and getting through parliament legislation born of urgent pragmatism as opposed to the popular will. What government in the history of this country has been forced to adopt a policy of reversing economic growth? But we all now accept that for humanity to have a fighting chance of surviving climate breakdown, we must drastically reduce energy consumption and exploitation of what remains of the earth's natural resources.

Now to the heart of the matter. We have introduced a raft of laws over recent years to significantly shrink the economy. Most of you here will recall such measures as imposing prohibitive taxes on motor vehicles of all classes, introducing a Universal Citizen's Income to drive as many people as possible out of productive employment, curbing the birth rate among most social groups and criminalising virtually all forms of human activity not conducive to preserving the planet as we know it.

From a personal point of view, enacting certain draconian and often anti-democratic laws has been abhorrent, but I am nevertheless proud to have to have acceded to the premiership at such a time of national emergency. Public opinion is slowly but surely swinging round to reappraise the hierarchy of crime. This reappraisal has been conditioned both by the harsh reality of environmental degradation and climate crisis whose destructive effects we see all around us and by the concerted re-education campaign we have pursued through the media, schools and by every other conceivable means.

We have witnessed the penal system and legal profession come to terms with the shift of emphasis from punishing the socio-economic criminal towards greater condemnation of the environmental criminal. Apparently, it is the dramatic negative economic growth which is largely to thank for the unanticipated drop in the conventional crime rate. Social scientists and criminologists tell us that the significant reduction in socio-economic inequalities has led to a corresponding reduction in social envy and unease. This in turn has led to less property crime. As one of you quipped the other day – there's hardly anything left to steal anymore! And to think that only a few months ago our worst fears were civil unrest and a complete breakdown of law and order!

Of course, we have to distinguish between the petty environmental criminal on the one hand and the irresponsible industrial-scale polluter on the other. This is only the same as taking a harder line with organised criminal gangs than with occasional opportunist crooks....'

Sir Robert Wallace continued his monologue for a further few minutes. He proudly referred to the imminent opening of eight new prisons up and down the country intended exclusively for environmental criminals. This was to encourage the growing popular perception of the qualitative distinction between ecological and socio-economic crime.

Understandably, there remained considerable unease about where violent crime was meant to fit into the reconfigured picture. Clearly, it was more serious than petty economic crime, as it posed a public safety risk, but how could this be measured against the public safety risk of certain eco-crimes whose effects may be initially 'invisible', but whose ultimate impact could be on a much larger scale. And where the perpetrators were fully aware of the effects of their actions.

The PM would have to address the implications of this issue before long with his minister for Legal Affairs, but the most immediate concern was a review of recently introduced measures to tackle the climate crisis with the fresh water shortage now being experienced by all. Added to this, was the growing land and property deficit which was apparent to anyone living in affected areas.

'Whether we talk about lack, shortage, deficit, scarcity, insufficiency, dearth, or search for even more synonyms, these words are the order of the day for us all and need to permeate the mentality of everyone working in all our ministries', the PM concluded, before opening up the discussion to his cabinet colleagues. He invited Sir John Beecham, Minister for Economy, Finance and Taxation to speak first and give a review of his department's work. Sir John spoke quickly, but confidently in a bid to get the pain over with as soon as possible:

'Colleagues from the ministries for Legal Affairs and Health and Wellbeing are also present today and will no doubt wish to deal with the substance of the various matters under discussion. I will, therefore, confine myself to summarising the outturn of recently implemented measures purely from a fiscal point of view.

'The New Year's Resolutions pledges have been taken up by an estimated eighty per cent of the population nationwide and have saved the nation an estimated two and a half billion pounds and an inestimable amount of energy, water and other resources. Our target is to draw a further eight per cent of the population into the scheme during the first quarter with a view to incorporating all but the most elusive members of society by January next year.

'From their introduction in November, fines for excessive and wasteful use of resources have brought in over 1.2 billion to the Treasury – a fifteen per cent increase from the previous quarter. Burial fees through licensing on private land and related fees are modest as yet, but since their introduction as recently as 1st December, there has been significant take-up and potential earnings come not only from the fees, but also from savings garnered from householders paying a modest tax on income generated.

'There have been considerable savings to the State arising from the wider application of the voluntary euthanasia legislation thanks to its growing acceptance among the public. In this connection, it is estimated that the NHS has saved upwards of £14 billion through the fall in demand for advanced age care over the past three years.

'The savings made from a wider acceptance of voluntary euthanasia has resulted in a reallocation of resources to other priorities within the NHS. For example, it has enabled us to prioritise treatment of productive members of society and, most importantly, to increase the preventive medicine budget. This is known in the medical world as prophylactics and is best described by the old adage: 'a stitch in time saves nine'. Next quarter, I look forward to providing you with further data to illustrate the success of the drive to better fund the business end of the NHS.

'Obviously, it is for my colleague in the Health and Wellbeing Ministry to allay any public concerns over ethical issues raised by certain policies and to tackle alleged abuses of any procedures.'

Sir John Beecham paused his address here, content to have represented himself on the high moral ground. He was not at all troubled by his secret desire to see his own ailing 88-year-old mother avail herself of euthanasia in order to bequeath him a substantial inheritance. He continued after taking a few sips of water and clearing his throat, consciously resetting his earnest expression which he'd tirelessly rehearsed in the mirror early in his ministerial career.

'I do, unfortunately, have to report a number of regrettable abuses which have come to our department's attention with regard to our policy to reduce economic activity. Clearly, the aim of the legislation was to curb the production and trading of goods and services whose manufacture is wasteful of resources and brings a negative environmental and social impact.

Hastily recruited and inadequately trained agents have in some cases run amok in parts of the country, closing down or heavily fining perfectly legitimate small-scale businesses and cooperatives. There have been cases of self-seeking agents over zealously imposing fines tempted by bonus clauses written into their contracts which incentivised such behaviour. I assure you that, working with my colleagues in Legal Affairs, this oversight will be addressed as a matter of urgency.'

In order to end on an upbeat note, Sir John reminded his assembled peers of the remarkable progress made by the technology and data teams in his department. These had made impressive strides forward in equipping inspectors with the capability to track environmental offenders' historical footprint in order to assess the severity of their crimes and impose the appropriate sanctions and penalties.

Sir John, feeling he had given a creditable account of himself and his ministry, gave way to Hazel Cruickshank, Minister for Health and Wellbeing, whose task it had originally been to justify to parliament and society at large the Voluntary Euthanasia Act from a medical and ethical point of view. If necessary, she could be relied on to reaffirm these arguments before her colleagues today while also addressing other current issues.

Hazel took the floor confidently and spoke with the level of decorous solemnity one might expect of a senior figure addressing so sensitive yet consequential a matter. Despite the inevitable press reports and complaints to the ministry about excessive pressure applied on individuals or their relatives in voluntary euthanasia cases, Hazel did not refer to these. She simply alluded to the need to proceed cautiously with further liberalisation of euthanasia regulations, as officialdom euphemistically expressed it. She was perfectly aware, however, of her government's intention to normalise euthanasia in the public mind to the point where opposing it would be seen as irrational and unreasonable.

Only a year ago, she had been required to justify to parliament the government's bill to introduce the age-related sliding scale of reductions of annual NHS expenditure. Its enactment attracted a degree of muted criticism in certain sectors, but very little of the opposition came out in public debate owing to media restrictions.

Hazel was grateful at the time that she was new to her brief as Health and Wellbeing minister and so largely escaped being associated with some of the more radical or, what some would term, regressive legislation. In addition, the immediate effects of environmental crises helped to steal the attention of more vocal members of the public away from an issue that was unlikely to affect them personally in the near to medium-term future.

Hazel finished her pitch on the thorny question of projected increases in prescription charges which, along with existing charges for medical centre visits, were intended to deter frivolous or otherwise unnecessary visits to GPs. Such measures were more politically sensitive as they had a greater impact on a larger cohort of citizens owing to their everyday nature. The average person might visit their doctor and pay for a prescription two or three times a year, but would probably only face the dilemma of unaffordable private medical care versus euthanasia for an elderly relative just once or twice in a lifetime.

At last, it was the turn of the Minister for Legal Affairs, Verity Shillaker. Although new to her role, she was the least nervous of all who had spoken. She had been fully briefed by her predecessor and talked everything through in advance with all relevant Cabinet colleagues, not least with the Prime Minister. It was too soon for her have experienced the stark contrast between theory and practice. In any case, she was able to relax secure in the knowledge that there were no journalists within a mile of the cabinet office.

'Ladies and gentlemen, I thank you all for presenting a comprehensive review of the situation prevailing in your respective departments. As we are well aware, all our ministries are interconnected on so many levels.

Now, to turn to my recently adopted new home: the Ministry for Legal Affairs. No society and certainly no civilisation, modern or ancient, has been able to function without a dynamic body of legislation supported by a robust legal and penal system. In recent years, as the climate emergency and environmental crisis have wreaked havoc throughout the globe, we have seen countless societies crumble for want of having the constitutional and institutional mechanisms in place to respond adequately to the rapidly deteriorating situation.

'Many nations around the world were surprised at our country's capacity to streamline our political and administrative organs of State in a way which enabled us to keep our heads above water – if not literally, as there is no refreezing of the icecaps – then at least figuratively. Yes, we initially faced criticism from our longstanding allies, former Commonwealth friends, trading partners and even the largely defunct International Court of Human Rights for seemingly turning our back on our democratic traditions. However, any discerning commentator today would have to acknowledge the wisdom of our difficult choice to curb certain civil liberties for the greater good of society. We see now how the majority of countries where this difficult choice was not made have descended into political, social and economic chaos, all of which has only served to undermine any collective efforts to tackle the environmental crisis.

'I apologise for such a long preamble, but I felt it necessary to restate the background to what I am about to put before you even though most of you are privy to the broad outline of my proposals.

The first thing, and I am sure no one among you would disagree with this, is the urgency of speeding up our judicial system and eradicating the backlog of court cases. In order to achieve this objective, on the spot fining will be introduced for a raft of environmental or 'eco' offences – a list too long to go into here – but a summary of these can be found in the detailed appendix in your agenda pack.

'Suffice it to say, that police, environmental enforcers and other guardians of public order will be empowered to impose fines up to a maximum value without right of contestation or appeal.

Any such resistance will be dealt with by summary arrest and a minimum term of imprisonment as yet to be determined. Offences deemed sufficiently severe to bring to a Magistrates court, as they are likely to attract a larger fine or a possible prison term, will lead, if proven, to the identity of the offender being published in the local press. In common parlance, this is generally termed *naming and shaming* and is already a common practice in many parts of the world'.

'On a more technological note, further progress has been made in terms of producing plausible historical evidence of environmental irresponsibility: frequent flying, second home ownership, extravagant consumerism and such like. It's all in the bank records, but new laws, of course, empower us to track past behaviour in other ways if the need arises.

'Obviously, as with earlier legal reforms, we've used the remaining media outlets to publicise the new laws and are working with journalists and broadcasters throughout the various networks to get the message across as constructively as possible and ensuring a helpful narrative is presented. This is what they're good at, after all! One thing which always gets the public on side is the promise of tougher laws and ramping up the severity of penalties, and we've plenty of good news on that front.'

Before concluding, Verity made a few more points intended to remind the assembly why such tough reforms were about to be introduced. She reminded the assembly of how low the crime rate was compared with recent decades when overproduction of consumer goods combined with rampant social inequalities had engendered the perfect storm of hardship and envy which in turn led to a high crime rate and public disorder.

She didn't mention the growing army of people made redundant from their jobs of choice and redeployed at just above the Universal Citizen's Income level in order to enforce the new laws. There were several other less palatable facts about the *Brave New*

World she was co-creating which would not have chimed so well with the general tone of the cabinet meeting. But these were for the most part tacitly understood by all present.

Before the cabinet meeting broke up, a few other matters were briefly discussed such as the progress of perpetual sex education reforms in Roger Mayhew's Ministry for Education, Culture and Spirituality. Hazel Cruickshank made a few comments in this regard by prearrangement with Maynard in order to stress the crosscutting nature of this policy area with her own Ministry for Health and Wellbeing. She also alluded to the pilot scheme to roll out universal free meals in Northern parts of the country, though the contraceptive aspect of this policy was not mentioned, as it was still felt by the PM to be imprudent to unveil this prematurely to anyone outside a tiny circle of trusted initiates.

Promotion of the New Religion was deemed worthy of a little discussion before all present agreed that the embedding process was proceeding at a satisfactory pace. Maxine Walker, The Home Secretary, despite having retained her status as second only to the Prime Minister, spoke last and for the shortest duration, though she did so with unparalleled aplomb given the enormity of what she announced:

As a result of the increasing frequency of unpredictable devastating storms, coastal dwellings were being swept into the sea or ruined at a rate faster than local shelters could be built. Therefore, the scheme already in existence to encourage residents in safer regions to open their houses to storm refugees for modest remuneration, was to be extended and made compulsory in certain cases.

Leaving the Cabinet Office, each minister attempted to assume an air of inscrutable equanimity which belied their own particular anxieties.

Roger Maynard: *Thank God my children are already grown up and married with families. Ten years later and they'd be sterilised!*

Hazel Cruickshank: *Thank God I know what's in the Kinder Juice and can tell my nephew not to drink it!* But then, she got to wondering about the implications of his being the only horny teenager among his peers.

Verity's most recent predecessor as Minister for Legal Affairs, now Minister for Transport: *Thank God we're seeing the demise of the permissive society at last! Tough justice is what'll save the nation. Roll on the day they bring back hanging – that'll keep any rebellious mobs at bay!*

Home Secretary Maxine Walker: *Thank God my second home is too remote from civilisation! At least I won't have to worry about giving half of it up to refugees!*

Prime Minister Sir Robert Wallace had been observing his ministers' body language and studied their styles of delivery over and above their actual message content which was well known to him already. He just wanted to get a truer sense of what these people were in and of themselves and which one of them was most likely to be standing in his shoes in six months from now when almost inevitably the political die would have been cast against him.

He was at least a little reassured that the present incumbent of the ministry for Legal Affairs, Verity Shillaker, was not as mean spirited and downright cruel as her most recent predecessors. This individual, now biding his time in Transport, had revealed a little too much of his warped soul one evening after taking a little too much drink at the members' social club.

Indeed, Sir Robert was not at all far off the mark: the current Minister for Transport was not at all gratified at the prospect of the worst environmental offenders being exiled with minimal supplies to almost certain death on an uninhabitable island. Justice had to be seen to be done, after all! He took secret pleasure in visualising creative punishments for environmental criminals. For example, he gleefully imagined a serial potato crisp muncher being put to death by asphyxiation in a bin full of crisp wrappers or a serial owner of petrol-guzzling prestige motorcars being crushed to death at a scrap yard inside one of his favourite vintage models.

In the meantime, he had to content himself with looking forward to the next round of tweaks to the retributive justice within the penal system. He had it on good authority that these tweaks would include broadening the concept of criminalisation by association. It was a logical next step to assume that family members who had lived with and benefited from the proceeds of an environmental criminal were implicit and hence liable to prosecution and sanction themselves. In this way, whole houses could be freed up for refugees from the south at potentially no cost to the exchequer.

On his way to Number 10 Downing Street, the PM made another attempt to hit upon a pun around his name Wallace which would connect with Walpole. *There must be some connection, however obscure, between pole and lace...,* he pondered. But as usual, he couldn't find one.

CHAPTER 13: ALL'S WELL THAT ENDS

Anne felt it strangely fitting that the letter from the Environment and Housing Agency should fall onto the hall door mat on Monday, 31st January – just over two weeks since the flooding and the momentous family decision which arose from it. Was this Fate's conciliatory way of rounding off the first month in what promised to be a tough year ahead?

Their application to receive a guest family had been accepted. There would probably be a maximum of three persons – an adult and two children or two adults and one child. This was the happy medium, as just two would mean less extra income than hoped for, and four would mean an overcrowded house.

The small family group in question was expected to arrive within the next few days having already spent over six weeks in a local shelter near Southampton where they had lived and lost their home through a combination of storm winds and flooding.

Anne had also decided on this auspicious day to hold a family meeting to discuss how everyone had managed their first month of acclimatising to their New Year's Resolutions. After bringing her husband and two children together for tea, which was no mean accomplishment in itself, she opened the review in the hope of breaking the ice on the potentially embarrassing topic of reduced washing.

'I must say, since I've started being more mindful about the way I use water when bathing, I've noticed I automatically use quite a lot less. Haven't you all found the same?'

Jenny decided to come in first with her distinctive offering and have done with it.

'The timing isn't terribly good for me, to be honest with my periods having just got quite heavy. I find I'm trying to hang on till I get to school where I can at least get a mini-shower and use loads of paper towels to get dry. Someone said they only have so much toilet paper and paper towels through an admin error, so it might be too good to last.'

It was John's turn next: 'Yes, it's the frequency that was the real issue at first. But I must say that two showers a week, one minimal and one proper one now seems adequate and normal. It makes me think how wasteful I used to be. And I can't believe how I've got used to washing my hair just once a week and how it feels better in some ways than when I washed it every other day. I reckon we owe a vote of thanks to mum for getting hold of those cheap slow-burning incense sticks. Just like snuff in the olden days – they really do cover the pong of body odour when someone's getting particularly ripe just before their shower day!'

Mike decided to change the subject to the heating, making the point that wearing an extra layer or two meant he was quite comfortable for the first two or three hours of the morning without the heating on. He was left wondering how much fuel and money they might have saved in the past had they only realised that up to half of the energy and water they used to use was for comfort rather than survival. If people had realised this and acted on it fifty years ago in the rich developed countries the planet might not be in such a mess.

'And at least cutting down has kept those awful inspectors at bay who have been hounding so many of our neighbours in one way or another!'

Anne empathetically went on to remind the others how older people feel the cold more and how deaths from exposure in the home had skyrocketed in recent years.

'No doubt the government records those deaths as involuntary but convenient euthanasia!' John suddenly gave in to the urge to further bolster his growing reputation as a reliable source of bad taste humour. 'Whereas I'd call it death by neglect,' he added for balance.

Anne resumed heedlessly: 'Come to think of it – when did we last check on the Watsons? I hope they've not had another nasty or even nastier visit lately. Apparently, the main culprit is that Nigel Crawley who paid us a visit over dad's workshop.' She at once regretted bringing up a subject still so raw for her husband.

Anne, who listened to the national news and weather reports more regularly and intently than anyone else, might have expected what came later that week on Friday, 4th February.

A second letter in an envelope identical to the first appeared early that morning in the hallway. It landed rather more awkwardly on the doormat than the first, as if to presage something untoward. Consequently, Anne took extra care in opening it as if this superstitious act might mitigate potential bad news.

The good news came in the first paragraph: a single mother in her late twenties and her two children aged twelve and eight were expected to arrive on Saturday, 6th February. *Heavens, that's tomorrow!* she thought, *they don't half work fast when it suits them in a national emergency.* She recalled that not so many years ago, it would often take several months to place a single child with a foster family, but now....

The bad news came in the second paragraph:

We regret to inform you that, in view of the exceptional circumstances arising from the national Storm and Flooding emergency and the sheer volume of housing loss the country has experienced in recent weeks and months, the National Rehousing Agency will no longer be able to honour in full the contract offered to guest families at the time of application. Hosting allowances will, therefore, be reduced by an average of 40 %. Rehoused persons will still retain 50% of their Universal Citizen's Income as originally provided for by the scheme.

There followed a table showing how these hosting rates had been scaled down from the original amount. It got worse still in the third and final paragraph.

The hosting allowances have, however, been calculated to ensure that the guest families' essential needs can be catered for from the budgets set out and should, therefore, suffice to cover the expenditure incurred.

We should advise you that as you were assessed by us as being in a position to host a family in need of shelter, you are now required by law to honour your commitment and that refusal to do so at this stage would result in a fine of £200.

'Bloody hell!' Anne exclaimed. She couldn't believe that after all the ingenious lengths she'd gone to bolster her family's financial security, her latest efforts looked like doing the reverse. How would she break this latest news to Mike and the children? She soon regained her sangfroid, however, and, with no one else yet up and round to distract her, she was able to sit down with the figures quoted by the National Rehousing Agency and make a few outline calculations of her own.

Anne felt her family had a fighting chance of at least breaking even provided the guest family's needs and expectations were moderate. She could be confident that essential heating costs for seven people in the household wouldn't be proportionately more than for four. There should also be other economies of scale. For example, preparing meals for seven would work out marginally more efficient that preparing them for four, though it might be tricky if the guests had different dietary habits!

Anne dwelt on these and other such reckonings until Jenny joined her in the kitchen. Like most parents in a similar situation, she decided to shield her daughter from the full extent of her anxieties and simply stated that they may not benefit financially as much as she had hoped from being a host family.

This was the line she would take with her husband and son too. She would need to be particularly careful in Mike's case, as he still tacitly in overall charge of family finances.

Next day, late Saturday morning, the guest family arrived. Single mum Chloe aged twenty-nine with her two children, Katie, 12 and, Christopher, eight. *A pity they couldn't have both been nearer to my children's age*, thought Anne in a first wave of disappointment, as she ushered them all into the hallway. However, being the only one available for the welcoming party, Anne appreciated the chance to process her own emotional response to the newcomers before having to introduce them to John and Jenny when they came home from school.

She would also have at least a little while to consider how best to break the news to Mike when he at last got up. He had taken to rising much later these past few days. They hadn't broached the subject directly since the house meeting, but Anne knew her husband was struggling with the concept of an alien family descending on and potentially merging with his own. He had had difficulty enough managing his resurgent depression since the uplifting effects of tackling the flood emergency had begun to wear off.

Jenny's diary. Monday evening, 7th February.

With the stress and excitement of the Lovells arriving on Saturday and settling in, I've not got round to doing my daily journal, so am now covering the last four days. At least looking back over a longer timescale makes you home in on the key events, as you can't recall the less important details in any case!

Chloe is aged late twenties and a single mum. I'm burning to ask her how she came to be landed with two kids on her own. She's so nice, I can't imagine why a bloke would leave her in the lurch. Or perhaps she just wanted to raise her children on her own. But she must have been so young when she had her daughter, Katie, that I can't imagine her making that choice unless it was much later. Perhaps she kicked her husband or partner out for being unfaithful.

Chris, the boy, is only eight and it's going to be hard for him to settle in as he's too young to mix naturally with the rest of us. If anything, it's worse for him now, as he's going to miss his school friends and even his sister's got less time for him, as she wants to spend more time with me – a girl closer to her age!

I can see mum's relieved that they will only need two rooms between them. If push came to shove, I suppose Katie could share with me, but though I think we'll get on, having some privacy in my own room is the thing I value most and would hate to have to give that up.

Dad has tried to make Chris feel part of the family and took him round the garage on Sunday, showing him his tools and the things he's made and repaired. I'm hoping they'll get on and it'll give dad something to do, but he seems to have forgotten how to talk to an eight-year-old. It's a long time since John or I were that age!

Today, I had to take Katie in to my school, as it's nearer than John's and the authorities obviously decided our closer ages would make it easier. She's year 8, I'm year 10. She didn't seem too nervous, but I reckon the others in her class will make fun of her because of her southern accent and I hope they're not too cruel.

Mum and his mum took little Chris to the primary school which both John and I used to attend. She waited there with Chloe for the first two lessons in case there were any problems, but all seemed to go well.

Wednesday, 9th February.

Well, it didn't take long for little Chris to find his feet. Mum got a call to talk to his teacher at the end of the school day. Apparently, he'd sworn in class, had a fight with another boy in the playground and then refused to go back into lessons after the lunch break. The teachers eventually coaxed him back into the classroom, but he'd refused to engage with the lesson and just sat at the back sulking till the end of the day.

Mum had to go in to collect him and discuss what had happened with his teacher, as Chloe was out most of the day. Then she had to explain everything to Chloe when she came back and it didn't seem right. Chloe didn't apologise or even say why she'd had to go out during the day and not be back in time to collect Chris in the first place. It's not far to the school and aged eight, Chris could manage to walk on his own eventually, but it was only his third day and you'd think his own mum ought to pick him up at least for the first week!

Friday, 11th February.

Disaster! Firstly, I thought Katie and I were getting on fine – and so we are at home – but today she walked away and completely ignored me when I went up to her in the school yard during break. I get that it's uncool to be seen mixing with other year groups and perhaps I was at fault, but it seemed a bit extreme. Perhaps you get real stick for mixing with other year groups at her old school down south.

Back at home in the evening, it was the opposite. She seemed to want to spend all her time with me and ignore her little brother. After over an hour trying to be nice and listening to her complaints about her old life and her impressions of her new school, I had to suggest we both needed time to do our homework.

Chris then kept bothering John for attention. John tried to keep him occupied as best he could with a few of his old toys, but obviously didn't want to spend all evening with him and so passed him on to mum. She was her saintly self as usual and tried to talk to him and interest him in some of our old books. Clearly, though, he wasn't keen on reading or even being read to.

At about eight, mum found Chloe in the kitchen frying up something she'd bought during the day. Chloe just suggested plonking Chris in front of the TV. Mum later told me she'd had to have a serious conversation with Chloe about the need to agree on meals and cook together to save energy and water owing to the new restrictions and threat of sanctions for breaking them. Chloe didn't argue but she didn't seem to take in what mum was saying either.

Saturday - Sunday, 12th to 13th February

Yesterday, I should have started my entry with 'A few problems' and left 'Disaster' to this weekend! Having been allowed to watch TV by himself last night, Chris came down early and decided to switch it on again this morning. When John came down next, he found Chris fiddling with the buttons on the set. The little brat had obviously lost the picture or channel he wanted by pressing something on the remote and then tried to fix the problem by attacking the controls on the set.

Dad was summoned but he couldn't immediately fix the problem and said he'd have to take the casing off to look inside. Meanwhile, Chris went missing, we assumed to escape having to face the music. We sent out a search party involving everyone but his mum who was out – again! This time, we found the little sod in the garage where he'd been playing with dad's tools. Thank god we found him when we did, as he'd already had time to squeeze into a plant pot a large amount of glue which he'd then used to stick odd bits of wood together and make what he called an army barracks. Needless to say, the unused glue had seeped out through the hole in the plant pot and stuck a whole load of dad's tools together into the bargain.

Dad's inner battle not to lose his temper with Chris was as plain as day. He wisely channelled his anger into trying to prise apart some of his tools which had been stuck together. Fortunately, Chris had used a tub of water-based glue so dad was able to soak most things in a bucket of rain water before it set hard. He drained this from the water butt outside and so avoided squandering our precious ration of mains water.

Unfortunately, Chris seemed intent on making himself even more unpopular today, particularly with me. He'd already had a session banging on the piano every day since he got here and even joined in uninvited when John and I were playing a couple of tunes together – John on the piano with me accompanying on the violin. He would either hammer away at the low notes or do the same on the high notes depending where on the keyboard John was mainly playing.

I should have known better than to assume Chris would confine his musical endeavours to making an annoying racket on the piano. This evening, I was in my room doing my homework when I suddenly heard a series of discordant scrapings on what could only be my violin. I rushed downstairs into the lounge and caught Chris in mid-performance. Unfortunately, my sudden appearance shocked him into dropping my violin on the floor. There was a nauseating cracking sound. Damage report: chin rest and one peg broken clean off and a six-inch crack along the body!

I stood in horror for I don't know how long. Rather like dad, though, I contained my anger just long enough to redirect it away from Chris, who came so close to having his face slapped, to the real culprit – the storm which caused the flooding and ruined our carpet. Together with the underlay, it would probably have cushioned the violin's fall sufficiently to prevent serious damage to my violin!

I did my best to show Chris I was cross with him, but forgave him at the same time. I would have suggested he help me fix the damage by way of atonement, but decided the risk was too great he'd only make matters worse.

Jenny ended her journal for the weekend here, proud of her carefully crafted sentences and judicious use of learned words such as *atonement*. Perhaps, in a bleak modern world of few conventional job opportunities, she might find a niche for herself one day as an author.

Also, putting everything down on paper helped diffuse much of her anger, even transmuting part of it into amusement. Later that evening, explaining to her mum what had happened, she joked that mother and daughter ought to work together to achieve joint sainthood.

Meanwhile, she would have a quiet word with dad and add her violin to his list of jobs to be done on top of repairing the TV and whatever else needed to be done in his beloved garage. Hopefully, Chris hadn't used up all the glue for his creative pursuits.

It was 14th February. Anne was painfully conscious that even in the present troubled times, this was a day many people associated with romance and celebrate, though it had never featured as such in her own life. From the start of their relationship, she and Mike had tacitly or explicitly - she couldn't recall which - agreed not to mark this or other occasions such as their wedding anniversary. It was all too corny and sentimental for intelligent, rational and unconventional people such as themselves.

Anne's regret at this naïve pact grew as each year passed, but so did the awkward barrier she would have to break in order to broach the subject with her husband. Today, however, just as she was on the verge of summoning up the necessary courage, Anne's resolve was completely knocked off course by events assailing her from all sides.

First, there was the low to middle-ranking trauma caused by little Chris's vandalism which, in varying degrees, had upset set the whole 'original' Greenway family. It was Jenny in the end, not her father, who stuck back the bits which had broken off her violin using what little was left of the glue. She announced that the sound wasn't much impaired by the unrepairable split along the body. John suspected she said this mainly to reassure her mum or maybe she just didn't have a good enough ear to be able to detect the difference.

Mike had successfully unstuck all his tools in the garage except for his cordless drill whose inner workings were irreversibly wrecked. He claimed to be optimistic about finding a way to repair the TV, but there was something about his tone which worried Anne.

John told his parents he'd run out of ideas on how to keep Chris occupied and out of trouble, but had so far managed to contain his exasperation. He'd taken the wise precaution of hiding his few prize possessions in the least accessible places in his room such as on top of his wardrobe and under clothes in his chest-of-drawers. He was even thinking about rigging up a lock for his room.

Katie had understandably been clinging to Jenny as the age difference between them was just under two years. On Sunday evening, Anne, with Jenny by her side for moral support, had taken the bold step of suggesting to Katie that she should do her share of playing with and otherwise occupying her little brother. The twelve-year-old seemed to get the message, though rather poignantly asked: 'And what about my mum?'

Anne at first interpreted this as *But, who's going to keep an eye on my mum?* before realising Katie meant that her own mum should take some responsibility for her little boy.

Her initial interpretation, however, was entirely justified. Since arriving ten days ago, Chloe hadn't stayed in her new home for more than an hour during the daytime except at weekends when she had attempted, much to Anne's irritation, to *do her own thing in the kitchen*, as she put it. She had even gone out every other evening without any explanation, leaving the Greenways in charge of her two offspring at dinner time.

Feeling increasingly uneasy about this pattern of behaviour, Anne decided to do a little detective work and follow Chloe on her daytime travels the following Monday morning. She chose the bathroom as the best observation post with its concealed view of the street where Chloe would have to make her exit from the front door. This occurred just before ten o'clock. Having established the direction Chloe was heading, Anne rushed downstairs already wearing her shoes and coat in order not to waste time and risk losing sight of her quarry.

She had even contrived to conceal her identity by donning dark glasses and a scarf covering half her face. The ruse worked, as she was just in time to follow Chloe to a bus stop. Anne waited out of sight behind a roadside tree until the bus pulled up and got on last, sitting at the front ahead of Chloe.

Two stops later, she followed Chloe off the bus for a final two or three hundred metres on foot. This took her as far as a seedy-looking building which bore clues as to its past life in various places on its façade. Anne clearly made out *Jimmy's Gym Club*, and, with a little more difficulty, *Marge's Massages*.

Anne watched as Chloe knocked three times at unnatural intervals and was admitted half a minute later by a squat gentleman looking even seedier than the shop front. Feminine intuition backed by her observations thus far would have justified Anne staying no longer at that point – all was as plain as day. However, largely out of a desire to satisfy her voyeuristic instinct, she decided to wait just a little while longer for one final piece of evidence. This came barely five minutes later in the form of a bald middle-aged man appearing outside the shop. This fellow also knocked out some sort of agreed code on the door and moments later was admitted by the same squat gentleman.

Later that evening, after checking Jenny was safely ensconced in her room, Anne caught Mike and John together in the kitchen and began her lament.
'Streetwalker, floozy, hooker, tart – it doesn't matter what term you use, the fact is we've now got a prostitute living under our roof, cashing in on the job and living the life of riley while we, her muggins hosts, are virtually on the breadline!'

'To be fair, not every term for prostitute would fit: *lady of the night* wouldn't do, as she's obviously at it mainly during the day!' As usual, John was the chief admirer of his own wisecrack.

'We should be thankful she's doing it discreetly and not under our roof. I just feel sorry for her kids. No wonder the little one is such a tearaway,' Mike contributed before withdrawing to the lounge to continue tackling the TV repairs and leaving his wife and son to continue the debate.

Anne and her son came to a pragmatic decision. They'd confront Chloe and suggest the fairest solution would be for the Greenways to retain all the modest amount paid for the guest family's upkeep while she would be free to enjoy her ill-gotten gains as selfishly as she wanted. Chloe conveniently came into the kitchen only minutes later *to do her own thing.* To their surprise, they found her completely compliant and amenable to the suggestion. She even seemed to accept Anne's tenuous explanation that she just happened to see Chloe enter the sleazy joint while visiting a shop further down the same road.

Having taken such care to protect Jenny from the uncomfortable truth about Chloe, Anne was shocked to learn that her daughter had ironically been the first to find out. She had innocently asked Chloe what she got up when she went out and received a direct and unashamed answer.
'If only you'd let on to us, I wouldn't have had to go through that rigamarole of dressing up and playing the amateur detective.' Anne scolded her daughter more in jest than anger.

Jenny's journal. Monday, 28th February

It's been one of the weirdest weeks of my life and I'm cross with myself for not keeping up with this journal as I'd resolved to do at New Year by making an entry every day. That's what the word JOURNAL means!
Can't be helped now, but at least it won't be so bad as long as I catch up on this, the last day of the second month of the year. I'll make this a people-centred account. Who do I start with?

John – he's been getting more obsessed with Mandy and has started talking about her whenever we catch up with each other in the kitchen. He said something really strange about how they were planning to 'get together' at Mandy's parents' house, as it was now impossible to get any privacy at ours. Surely, he doesn't intend doing anything physical with her after all the sessions we've had at school on sex education. I want to talk to mum about it, but fear she'll wrongly suspect I'm using the conversation as camouflage to cover what's going on in my own life.

On a more 'prosaic' level (I love that word which I learned the other day in English. It's even better than 'mundane', which means pretty much the same), poor John's new and long-awaited shirt got terminally stained when he was walking through the Technology Department earlier in the week. He suspects some envious student deliberately splashed a corrosive substance on him as he was passing. Added to that, the second pair of soles dad fixed to his shoes have already badly worn despite assurances that they would be hard wearing and one is coming unstuck and starting to comically flap as he walks. How uncool! I'm going to give mum and dad a pleasant surprise when I get into the sixth form and just ask for a second-hand 'new' top and skirt. As long as they're reasonably smart, they can save the money!

Dad – he's looking and sounding more and more like a lost soul as each day goes by. The most humiliating thing was mum having to get someone else in to fix the TV after Chris's antics the other week. And even now, the picture flickers at times and makes it hard to concentrate and gives mum a headache. A constant reminder of dad's failure. Telling him not to worry about it just makes him feel worse, so we pretend not to notice it now.

On the bright side, it means we have been doing even more of our own home entertainments and invented a couple more parlour games which even Chloe has joined in. In some ways, she seems closer to my age than Katie and – when I can catch her in - I quite enjoy talking to her, as her life has been so different. We don't talk about what she gets up to with the men she meets during the daytime. I agree with mum that it's better not to know. Who are we to judge anyway and Chloe has actually been quite generous with the money she makes 'at it'.

On a practical level, we are managing Chris a lot better between the four of us 'women'. We kind of do shifts and specialise in different things. Chloe takes him to school where he seems to have settled at last and mum picks him up even though she resents it and says he's old enough to come home on his own by now. But she feels extra responsible for someone else's child and wants to keep the peace with Chloe, who surprised us all the other day by saying 'thank you' to mum.

I keep him occupied for about an hour every evening and Katie ensures she gets him ready for bed and reads to him even though her own reading skill isn't up to much. I may try and suggest we swap roles or shifts so I can read to him next week for a change. I'd also like to help Katie with her English too, but will have to be tactful in the way I go about it.

But back to dad, as he's our real concern now because, whereas we're all managing life better, he seems to be going in the other direction. He very rarely talks to any of us and often leaves the room if anyone walks in on him. We've even stopped trying to find him odd jobs to do, as that just seems to make him more depressed, as he can't motivate himself and if he does, he seems to expect to fail even with the simplest things. For example, on Wednesday, he even got frustrated trying to fix the draft excluder on the kitchen door which leads into the yard. He gave up in the end and disappeared into his bedroom upstairs.

Mum is putting a brave face on everything and trying to keep up a strong exterior for our benefit, but I can sense it may take only one more crisis to give her a nervous breakdown. She behaved in the oddest way yesterday in the kitchen. I at last worked up the courage to mention how John keeps talking more and more about Mandy. She smiled awkwardly and immediately changed the subject to ask what I thought of school meals these days. She even asked my opinion on the Kinder Juice she'd heard we teenagers are being encouraged to drink these days! That made me wonder if kids at primary school get it. I innocently asked Chris what he thought of Kinder Juice and he clearly had no clue what I was talking about....

Enough about people. It's hard to believe that we've only just got used to surviving the horrible cold, wind and rain of the winter season and on the news they're already talking about likely freak hot spells from mid-March with possible droughts as early as May! True, we did have a heat wave in April last year which even led to wild fires getting out of control in the south and East Anglia. The climate is in a complete mess and there seems no prospect of finding anywhere for our guest family to go any time soon.

Tomorrow after school, John and I have agreed to celebrate 1ˢᵗ March – the first day of meteorological spring – by having a walk around the neighbourhood together.
I've been writing this diary for over an hour now and I'd better check how Katie's got on with getting Chris to bed and then see to my homework. I feel like a surrogate mother sometimes.

Jenny and John didn't get to go out for a leisurely walk to mark the start of meteorological spring. They both received a message shortly after 2pm via the school receptionist to go straight home after their last period.

Anne was waiting in the hallway as usual to greet her children, a habit she'd learned from her own mother. She always remembered the comfort and sense of self-worth this act of love used to give her. She wouldn't dream of denying her own children the same consideration. This was especially important today, as she had to break the news that their father had taken his own life. Her only dilemma was whether to talk to them together once they were both back home or individually, as each arrived. She was still agonising over this painful decision when Jenny appeared at the front door.

Jenny had intuitively sensed something was seriously wrong the moment she was told at reception to go straight home and this was only confirmed by her mother's demeanour. In the event, very few words were needed to convey the facts and, after a remarkably brief outpouring of emotions, both felt stronger and ready to meet John together less than half an hour later. John had not read anything alarming into his school receptionist's message and therefore the news of his father's death came as a complete shock. On hearing the dreadful news, he marched straight up to his room and broke down.

John cried inconsolably well into the evening. Mother and sister took it in turns to stand outside his room until the sobbing died down and they felt it was appropriate to enter and try to comfort him.

Mike had placed his suicide note in the top drawer of the bedside table where Anne also found the half empty whisky bottle and completely empty paracetamol tablet box that morning as she awoke by her husband's limp body. She immediately called for an ambulance which arrived just under an hour later. The crew at once ascertained that Mike was showing no vital signs and he was pronounced dead on arrival at the hospital.

His suicide note read:

Dear Anne, John and Jenny,

For some time now, I've been contemplating this step. I've done my best to 'keep my chin up', as they used to say, but since losing my role at the repair shop, (even that was a poor substitute for my old 'proper job'), I've literally lost the will to live. In a world of increasing shortages of everything, I think the best contribution I can make is to check out. At least there'll be more resources and space for everyone else. I mean society in general and this family and guests in particular.
If there's nothing after this life, I'll never know. If there is something, it can hardly be worse than this degenerate life I've been leading. Perhaps the new religion is right and I'll be reincarnated into a better

world.
Don't anyone blame yourselves. I'm proud of you and am sure you'll
all make out fine.

Mike, Dad.

Although Anne's predominant emotion towards her husband was anger, she was grateful that he had articulated a plausible explanation and justification for his irreversible action. This would at least assist the process of *closure* in the sense coined by those awful so-called cousins across the Atlantic.

The note satisfied John more than it did Jenny, although she was not angry at her father – just desperately sad that he had gone.

Remarkably, John and Jenny's spring walk was put back just two days after this latest tragic event. So, after a quick tea together on Thursday night, 3rd March, the two, as befitted the name of the month, marched out of the house together into the crisp evening air. Their first stop was just across the road where they visited the Watsons. Mr Watson, or Terry, as they now called him, had been ill with a virulent form of flu through much of January, but they'd heard a couple of reports since that he was doing much better. Oddly, it was only as Mrs Watson opened the door that it occurred to John and Jenny that they'd not yet discussed what, if anything, they would say to anyone they met about their father's passing.

As it turned out, they mentioned nothing, as Joyce clearly had sufficient cares of her own to occupy the communication space. Owing to two brief spells in hospital last year which nearly used up Terry's treatment allowance, they had avoided involving GPs or the NHS as far as possible for fear of incurring any unnecessary expense this year. They were unsure if and how such visits to the surgery were costed against their allowance and Jenny promised to find out on their behalf. The Watsons were now feeling quite buoyant with, they hoped, the worst of the cold weather behind them and only a few pounds to date spent on prescription charges to treat Terry's flu.

Joyce was frankly more worried by the prospect of another visit by that terrible Mr Crawley and his partner in crime, whatever his name was. The Watsons hadn't personally been troubled by them again so far this year, but in the neighbourhood there were at least three roads where they had heard first or second-hand accounts of unpleasant encounters with the diabolical duo.

After an hour or so, the siblings returned to the end of their own road where Jenny decided she needed to get back home to catch up on her homework and so left John to wander a little longer on his own. He decided to take a walk down two of the roads mentioned by Joyce which appeared to have been descended upon most recently by Crawley and his side-kick, Jones. Just as he turned into the second of these, he caught a glimpse of two familiar figures about a hundred yards away. Crawley and Jones appeared to be comparing notes by the drive of a distinctive-looking house. John crossed over the road to avoid entering either man's field of vision and crept up closer until he was able to stand behind a pavement tree almost directly opposite the couple, hidden from view but within earshot.

As usual, Crawley was doing most of the talking:
'Jones, I keep telling you – the rules of the game have changed since that new directive came out. No bloody bonuses for fining businesses even when they're in breach of environmental law! And they've barely even put our pay up - bastards! That means we've got to work extra hard at the softer targets. You posing as good cop and looking all sympathetic as I act Mr nasty piling on all the historical consumer crimes may be great psychology at the start. But you've got to let me have the final word. No damned good saying as we're leaving like you just did now: 'Don't worry Mrs Parkhurst, I'm sure this can all be sorted once your husband gets in and you can talk it all over together.' No, it ruddy well won't all be sorted – he's the blighter we're out to get

arrested!'

John had stopped listening beyond the reference to fining businesses. What he'd suspected all along had just been confirmed – that these two, even if they'd been acting within the law at the time, were motivated by greed. By the time he had refocussed his attention on the two men, the quieter one, Simon Jones, was already walking away from Crawley. It appeared that the working day was over. Crawley stood for a while, casting glances in various directions as if to decide which homes he would need to revisit in order to wreak further havoc on decent people's lives, or to assess what rich pickings he might extract from new victims on his next sortie.

At last, Crawley moved off towards the darker end of the road where one of the street lamps had failed. John followed stealthily behind his quarry, hoping his homeward path would lead to somewhere altogether out of view. For some reason, he'd naively assumed that Crawley would be making his way to a bus stop on the main road and began to despair of ever coming to a secluded spot. However, just as he was about to give up hope, Crawley turned off into a dark alleyway where he had parked his car.

Of course, thought John, a despicable slime ball like Crawley would always find a way of clinging on to a private motorcar – a treasured possession which virtually all the humble folk he persecuted had long since been forced to relinquish if they'd ever had one.

John made his move as Crawley leaned on his car with one hand while fumbling in his pocket for the key with the other.

'You killed my dad, you bastard!'

The environmental enforcement officer involuntarily released the car keys he was about to pull out of his trouser pocket and transferred his grasp to the mobile phone beside them. He then invisibly pressed what he prayed was the emergency key to summon the assistance he instinctively knew he was certain to need. For the next few minutes, he just needed to keep this kid talking.

'I think you must have confused me with someone else, lad,' Crawley began. Another instinctive impulse prompted him to be employ elaborate speech, drawing out his vowels as long as possible in order to play for time.
'I bet I've been doing this inspector's job since before you were born, lad, and I can assure you I don't get paid enough to go around killing people!' He then realised his mistake. This was not the time to be making light of a murder accusation when it was obviously sympathy and empathy that the boy needed.
'Listen, I can see you're terribly upset and angry. Anyone would be if they'd lost a parent, which I'm sure you have. I mean, I'm sure you're not making it up. If there's anything I can do to help...'

John simply lunged forward and thumped Crawley squarely on the forehead. He then opened the car door on the driver's side, lifted the dazed man half way up into the opening and slammed the door shut simultaneously trapping his left arm, chest and head.

As John slammed the car door on his victim for the second time, community police officer Margaret Warwick, appeared in the blind alley. Despite the growing darkness, she immediately recognised John from their two previous encounters. Stepping closer with her torch, she also identified Crawley whom John had begun to alternately kick and punch after he had slid out of the car. Margaret's training should have prompted her to verbally intervene as soon as she observed the violent scene, but something held her back until she had run to within just two metres the car.

'Young man – stop right now!' This came out sounding more like a polite request than an urgent command. John, completely absorbed by his violent treatment of Crawley, only fully registered Margaret's presence as she came close enough to grasp him by the left arm. Even then, he continued kicking Crawley's limp body with his right foot as he lay on the pavement by the car. Gradually the kicks became weaker and finally came to a stop.

Margaret shone her torch onto Crawley's contorted form. He was almost completely surrounded by a dark red pool with fresh blood still oozing out of visible parts of his body.

Little by little, John became aware of the enormity of his predicament and stared in horror at the community policewoman who had unmistakably witnessed his violent attack on a man who, in the eyes of the law, may not have even technically committed an offence.

Margaret stooped down to study the victim more closely.
'He's badly hurt, but seems to be breathing still. Do you think he'll live?' John asked Margaret, sounding more like a concerned bystander than the brutal assailant himself.

'No, he won't survive,' she replied impassively as she reached into the car through the still open door and found the boot release button. She pulled out a blanket.
'This'll do,' she muttered as she methodically folded it twice, draped it over Crawley's face with an overlap of about eight inches resting on the pavement either side of his head. She then stood firmly with a foot on each overlap and resumed talking quietly to John.

'Over the past two or three months, this monster has called me out several times to assist in arresting mainly older lonely people for minor or trumped-up environmental offences. I've observed enough of his intimidating tactics to get the measure of the man and many a time, I've felt sullied by my connection with him. What he didn't bargain for was that working with the local community, I've got to know some of the perfectly decent people he's had carted away and thrown into prison cells.

'What really turned my dislike of the man into pure loathing was when I learned from colleagues that he'd been disciplined by his superiors for fabricating cases against people such as your dad, for running perfectly legal outfits which benefited the community. Even after being disciplined, he was still allowed to carry on in his job interrogating innocent and vulnerable victims for far too long. The irony is that had you not come on the scene this evening, I would have arrested him. The warrant came only this morning....'

Up to this point, John had been listening intently, but during the brief pause in her speech he looked down and noticed the policewoman was still standing with her feet firmly on either end of the blanket pressing down on Crawley's face and pinning his head to the ground. She also glanced down momentarily before tentatively stepping back and removing the blanket. He lay completely motionless just as before. The difference was that now both his bleeding and breathing had stopped.

Margaret broke their brief shared contemplative silence by motioning John to step well back from the scene and quietly explained herself as they walked away together.

'If I had let you continue kicking him, he may have died purely as a result of your assault. Then most of the guilt would lie with you. If I'd just stopped you, he would probably have recovered well enough to identify you and bring charges for grievous bodily harm. I'm not a lawyer and couldn't say whether what he did to your father and others would have had much mitigating effect in court.

'What I *am* confident about is that with him dead he can't identify you and, given limited police resources and the fashionable focus on environmental crime these days, it's unlikely there'd be a serious investigation. Twenty years ago, it would have been a different story with a big forensics team on the job. But that was then.'

By now, John had got over the initial shock well enough to speak.

'How did you come to be around just when it was all happening?'

'He somehow managed to call me, just as he'd called me out to all those cases I was talking about. And this is my beat, so I was only two streets away.'

'So, won't they know at the police station that you were the one called out and won't you have to send in a report?'

'Actually, no: the call went straight to me and there's no problem with me reporting that bit truthfully anyway. He called me and when I got to his car, he lay dead. These days, they may not even carry out a post mortem and just assume he succumbed to the injuries caused by his beating. They'll know I was about to arrest him for his corrupt dealings with the public he was meant to be serving. I'm ninety percent sure it will rest there. Given his dishonest behaviour, they'll assume it was a punishment beating carried out by one or more aggrieved residents...'

'Well, that too would be true, then...' The enormity of his crime had now fully dawned on John.

Having called there once before, Margaret knew where John lived and had purposely ensured they were moving in that direction. About two hundred metres from his house, she stopped, feeling she owed John some further reassurances.

'These days, only about 10 percent of CCTVs are loaded and many of those aren't in working order. And I doubt if you've gone past any on your route today. Certainly, there won't have been any operating within five hundred metres of that place.'

They continued walking together in silence for another minute until they reached John's road. The most important part of Margaret's conversation with John had to be now.

'John, if we both stay calm and rational over the next few days and weeks, you're – we're – pretty certain to get away with this. We've also both got a conscience to deal with, however. For my part, I'm prepared to deal with mine and suffer any karmic consequences. From what I've seen, I'm confident you will manage that too.

'The new religion teaches that there are some cases when higher laws outweigh society's manmade laws. I think this is one of them. In extreme situations people have to act on impulse or instinct without the luxury of being able to weigh up all the pros and cons and rights and wrongs of what they're doing. I'm sure you've learnt a lot about that at school in your RE lessons. If we have to compensate for our actions later in this or in a future life, then so be it.'

Margaret had in fact felt almost completely in control of her own actions this evening and was as sceptical about the new religion as the teenager she was lecturing. However, this was the best message she felt she could leave with John as they parted.

'Now go inside, get washed, check your clothes for any... stains. It would be too risky to give you my phone number, but, for the next couple of weeks, I'll aim to stop here for a few minutes every day at about 5pm in case you need to talk about... whatever.'

EPILOGUE

Jenny's Journal

Thursday, 3rd March
Glad I came home early this evening as I had so much damned homework to catch up on. At least Katie has got Chris off to bed and read him his story. John isn't back yet. For some reason, I've got a sense of foreboding which I know won't pass until I hear him get

in. They say when you've lost one family member – and we've lost three in less than a year – you naturally get paranoid about losing someone else close to you. Logical, really.

I'm still in a daze over dad's death and don't know whether to feel guilty or proud of myself for not being paralysed by grief. Mum too is still being so strong. I only heard her cry quietly to herself once the other day.
There – I've just heard John come in now. What a relief! I'll talk to him tomorrow about what he's been up to since we split up an hour or so ago.

Saturday 5th March
John has been acting weirdly and didn't want to give an account of what he got up to after we went our separate ways on Thursday evening. Perhaps he had a secret rendezvous with Mandy. Or just found a quiet corner to grieve. I'm not even sure he's told Mandy yet.

Sunday, 20th March
It's all over then. Mum arranged the funeral and burial. So, dad's finally come to rest at the bottom of our garden, though not quite the bottom, as with five graves there already over four plots, he's had to join the second row so he's that bit closer to the house. It seems appropriate somehow. Mum said we might apply to host another two graves – one to complete the second row and the other to start a third row. I almost said – but what about leaving space for the rest of the family? But then thought better of it. We don't want to tempt fate: let's hope the fifty percent of us remaining Greenways will get to live a good few years yet in our present incarnation!

Thursday, 31st March
Mum told me and John today that there was good and bad news. The good news was that the Home Office had sent us fifty pounds compensation for that awful Crawley man's illegal treatment of Dad at the repair shop.

The bad news was that the letter was dated just one day before dad's suicide. If only he'd known he'd been vindicated, surely that would have given him the strength to go on.

On hearing the news, John went pale, but then smiled strangely, saying that he'd heard from the local community police officer that a warrant for Crawley's arrest had been issued shortly after this. Then, when she came out to arrest him, she found him lying dead in a pool of blood. He'd obviously suffered a well-deserved punishment beating by some of his victims.

I was shocked he could take pleasure in this miserable man's death and told him I thought violence and disproportionate revenge wasn't justified. He stared at me coldly and said the police officer had told him he'd terrorised half the local community with his false or exaggerated accusations and some had gone to prison and no doubt Dad wasn't the only one who ended up taking his own life. I had no answer to that.

Tuesday, 26th April
Will our woes never end? This first heatwave of the year has had terrible consequences across the country and right here in our own community. On my way home from school today, I got this sudden intuitive impulse to go round to the Watsons' even though my aching head and parched throat were telling me I needed to get a drink urgently before I collapsed from dehydration. Joyce took longer than usual to get to the door after I'd knocked. She solemnly and distantly announced that her husband Terry had succumbed to the extreme heat earlier in the day and she'd be in touch about the funeral in the next few days.

It occurred to me later that, as the Watsons don't have much of a garden, Terry could have his grave next to Dad's and then Joyce would be able to visit. I mentioned this to mum who frankly told me that she might have to be hard-nosed about the need to use these two potential extra plots to earn extra money. It would be awkward to take money from poor Joyce. But then mum relented and suggested we compromise and offer to arrange this for her via the ministry, but that we wouldn't take payment. Joyce may insist on paying anyway and we'd still have the second plot we could charge for.

Wednesday, 6ᵗʰ May

We've come to a bizarre arrangement with Chloe. She's agreed to take all her showers at the place where she works most days, as there don't seem to serious water restrictions there. This has slightly increased the allowance for the other members of the family and we've already noticed the difference. Also, Chloe seems to have grown up a bit and is now staying in to spend time with Chris at the weekends and one weekday evening. He is now behaving a lot better both at home and school. Katie too is clinging to me less and getting on better with her little brother. She has even taught him some of our easier parlour games which he seems to enjoy.

Saturday, 9ᵗʰ May

I've been talking to Chloe again. Somehow, no one had thought to ask her about how she came to be on her own with two children. We all seem to have assumed she had always been a single mum because of how she makes her living.

She told me today that she was reasonably happily married until Katie started school. Then her husband signed up with something called the Coastal Defence Service. He didn't tell her anything about this work and she imagined it was to do with combatting the effects of coastal erosion. He'd only been doing the job for about nine months when she received a surprise visit. A stern gent in military uniform solemnly announced that her husband had been killed in the line of duty and had been awarded a medal for bravery in the Territorial Army defending the homeland against a horde of armed illegal immigrants. The small one-off bereavement payment she received soon ran out and, with Chris on the way, Chloe had to take desperate measures to make ends meet.

Thursday, 14ᵗʰ May

I met Joyce in the street. She told me a week after Terry's death she'd accepted an offer to swap her three-bedroom house for a pre-fab 'modular' grannie flat in the next town. They're hardly giving her anything to cover the extra value of her own property, but she will get a slightly higher pension, so a bit more cash to cover day-to-day living, which is what she really needs. Another refugee family from the south will move in the day after she moves out. She's had Terry buried near her new home where there's still room in an abandoned church graveyard. So, I'm glad we never got round to offering her a grave for her husband in our garden after all.

Saturday, 27th June
Mum received a letter today saying that host allowances are being raised by half a per cent from the end of July. This sounds very little, but they reckon there's been about one per cent deflation this year so far, so it's actually an increase of more like one and a half per cent. So, they claim anyway, but not sure we can trust the official deflation figures!

Some economist was on the TV and said this level of deflation was good for the negative growth economy, as seeing prices come down and their money go further, people tended to delay making all but essential purchases. So, less demand, fewer things produced and better for the environment.

A sociologist was on too, saying that people are reporting higher happiness levels as they realise how better life is without the mad rush to earn more and more and be forever buying things they don't need. There may be something in that, but most people I know are worrying about getting hold of enough basic food and keeping warm and clean through the winter. Or wildfires in and out of season burning down their homes as well as destroying farmland and crops in a country where we are still less than fifty percent self-sufficient in food production.

Friday, 24th July
Today, the government's announced that households living in 'climate safer' areas and with suitable spare accommodation will have to take in refugees. As it's an emergency, there's no payment, just a meagre allowance for food. They are citing evacuation during the mid-twentieth century world war. This was when children were

sent away to live with host families to escape the bombing of industrial cities. Nowadays we don't need a war to displace people, just the climate we've managed to mess up during peace time.

Mum was so smart arranging for us to get our guests when she did. Trouble is, there's no guarantee the ministry will continue to honour its deal with our family...

Tuesday, 18ᵗʰ August
Just when we thought Chris had settled down and put aside his mischievous ways, he's caused all-round grief by leaving the front door open and letting Jock run off somewhere probably never to be seen again. We can only hope he's picked up by a rare dog-loving family and they'll read our address on his collar. More likely, someone will call the wardens and he'll be put down and, knowing our luck, when they trace him back to us, we'll get a fine into the bargain.

Friday, 21ˢᵗ August
Our worst fears have been confirmed. A neighbour told us they'd seen a warden bundling a dog which answered Jock's description into a ranger's van. It's a sad fact that none of us in the family really bonded with the poor dog. It's as though because he was intended to keep nan company and she put an end to her life on the very day I brought him home, he kind of belongs with her. Only he'll get no grave.

Wednesday, 9ᵗʰ September
I could hardly believe it at first. Our family passed the water consumption inspection which all households now get, starting this year. I naively suspected that the inspector, who was less officious than I'd expected, made a more generous allowance in our case, as we're a host family.

Mum then told me that she'd asked Chloe to be at home when he came and work her magic with the inspector if required. Her tone and expression left me in no doubt that it had been required.

Let's hope we do as well next month when we're due an energy consumption inspection. I've never understood why this is so vital now over 80 percent of the country's energy comes from renewable solar and wind power. Of course, they can read our meters remotely, but they just want to send someone round to intimidate us and stick their noses into how we use our appliances, etcetera.

I also can't believe that I started today's entry with the damned inspection instead of my first day at school of the new year! To be fair, not a lot happened except all the rigmarole of being given our new timetables for year 11. John started back too. He's in year 13 and he's taking an extra course in Karma and Reincarnation. I should have thought there was enough compulsory RE in the curriculum without voluntary extras, but he said mysteriously he has a special reason for wanting to learn more about this. I suppose it's to do with wanting to know more about what awaited gran and dad in the Great Beyond.

Friday, 23rd October
I never thought I'd live to see this day: Mandy has at last put her foot down with her parents and is coming to stay with us over half term!

I was so pleased for John, until I realised I'd have to move in with mum or she'd have to move in with me for the week. Then, just as I'd conquered my selfish side, mum announced that Mandy was going to sleep in John's room – with John! I honestly don't get it after that discussion John had with mum only six months ago. Surely, if he's suddenly discovered his sex instinct, he wouldn't be so stupid as to act on it?

Sunday, 8th November
All six of us went out to picnic at the bottom of the garden this afternoon. It was another nice warm sunny day which meteorologists keep spoiling by telling us they shouldn't be happening in mid-autumn, but with so much climate chaos across the world, you just have to be grateful for whatever bit of pleasant weather comes your way.

We've decided that with the two new guest graves instated, making a total of five, we're going to take it in turns to offer visitors tea and homemade biscuits for pre-arranged visits. John has fixed a small collection box on a post to the side of the plots in case people want to make voluntary donations towards the refreshments.

Mum says the refreshments are meant as a nice touch and not to make money, as our finances are on a pretty firm footing these days with the income from the graves and the small extra allowance we get for hosting Chloe and her family.

Tuesday, 17th November
Something quite shocking dawned on me this evening when talking to mum. I was thinking how she's only just over forty and how lonely she must be with dad now gone for nine months. I summoned up all my courage and asked her if she might one day get married again or consider looking for another partner.

She said quite convincingly that she has enough people in her life with the two of us and the refugees who are beginning to feel more like our own extended family.

Then I was even bolder and asked her if she missed having a man in her life. She paused, and then, looking equally embarrassed and wistful, told me she no longer had any needs in that department.

Tuesday, 1st December
The weather has turned desperately cold and of an evening we're having to huddle together in the lounge – the only room we can normally heat if we're to keep within our allowance or even just afford. I've had the strangest idea that when it's our turn to wash, we ought to boil up just enough water to bathe in the lounge, as we can't heat the bathroom and I don't fancy freezing to death while showering. But then, where would everyone else go to give the bather privacy? I suppose they could manage for ten minutes or so wearing coats in the kitchen or even go to their rooms.

I don't dare think what's going to happen when, like this time last year, mum calls a family conference to discuss New Year's

Resolutions. I literally can't think of what more we could do to save energy or world resources. There's talk of a new law to impose a one-year ban on buying any new clothes intended to force everyone to learn to 'mend and make do'. The trouble is, if that became a law then it wouldn't be admissible as a New Year's Resolution and it's the only thing I've thought of so far that wouldn't be too irksome.

Wednesday, 9th December
I overheard a mysterious conversation between mum and John in the kitchen this evening. They were talking about Mandy coming to stay over for the Christmas period. Mum seemed OK with the idea, as Mandy seems to have come out of her shell since putting her foot down with her parents and becoming more independent. She and I got on fine and she and John sharing a bedroom together wasn't so embarrassing last time. So why not have her again at Christmas and get her to join in our family games?

But then out of the blue, John announced 'I've managed to sneak out of school a few cartons of Kinder Juice for you. Where do you want me to store it – in the garage in the usual place?'

Mum's obviously using John as a conduit for stocking up on some nice drinks to treat us all with at Christmas. I don't suppose it's exactly illegal to bring the Kinder Juice home from school, except I know it's intended as a healthy free drink for teenagers, so it would be against the spirit of the government's scheme to hoard it for just anyone to drink. It seems a bit unfair on John having to do all the smuggling. I must ask him if he's having to give up his ration or do they give the kids in his school as much as they want. Mum just reminds me every now and then to make sure I drink the stuff regularly.

After completing her journal on 9th January, Jenny had little homework to do, as the term was winding down. Finding herself at a loose end, she decided to satisfy her curiosity and seek out John's stash of Kinder Juice in the garage. She wondered how soon it would take her to find the hiding place and how many cartons he'd managed thus far to smuggle out of school.

She hadn't been in there since trying to help her dad salvage his tools after Chris's escapade nine months ago. She turned on the light and immediately felt a pang of guilt at this extravagant use of her family's energy ration. She quickly scanned the shelves and imagined herself in John's shoes. Where would he have hidden the cartons, bearing in mind they would increase in number over time? Somewhere out of sight, but easy to reach and not too far from the door, as the risk of someone coming across them was very slight with no one having cause to use the garage.

Using these powers of deduction, Jenny quickly settled on a cardboard box which she carefully took down from a shelf at chest height next to the work bench. She was right... but there were only two cartons there! From the way John was talking, you'd think his smuggling operation had been underway since October half term! She checked out a few more containers in the garage before concluding that this was the only hiding place. She would have a word with her mum.

It was after seven o'clock when Jenny came back into the house and into the lounge where Anne was sitting with the rest of the extended family. There was very little sound, as the rule was that with so many people occupied in different ways, the TV went off at six and only came on briefly at nine again for the news. Jenny sat patiently, waiting for her mother to leave the lounge so she could follow her out. She didn't want to bring up the smuggled drinks business with her mum in front of the whole assembly in case it spoilt her *Kinder surprise*.

The half-English, half-German term for the drink meaning 'Children's Drink' amused Jenny's creative mind. Unaware of the ulterior purpose of the drink, she didn't cotton on to the play on words intended by the inventor of Kinder Juice which could literally be taken to mean *kinder* in English.

At last, Anne left the lounge with Jenny discreetly following behind. Just as she entered the kitchen, she caught her mother in the act of retrieving a carton of Kinder Juice from a cupboard at head height.

'Mum, what on earth is it with this Kinder Juice? Yesterday, I heard you talking to John about him bringing home a supply from school. What is this stuff – the elixir of life? I know it's meant to be good for teenagers, but are you on a quest for eternal youth or something?'

Anne blushed and Jenny recognised an expression on her face akin to the one she wore last month when she claimed to have no needs in the men department. However, her mother took only moments to compose herself and provide a dignified response.

'It's complicated and yet very simple. John is in love with Mandy. I believe she's good for him, so I want to encourage their relationship to blossom. There's precious little in this life to enjoy these days. You were right about me: in my early forties, I'm still quite young myself and the idea of male company is still quite appealing. But the situation is different for me. And you're still too young to be thinking about boys. You've said so yourself.'

Anne pushed the carton along the kitchen work surface towards her dumbfounded daughter.

'And yes, this is a very healthy drink specially designed for teenagers. But, as I've suspected for a good while, it's also a libido suppressant or inhibitor.' Anne looked hard into her daughter's eyes for reassurance that she had understood and that there'd be no need to invoke the ugly term *sex drive*. Thanks to Jenny's extensive vocabulary, her prayers were answered and they were both spared further embarrassment.

The two stood staring at one another for a while until first Anne, then Jenny burst out laughing. But then Jenny felt very sorry for her mother. Anne felt the same for her daughter, her whole family, living and dead, and for all humanity on this godforsaken planet. And as amusement turned to sadness, so laughter turned to tears.

THE END